KING OF THE DEAD

A ZOMBIE ROMANCE

RYANA HUNTER

Black Rose Writing | Texas

This is a work of fiction. Names, characters, businesses, places, events, and incidents are either the products of the author's imagination or used in a fictitious manner. Any resemblance to actual persons, living or dead, or actual events is purely coincidental.

ISBN: 978-1-68513-580-5
PUBLISHED BY BLACK ROSE WRITING
www.blackrosewriting.com

Printed in the United States of America
Suggested Retail Price (SRP) $20.95

King of the Dead is printed in Garamond Premier Pro

*As a planet-friendly publisher, Black Rose Writing does its best to eliminate unnecessary waste to reduce paper usage and energy costs, while never compromising the reading experience. As a result, the final word count vs. page count may not meet common expectations.

Edited by Joyce Fernandez, ReJoyce Literary Editing Co. (Rejoyceliteraryediting.com)

Praise for
King of the Dead

"A fresh take on the zombie romance, leaves you hungry for more."
–Torri Heat

For those that enjoy orphic tales.

KING OF THE DEAD

New York
Springfield
Boston
Massachusetts
Connecticut
New Haven
Pennsylvania
Long Island
Albany
New York
Maryland
Philadelphia
Baltimore
Boston Necropolis
Horde
?????
Survivors
?????
N
E
S
W

Prologue

Renee dragged herself up and placed her palm against the windowpane. The bloody scene in front of her wasn't any different from anything she'd seen in the past, but it still left her heartbroken. People ran and screamed, trying to escape them. Some shot and took the slower ones down, the shamblers. Humans dressed in military fatigues fared better, seeming to have gotten away and moved out of her vision. Most humans died horrible and bloody deaths; their limbs torn off as the hungry horde surrounded them.

No escape. Even Renee knew her time was up. She got away because they'd assumed she was already dead and had moved on to the still-live prey. They preferred meat with a heartbeat. Eventually, once they ate their way through a city, they'd go back and scrape the bones clean until there wasn't anything left of the living.

Renee had fallen and hit her head on a concrete curb just outside the hotel she was hiding in. She only managed to make her way two floors up because dizziness was overtaking her sense of direction and ability to balance. Her fingers gripped the windowsill of the window in the room she was hiding in while her palm, flat on the glass, kept her from swaying. Something tickled the side of her face, but she ignored it, unable to look away from the death in front of her.

Maybe it was better she couldn't hear the screams, gunfire, or explosions. Her cochlear implants had been acting up for weeks, and the hit to her head against the concrete seemed to have taken what little hearing she had left.

She'd lost the hearing in her right ear when the transmitter and speech processor had been ripped off in a narrow escape from one of the undead. The left external processor needed new batteries.

It was one of the only reasons Renee thought *maybe* going into a city was necessary. Now she was back in the silence that filled her early years, only this time, it was a relief. Never could she have guessed she'd want to be deaf, but at least this way the last sounds she heard wouldn't be the screams of terror that haunted her days and nights.

Renee shivered. Most places had no power, and it was only fall, so she shouldn't have been as cold as she was. It was just after nightfall. She closed her eyes even though it was stupid to close them, leaving herself open to attacks, but what did it matter anymore?

The city was overrun. All of her family and friends were long dead. Any new alliances she'd made - gone. After fighting so hard over the last seven years, she was alone again. The last of her food was depleted days ago. Out of water. No reason to try anymore. Humanity had lost.

For months, she and some other people she'd met chased a dream of reaching Nantucket. Supposedly it was a safe haven, and it was the only reason they'd been foolish enough to enter Baltimore. They wanted to go around the city. All cities were dangerous because there were always undead around, but they'd been desperate. They didn't have enough supplies to make it if they went around the large city. Going straight through was their last hope.

Her small group had joined up with a scrappy militant group Renee didn't trust, along with an insane posse of scavengers. All scavengers seemed to have a death wish, at least in Renee's opinion. Who else would venture into cities for supplies regularly? As soon as they stepped foot in Baltimore, Renee knew they'd made a colossal mistake. It was too barren, too quiet. She swore she even felt the undead watching her. It didn't make sense - zombies didn't watch anything; they didn't plan. They came in waves and devoured everything until only piles of bones remained.

The image of the tall, menacing zombie filled her mind. Renee had seen him in the shadows just after she got to the heart of the city. At first, she hadn't realized he was undead because the dim light obscured his features.

Even after, when everyone was running for their lives and she'd seen him again, he didn't look quite dead. He was too clean, too fresh looking - almost human. If it wasn't for his deathly pallor and the way the other zombies hurried away from him like they were making room for him, she might have mistaken him for a human survivor.

Renee put her forehead against the glass and gripped the windowpane tighter. Nausea threatened to make her throw up what little fluid she still had left in her body. The hair on the back of her neck stood. She bit her lip. They were here. Only a matter of seconds until it was over. She might not hear them, but she could sense the zombie's approach. She refused to open her eyes.

I'm a coward. I should face my death, or at least fight back. She squeezed her eyes tighter. A light touch on her back made her stiffen and tremble. It was a hand, a chilly hand. It slid up her neck and gently squeezed. Renee froze. It wasn't a zombie. Confused, she opened her eyes and looked at the reflection in the window.

Chapter 1

Renee yawned as she stood on top of a crushed car and leaned against the utility pole the car was wrapped around. She was not thrilled with her new group, but what choice did she have? Humans that traveled alone were an easy target for zombies and humans alike. The undead would eat her, and the humans... well, it largely depended on who found her. But she'd learned early on what happened to people traveling alone who were unable to defend themselves.

She shivered from the memories of witnessing people die. The world was a harsh, horrific, never-ending cycle of death. Renee sighed and pushed her long, brown ponytail behind her. Had to stay focused. Her only job tonight was to stay awake and watch for threats. Mark said she wasn't useful for anything else. Mark was a tool.

Iris told Renee she slept better when Renee was on watch because Renee caught things others didn't. Renee scrunched up her face. She understood they weren't friends, but she wanted them to be. She wanted *someone* to like her.

I like you Renny, her brother said beside her.

Renee stiffened and wouldn't allow herself to look in his direction. If she did, he'd fade away, and she was feeling pretty lonely again.

I think you have to, Liam. You're my brother, she replied in her mind because she knew he'd hear her since that's where he lived.

Untrue. A lot of brothers, especially ones like me, who are a lot older, don't like their little sisters. But they're jerks and I'm the best, he laughed because that's what she always told him, but he never believed it.

You are, but I can't get distracted. I have to make sure nothing sneaks up on us. We're too close to the city now, and if I make one more mistake, Mark said I was out. How was I supposed to know he was going to let those scavengers join us? Renee grumbled and scanned the area again.

Even if you didn't, you probably shouldn't have charged into camp screaming that you were being attacked. His tone was gentle, but his words still stung.

Well, any other time, that's what it would have meant! She snapped and frowned. Typically, if you were already in a group and another gang of similar size approached, it rarely meant they wanted to team up. It meant they wanted your stuff. Some groups were willing to trade or help each other, but many would fight to get what they wanted.

She took a deep breath and peered into the darkness. Tuning everything out, returning herself to the childhood state when she leaned on her abilities to perceive things with her senses of sight, touch, taste, and smell, to tell her if something was wrong. There was a chill in the air that left her skin feeling damp. The light breeze carried an odd mixture of scents to her nostrils. Pavement, decaying foliage, mold, people that needed to bathe, a musty fragrance she couldn't place, and a trace of something fresh that reminded her of sunshine.

Citrus? She blinked and squinted her eyes when she saw what appeared to be glowing stars in the sky, only they were too close to the ground. Renee leaned closer and tried to keep her heart rate down. There were so many small glowing orbs that her mind couldn't register the sight. Fear lanced through her and made her limbs lock into place.

She'd heard stories over the years talking about the zombies once they started to group together. She suspected the stories were nonsense. It was said right before the undead attacked, people on watch would sometimes peer into the darkness and witness a sea of lights too close to the ground to be stars. It was almost beautiful in an eerie sort of way. Just the idea of a glittering mass of stars made her think of her books. Only in those stories, it wouldn't be a sign of danger. Instead, the two romantic leads would have an important scene, the stars, a magical backdrop, and the characters might even kiss.

She shook her head. Not sure what the connection was between the sea of lights and the horde of undead, but it was clear enough from the stories, if someone witnessed it, they were slated to die.

No escape from death. There was never a way to avoid it.

With shaking limbs, she eased down off the side of the car as quietly as she could. She pulled her lips into her mouth to hold in any sounds that might escape and tiptoed back to camp. John, from the militant group traveling with them for weeks, and Jules, who had arrived with the scavengers, were still awake.

"Where's Mark?" Renee whispered. They leaned forward, and Renee reminded herself to speak up, repeating the question.

John pointed to a dark sport utility vehicle. "Why?"

Renee resisted the urge to touch her transmitter. No voice sounded exactly "right" when someone spoke to her. At least from what she'd been told. Since she hadn't been able to hear before her implants, except for extremely loud noises, Renee didn't know how voices should sound. Human speech, to her, always seemed what she imagined something robotic or mechanical would sound like. Certain types of voices didn't get picked up as well as others, and she'd rely on her early acquired skill of lip reading. John's voice sounded strange, but she couldn't adjust her remaining implant to pick up on his voice better; due to minor damage accumulated over the years to her transmitter and speech processor, which prevented her from adjusting the volume.

Ignoring the fact she might have missed some words, she hurried to the SUV. "Something's... wrong. We need to move." Renee said, not waiting for their responses. The residual fear of being ostracized by another group of humans made her pause, but she took a breath and straightened her spine. She wouldn't fail this group like she had all the others. She knocked her knuckles against the vehicle's glass window.

Mark's face popped into view. No one, except maybe those in the fabled safe zones, slept soundly anymore. Any tiny noise would wake them. It was the only way to survive. His expression shifted into disapproval before he opened the door.

"What?" Although alert, his voice sounded groggy, the dark circles under his eyes further showed his exhaustion.

"We have to move... there are... zombies. I think," she mumbled the last words, hoping he wouldn't catch her lack of confidence.

Mark stared at her for a moment, and Renee wondered if he wouldn't listen to her.

"Is this like the last time?"

She shook her head. "No. That was different."

"You're not using this as an excuse because you screwed up finding what we needed? This isn't some childish distraction?"

Renee clenched her teeth. Okay, she'd made some mistakes, but this bastard held them over her head like a guillotine, ready to drop the blade at a moment's notice. For someone who had been shy most of her life, after the eighth group of people who had died due to her inability to conquer her fear, she'd made a choice. She would speak up more often, be more aggressive if people weren't heeding her warnings.

It didn't say much, having survived the multiple groups she'd traveled with. They were all dead because of her - her dumb panic attacks left her incapable of doing anything other than curling into a ball. But Mark didn't know any of that. He only knew that she was more outspoken, an annoyance who questioned his ideas. Perhaps she didn't have his military background or skill set, but she'd survived just as long - and often by herself.

It took all of her self-control not to snap at him. She had never given any of them a reason to think she'd lie about something so important. Why the hell did he even want her on watch if he wouldn't believe her?

"No. I saw the sea of stars." As the words tumbled from her mouth, they sounded dumb, and she wished she had phrased it differently.

He clicked his tongue against the roof of his mouth before he answered. "You woke me up for this?"

Couldn't he sense something wasn't right? She hadn't detected it before when she was by herself, but there was a weight to the air, it seemed to press down on all sides and caused her stomach to knot. Renee had felt it before... right before they encountered zombies.

"I get you don't like me, but I'm telling you I *know* they're nearby. If we don't move-"

Mark put up his hand. "Then why hasn't anyone else reported the same?"

"Because... I was the only one to the south."

His face bunched in irritation before he breathed out and relaxed it. "Look, I'm glad you're... paying better attention, but the horde Ty spotted earlier in the week was massive. Larger than most of us have seen, even those from out west. It was thousands, Renee."

"I know that." She mumbled.

"If it was that massive horde, everyone would report in. It could just be shamblers. Did you get visual confirmation?"

Damn it, I don't need visual confirmation, she thought sourly. After so many people had died who had been traveling with her, she recognized when the zombies were close. Many humans had developed an uncanny ability to sense when zombies were near, but Renee's was remarkably accurate. Renee pulled her shoulders back. She refused to let this group die like the others, even if she had to fight Mark to save the rest.

"We shouldn't go into the city. I swear, that's where they're headed." She sounded confident, even with him eyeing her. When Ty saw the horde earlier, he said it looked like they were also headed for Baltimore. Even if Mark didn't believe her, he'd believe Ty, right?

"That's not as much of a risk anymore. There's always undead in the cities, but they're just one-offs. Hordes that big don't go into cities. Why would they? Unless humans try to settle somewhere, they wander around looking for food."

"But Ty-"

Mark put his palm up to stop her. "I know what he said. That's why we avoided the horde he saw and let them pass us, but I doubt they'll enter the city." He adjusted in the bench seat.

"You saw them?" Iris asked, sidling up next to Renee.

Damn it, she moved quietly. Renee didn't hear her coming. Of course, it was on her bad side. Plus, what most people didn't understand was that cochlear implants' primary purpose was to process speech, not environmental sounds. While they did pick up on most sounds, the processor interpreted those sounds, sending them to the brain's appropriate auditory channels. Those channels were set up for speech, not ambient sounds. So sometimes she'd miss things or misinterpret noises.

Iris was tall, around five foot eleven inches, and muscular. Before the world ended, she was a police officer. A few weeks ago, she showed Renee her badge. She'd kept it all these years because it still meant something to her. She even told Renee she still believed her mission was to protect and serve.

"She didn't see anything." Mark waved his hand dismissively. "If she had, others would have too, or worst-case scenario, we'd be in the thick of it right now."

"But-" Renee took a step toward the vehicle.

"Don't." Mark's tone switched to the short, nasty one he mainly used when he spoke to her. "You almost got us killed when the scavengers joined us, you didn't find the medicine like you promised you would, you dropped days' worth of rations because you ran, you're a shit cook, and you can't even hear out of your right ear. The only thing you seem capable of is being on night watch so the useful people can rest."

Renee's lips trembled. What an asshole! It wasn't her fault that most of the medicines were gone now. For the first few years of this mess, she'd been an expert at finding all kinds of pharmaceutical medications. Mainly because she always needed to stock up on batteries for her implants, so she was always searching around in drug stores and abandoned urgent care buildings.

She couldn't refute the part about the rations because that happened exactly as he said it did. A smaller horde of zombies closed in on them, she panicked as usual and ran. In her rush, the bag slipped off her shoulder and she was too scared to go back for it. By the time things had calmed and she found it, everything was ruined.

Before the apocalypse, Renee had no reason to learn to cook, her parents had taken care of her and her brother. Now constantly on the run, everything had to be cooked over a fire, which was totally different from what she'd seen her parents do. She could have made cupcakes from scratch, if there had been a working oven, that had been a hobby of hers in high school.

It was a low blow to mention her hearing, but Mark didn't see the point in holding back. It infuriated her, but also shut her down. As furious as she was, the word *stupid* kept repeating in her head so loudly that she couldn't organize her thoughts.

"She *is* alert at night, Mark. Don't be a dick. She was the one who told us about the wandering group of undead three weeks ago that saved our hides. Renee was also the one who realized a pack of coyotes were tracking us." Iris crossed her arms and shifted her face into the *don't fuck with me look* only Iris could pull off with Mark.

Mark leaned forward and locked his gaze on Renee, but still spoke to Iris. "I told you before, Hernandez, she's *your* problem. You decided she should stick around after fucking up - so deal with her." He backed into the SUV and closed the door in their faces.

Chapter 2

"Prick," Iris muttered under her breath, leading Renee back to her post on top of the mangled car for the night. Iris' dark brown eyes stared right into the location where all the lights had been, but now it was only darkness. "I heard you say something about the sea of stars," she said in a hushed voice.

As much as Renee felt like her parents hadn't been supportive of her and navigating life with an impairment, her parents did have *the best* of the cochlear implants at the time surgically inserted. She couldn't recall the details of the procedure but was told the length of the array and the sound encoding surpassed the quality of all other implants at the time. The surgeon had assured Renee her hearing was as close to natural as possible. Renee always thought her parents had supported the surgery because they couldn't accept their daughter was defective. Since they had paid top dollar and got her cochlear implants that were years ahead of other options available. Now she was able to manage even in the middle of an apocalypse, sometimes picking up on hushed sounds and voices.

Renee wasn't feeling confident anymore. Part of her wondered if she had lost her mind or imagined it. "Yeah... I saw..."

Iris turned to her. "Mark is an ass, but he knows about the stories. It's only been a couple of years since sightings of the seas of stars started, but each time there's a survivor, it's always the same. They, or someone in their group, witnesses it and then they all die."

"Then why did he ignore me?"

She stretched her neck, popping it before she replied. "He thinks you're either pathetic or nuts."

"Why would I lie about something so important?"

Iris patted her shoulder. "He doesn't see you as anything but a kid. You're younger than the rest of us, and you're... different. Most people still alive aren't the greatest people, Renee. They're all hard and cutthroat, they had to be to survive this long. You're not."

"I don't see how that makes any difference." Renee wasn't sure if Iris had just insulted her or not. While Renee didn't want to be considered 'cutthroat,' she knew she was a survivor, she had to be given the world's current condition.

"It means when you see something violent or bloody, you still react like it's the beginning of this mess and freak out. If you see someone hurting or alone, you want to help. Even when you understand they might be setting you up for a trap, and then you spoke about the books..."

Renee gritted her teeth. Again, people were judging her for what she liked to read. Why was it so terrible that she liked romantasy? People made jabs at her attempt to escape the terrible reality they were all living in.

The world was horrible.

All day.

Every day.

She couldn't fathom that no one she'd met didn't want to lose themselves in a book. Especially books with not just beautiful characters that were better than people, but were located somewhere else, not in their bloody and broken world. Usually, the setting of the books she enjoyed was a different realm or planet with wondrous things that didn't exist in the hell she lived in.

Iris made a cross over her chest and whispered something in Spanish, but Renee didn't speak the language. However, her tone of her words sounded like a prayer. "The only book anyone still talks about is His word. We're all forsaken, made to exist here until He returns. I hope to be worthy this time."

Renee frowned. She understood Iris was very religious and believed that her sins caused her to live through what she called *trials and tribulation* to prove to her god she should be taken when he returned. Perhaps Renee was too cynical, but she was fairly certain that no gods existed, regardless of religion, given the atrocities she'd witnessed over the years. But Iris was her almost-friend, and she didn't want to take Iris' spiritual source of comfort from her. Even though the others had mocked her about her fantasy books with fae and magic, Iris hadn't. She hadn't commented at all. Renee liked to believe that it had been intentional, versus her being at a loss for words.

"The horde Ty spotted... I've seen them. I passed them a couple of years ago when I came east. It was big, even then." Iris said as her features sharpened and her gaze became intense, studying the darkness.

"How do you know they're the same group?"

"You've heard of tailgating, right?" Iris glanced at her.

Renee nodded. It was a brilliant but dangerous idea that some survivors did when traveling long distances. A person would identify a larger group of undead and follow them. It helped mask their presence and cover the things that might get them caught by other zombies or humans. They'd follow just close enough not be seen or draw the horde's attention. When done correctly, the person could follow for long stretches and stay relatively safe. If they buggered it up... they became a snack for the zombies.

"I followed them for weeks."

"But how do you know it's the same horde of zombies? Wouldn't they have decayed by now?" Renee cocked her head to the side.

Iris narrowed her eyes at the darkness. "That's the thing I found out. No." She turned her head and leveled her gaze at Renee. "I don't know why, but the entire time I followed, only a few of the shamblers dropped. The rest remained. The group was ..." She grimaced. "They found people often and never, ever left survivors. Sometimes they'd eat until there was nothing but bones and then, occasionally, for whatever reason, turn on each other."

Renee shivered. The group Iris was talking about *had* to be the same one. Except all those years ago... no. It was a coincidence. "Isn't that what all zombies do?"

Iris shook her head. "Before I found myself on the east coast, I traveled with many groups, saw a lot of zombie hordes - they were... disorganized compared to that one. That one seemed," she paused and shuddered, making a cross again. "Evil leads that one. A demon controls it, demanding nothing remains but bones and dust."

"But how can you know that?"

"I don't, but He," she pointed to the darkness above them, "agrees. That group is more dangerous because they aren't *just* zombies, not like the others. They have an intelligence about them."

Renee pinched her lips. She was pretty sure no god talked to Iris. However, if Iris was right... that was the group that had been there the same day her parents... her brother. She shook her head. There were so many undead at that time and they hadn't started grouping up yet. It was only a coincidence. There was no way the bodies in her hometown could have been ravaged so quickly, and this specific horde... it couldn't have existed yet.

Not ready to ponder the circumstances that landed her in her current situation any further, Renee changed the subject. "How many groups have you traveled with?"

"This is the sixth."

Damn, about half the number of groups Renee herself had been a part of. Knowing Iris, she'd fought until she couldn't any more to protect her groups. She probably hadn't run like a coward every time, or anytime, for that matter.

"Why?"

Renee lifted a shoulder.

Iris stared into the inky night. "I don't see the stars... but I did once when I followed that group. The sound of their attack when they found a small settlement," she swallowed. "I'll never forget. Part of me wanted to help, but by the time I'd put it all together - it was too late."

"Do you think it's the same group? Do you really think we accidentally caught up to them? Ty was making sure they were farther ahead." Renee's stomach twisted with her words.

"I think... they sensed us because there's too many of us."

"Then we have to run." Renee reached for Iris' arm.

"No. I think they've moved, or we would have seen, heard, or smelled them. It doesn't make sense, but maybe they're headed to the city."

Renee hugged herself around her stomach. "We're supposed to go into the city tomorrow."

"I'll talk to Mark when we switch shifts for night watch. I know we need supplies, and I can't figure out why they would be headed to the city, but my gut is never wrong."

"We'll die if we go there after them," Renee whispered.

"Yes, but I'll make sure the scouts check the perimeter before we move towards the outskirts. The zombies don't hide or plan, so it will be easy to spot them." She patted Renee's shoulder. "I know a devil leads these undead, but it's not like when we encounter a group of violent people who can use weapons and plan strategy." Iris' voice softened, which was meant to comfort Renee, but the knot in her stomach wouldn't go away.

"I don't want to be with another group." The words tumbled from her lips before she could stop them. Although most had talked about their pasts over the last few months of traveling together, Renee had never admitted how many groups she'd traveled with or that she was always the lone survivor. And she knew Iris was *so* close to befriending her; she really wanted to have a friend in her isolated, tiny world.

"It will be alright. We will be cautious and make it to the safe zone. Perhaps there we can both be something different, something better, than what we are now." Iris's features shifted as a contemplative expression covered them.

"Better than what we are?"

"Yes. If we get to Nantucket and surround ourselves with other humans, we will be safer. If there isn't a church there yet, I'd like to start one, so that all can find salvation and comfort in His grace."

Iris wanted to start a church? Considering how important her god was to her, it made sense, but it also seemed like such a huge thing to do. Renee frowned; the only plan she'd had since this began was to find a secret that would eradicate the zombies. Beyond that, her only aspirations were to find an untouched library or bookstore, take a huge amount of food and water in with her, and set-up her new home. She wouldn't mind being alone so much if books surrounded her.

"Finish your watch. Lila will be here in a few hours to relieve you. I'll make sure the scouts check the outskirts before we go in. If everything goes to plan, we should be in Nantucket in two weeks. Focus on that." Iris gave her a small smile before she retreated.

Renee climbed back onto the wrecked car, leaning against the pole again.

Liam, I... don't want to be alone. I'm afraid of where my thoughts are going to take me. Stay with me.

Of course, princess. I'll never leave your side. I'm your knight commander, remember?

A tug pulled the corners of her mouth up despite him mentioning their childish games. Maybe she was pathetic and not cut out for this world. Or perhaps she was a genius who had found a way to cope in a way others hadn't.

Chapter 3

Renee tiptoed into the city. Her hands shook as she tried to hone in on any sounds, but she only had one good ear because her right cochlear implant was gone, lost to an undead weeks ago. She understood why she had been one of the first sent into the city. Although she'd been traveling for a few months with this group, they didn't seem to like her. Most people didn't. Mark wasn't the only one who tolerated her.

She was annoying and immature, but she didn't know how to necessarily grow up. Her best guess was that the trauma of the world ending when she was in high school had frozen her into a perpetual teenager, which in an apocalypse wasn't ideal. Only a few people were okay with her being friendly and perhaps clingy. Even though she herself wasn't fond of clingy people, she couldn't help it. When she was sixteen, she had just started to be more independent, but then everything turned into a nightmare and she'd reverted to seeking approval from those around her.

It's just like you practiced, don't just listen, Renny - watch what's around you. Pay attention to the scents you pick up when the wind blows. That's what will keep you safe.

The corners of her mouth tilted up. Even dead and nothing more than a ghost in her mind, her brother was the absolute best. He always looked out for her. Before getting distracted, she swallowed the lump in her throat and sniffed the air.

The stench of rot wasn't far away. She took light steps in the opposite direction of the smell. It might not be the zombies. Any time humans came within miles of a city, the awful scent of death wafted out, even if it wasn't filled with the undead. Decaying bodies and organic matter were never pleasant smells.

She'd been sent in to find medicines again. Oddly, it was one of the few things she excelled at. Not scavenging per se, but when she searched for items, more often than not, she would find over-the-counter or prescription medicines that helped those around her. She figured it was because she had to keep looking for batteries for her cochlear implants, which were stocked in most pharmacies.

I don't feel good about this, Liam. It hasn't felt good since we got close to Baltimore. Something's off, even if the massive zombie group isn't here, she told him in her mind as the memory of blackness with tiny dots of light surfaced.

I think you're just worried about Mark, Liam commented.

Renee paused and scanned the empty street in front of her. There were tons of discarded objects and cars, but no signs of life.

He's a jerk and shouldn't be in charge. He acts so superior to everyone because he was in the military. Who cares about that anymore? Iris was a police officer and just as capable. She's smarter too, Renee grumbled.

You can't keep stirring up trouble when you find a group. It's too dangerous to travel alone. Liam chastised.

I know. I know. But he's been shitty to me since I first showed up. He said I was a liability because I lost my right implant. I feel like he's been trying to get rid of me since I joined the group. Renee kept the whine from her tone.

She crept into an abandoned pharmacy and discovered it was like the others. Anything of value was already picked clean, but... she rounded the open door to the pharmacy area where workers would have been. The door being ajar wasn't a great sign, but every once in a while, she'd find something. Bingo!

She snatched the two bottles that had rolled under the cart and read the labels. One was hydrocodone, which would thrill her group, and the other was omeprazole. That wouldn't make as big of an impression. Renee wasn't even sure what omeprazole was or what it did. She only knew about hydrocodone because they'd told her specifically to look for it as well as antibiotics.

Her spine tingled as she stuffed the bottles into her pockets, eyes darting around to catch any movement in the empty building. She took rapid breaths and flexed her hands to get them to stop shaking.

Everything was fine.

She refused to lose it again and drop into a fetal position. If her group caught her one more time like that, she'd be out and she knew it. Damn it! Why was the world like this now? Inhaling a long breath, she forced it out slowly before repeating the breathing exercise ten times.

"I wish you were here. I hate this," Renee whispered out loud to Liam. She shuffled to the door and leaned against the wall, tilting her head to stare at the off-white ceiling tiles. Her old high school had those same tiles. She'd stared at them in class the day the zombies rose up.

High school had been hard for her. While she managed to make a few friends, they weren't in many of her classes, and she got picked on a lot. She'd hidden in her books, like she had been since middle school. Only her books were so much better in high school. She'd discovered a whole genre that seemed like it had been penned only for her. Filled with mystical creatures from another realm, magic, and the most romantic relationships that couldn't happen in reality.

It was ridiculous how many book boyfriends she mentally cataloged and also quite sad how many actual boyfriends she had during her teenage years. Zero. Right before the beginning of the end, her male friend Blake had given her the third book in the series she'd been reading when the zombies first appeared. She was ecstatic about the series but unsure why he gifted the book to her until Rebecca and Carla, her only other friends, explained it was because Blake had a crush on her. She frowned. If the zombies hadn't ruined everything, she might have finally had a real boyfriend.

It's been over seven years. You need to let go of that. Liam reminded her.

Her brother sounded as though he was right next to her. Tempted to turn her head and give him the stink eye, she refrained, knowing if she tried to look at him, he would not be there. Being alone was scarier than having your ghost brother haunting your mind.

Sorry I'm not wise and mature like you are, she snapped.

That's not what I'm saying, and you know it. You can't be a good queen, a good ruler, if you're always looking backwards, Renny.

She pressed her lips into a line. For a moment, she considered bickering with him, but the nagging sensation that someone was watching her made the hair on her arms stand up.

I like to think about my books, the stories, the happily ever afters of the characters. It's better than this crap.

She crept out of the back and into the main area of the store, checking the shelves for any first aid supplies, food, batteries, and any other useful items. What she really wanted to do was find a bookstore to see if she could find the series, she left off reading when the apocalypse began. Books were easy, yet simultaneously difficult to come by. The ones found with little effort were ruined because they were in the outside elements too long. The rain or sun would destroy them over time. The pristine copies tended to be behind locked doors, often with their former owners, now zombies.

Renee had found a couple books in series she thought she would enjoy, never the first one. It was always the second or third in a series, but she considered them precious cargo. Her expression soured. Precious cargo that she no longer had.

Never sure why her peers didn't like her, the trend continued, even when the world ended. Maybe she had a resting bitch face like her mother. Something scraped against the front windows. Renee ducked behind one of the shelves. Her lips and knees trembled. She reminded herself it could have just been the wind blowing garbage around. No stench floated in from the broken glass door.

Still, she couldn't be too careful as she tiptoed to the back door and put her good ear against it. Nothing. he wouldn't be able to hear anything through the steel door, but she pressed herself against it as if the door would give her some measure of safety. Feeling deflated, Renee had found items her group wanted, but there wasn't anything she wanted or needed, like her cochlear implant batteries.

With a deep breath, she turned the handle of the steel door and eased it open to the back alleyway and peeked out. Relief made her stiff shoulders drop. She wiggled through the opening and pressed herself against the brick wall behind the building. A crease formed between her brows as her eyes darted around. She rested her palms against her filthy jeans and took a shallow breath. Renee was always filled with nerve-racking anxiety in a city, even more so if she was alone.

In between groups, there were times when she traveled alone and it was terrible. As much as she might not like how most people behaved, it was always smarter to be with a group since they were almost as violent as the zombies. Being in a group meant more people to attack the undead, or other human groups bent on taking their supplies. She could barely sleep if she was by herself. Over the years people talked about going into the countryside as it had fewer zombies, but she'd always lived on a golf course in Timonium and didn't have a clue how to make it in a rural area. And unlike most of the people in her high school who had life skills, she had none.

Renee's mother always treated her like she was stupid and could never manage on

her own as an adult due to her lack of hearing. Each time Renee attempted to learn a skill, her mother would sweep in and tell her she wouldn't need to know it. Then her mother would complain about what a burden Renee had been since she was born. She'd been deaf before her implants, *not* incapable of learning.

Renny... you need to get moving. Her brother's voice said next to her good ear.

Do you feel it too? Like something's out there. Over the years, all humans had adopted an almost sixth sense for danger because if they didn't, they were killed. A gentle breeze carried a light citrus scent down the alleyway. It was the most pleasant scent she'd encountered since entering the city. It was like a siren's call, because what could smell so good?

Her feet carried her in the direction of the smell as she kept her eyes peeled for any movement. As she rounded the corner, she stopped dead in her tracks. Across the street, in another alley beside a four-story building, obscured by the shadow of it, was a man clad in black. He had long, dark hair and a proud stance that suggested he was someone who held some sort of authority.

Perhaps there was another group of humans in the city besides the one she was with given she did not recognize the man in the alley? Her stomach twisted. Most times when she met another human group, it was tense with an air of violence threatening to combust with the smallest spark of discord. Everyone always wanted what someone else had, and no one wanted to share.

Still, she gravitated toward the man in the shadows. He reminded her of someone... she couldn't put her finger on what was niggling at her, why he felt familiar. He couldn't be someone she met since the world had gone to hell, but maybe he was from before. Perhaps she'd gone to school with him? Passed him in a store?

As if he sensed her, he turned his head almost pulling his face from the obscurity of the darkness. His face was still shadowed but she couldn't help but spot his sharp cheekbones. She froze at the intersection between the buildings, almost outside of the alley. Her heart raced as the heat left her face. Her sense of danger was setting off alarm bells in her mind. She didn't know why, but the unfamiliar, familiar man was a threat. Renee turned on her heel and took off, racing back in the direction she'd come.

Chapter 4

Her legs screamed in exhaustion. She'd been running for what seemed like forever. Every time she paused to catch her breath, she heard the low moan of a shambler or glimpsed an undead that seemed to speed right by her. Stupid! After getting spooked by that man, she took off and got turned around. Although she'd been to Baltimore dozens of times before the uprising, she only visited specific areas, and because she'd panicked, she had run the wrong way and gotten lost.

She sniffed the air, trying to latch onto the awful, pungent smell of the river. Similar to sulfur, because of the algae and stagnant water, it wasn't hard to figure out the direction she needed to go as long as she wasn't cut off by zombies again. In the distance, random gunfire popped, which meant either her group had entered the city, or a different one was already in hiding.

Renee racked her brain as she tried to recall how to get to the baseball stadium from the harbor. Oriole Park, where the Baltimore Orioles played, was only a couple of blocks away, past the Baltimore Convention Center. Her chin tilted to the sky. It was growing darker by the minute. She dashed down the street to get closer to the inner harbor to help herself get her bearings and she spotted *him* again. The tall, intimidating man.

She'd spotted him on the roofs as she ran and near the building's alleyway. Each time, he appeared to be staring at her, which made her even more frightened. There were horror stories of people kidnapping others to satisfy their carnal cravings, but something still felt *off* about him. Renee wanted to slow down and get a better look at him but understood it would only bring trouble, so she kept evading him as best she could.

Exhausted, she pressed herself against the brick wall of a towering apartment building and tried to catch her breath. She shuddered when she spotted a few zombies zoom past her, chasing one of the scavengers that had teamed up with her group prior to entering the city. Shit. That meant her group was probably being massacred.

You can't keep up this pace, princess. Pick a spot and hunker down until things calm, her brother told her.

Iris was right. She told Mark it was too risky. Even when he argued, the scouts had seen nothing. Now both of them are going to die... or maybe they are already dead, she replied.

A scream bounced off the buildings to emphasize her point. The somewhat metallic sound of the scream, because her implant battery was low, did nothing to make her feel safer, even if it did mean there were other humans. When she'd first started hearing environmental sounds as a child it frightened her, but surprisingly her brain quickly adjusted to them. Ambient sounds faded into the background, and she mostly ignored them, the way others could ignore a dog barking. But voices - no. That was the main purpose for her implants. The ability to speak and be spoken to. Communication. At the moment, she didn't want to hear any human sounds, words, or utterances, especially from those screaming out.

The only reason they'd been dumb enough to enter the city was for needed supplies. She didn't believe there was a zombie-free zone and hoping there would be was nonsense, but after all her failures, she wanted to get one thing right, so she took a risk, knowing it was probably taunting death.

Renee hadn't told anyone, but once her group got closer to Nantucket, she was going to leave because she had unfinished business. There were many large groups of zombies. Initially, when everything hit the fan, it hadn't been like that, but over the years, they seemed to group together for reasons unknown to the surviving humans. If a horde found your encampment, surviving was almost impossible. No one could figure out when the hordes actually began to grow in number or why it continued, but there were upsides to the changing dynamics. Humans spotted groups of them much more quickly, allowing themselves a chance to escape.

Despite her cowardice, Renee didn't want to escape. Not exactly. She didn't want to fight them herself since she abhorred violence and death, but she *did* want to watch the undead and try to find a weakness or discover *something* that would help humans win this war. Because that's what it was. A war to the death but not for land, money or resources - it was a war to live.

You're not made for vengeance. You don't even have a plan. Her brother said close to her ear as she panted.

She hoped when she found information that could destroy the zombies, they would be in larger groups so they could be decimated en masse, giving humans a real chance at mending the world. She hadn't found the right group of people, but she never gave up. She wanted to find others who wanted to use whatever leverage they had against the zombies; the longer she searched, the better her chances of finding other people with a similar mission. It was obvious fighting the undead in small groups or with weapons wasn't dwindling the numbers fast enough, and if humans didn't come up with something else and soon, they were all doomed.

That still isn't a plan, Renny.

Liam, stop! I don't need this right now. I'm not a fighter, a scientist, or a doctor or anything that would be useful to come up with a smart plan on how to fix everything. Renee balled her hands into fists. *But because of my disability, I pay attention. More than most people. I might see or hear something that would really change things. I know Mom wouldn't think I could make a difference, but I want to believe someone could, and so, why not me? What if it's like that old book I read?*

Not The War of the Worlds again... Liam grumbled.

It could *be something like that! Maybe not a disease, since I think that's what they have, but maybe a virus? I think that's kind of like a disease, but different.*

I think you should be more worried about you right now. Liam's voice grew soft as the thundering of feet thudded towards her.

Renee gritted her teeth and forced her body to move again. Dead. They were all going to die. Or worse, history was about to repeat itself for the thirteenth time, she'd be without a group... again. She rounded a building and almost stopped when she spotted the same man from earlier, the one she'd been catching glimpses of as she tried to traverse what was left of the once great city of Baltimore, Maryland. Only this time, there was enough light for her to realize he wasn't alive. Although he wasn't disheveled or stunk like many of the other zombies. Even running, Renee spotted his alabaster skin that was almost translucent, showing the visible veins and arteries beneath and the strange washed-out irises all the undead seemed to have.

The hungry, animalistic sounds grew closer. She stopped staring and picked up her pace. Damn it, there were broken-down cars, scrap, and signs that had fallen blocking her path. Her only choice was to pass the man - no zombie - who had been following her. For a split second, her mind wandered to what that might mean, since zombies didn't seem to pay attention and strategically follow prey. Unless he moved, she would be just out of arm's reach.

The cool breeze picked up and citrus filled her nostrils again. Pleasant, considering it might be one of her last moments. The undead were on her heels. Squinting her eyes, she focused and pushed her legs harder. Sweat dampened her back even with the mild temperatures.

Shit. Shit. Just as she was about to pass the man, he reached out. The tips of his pale fingers grazed against her sleeve. She almost peed her pants in relief, understanding he must have been one of the slow ones.

An upscale, tall hotel loomed to the left of her as her feet thudded against the concrete. Surprised to find Mark fighting two zombies about fifteen feet away, his presence confirmed her group was there. Seconds later, Tom, one of the militant people who had joined them a few months ago, sent a battery of shots toward zombies seeming to have appeared out of nowhere.

Renee shuddered from the sounds that were loud enough she felt them as pops in her chest. Her steps slowed, and she risked a quick glance behind her. She was being pursued, but not by the numbers of undead like she anticipated. The sound of their steps was less like thunder and more like people rushing to enter an amusement park when it first opened. Stupidly, her mind recollected she'd only ever been to two theme parks before all this happened.

Continuing forward but staring back, her steps were erratic as she gasped for breath. Her entire frame shook as she struggled to put one foot in front of the other, forcing herself to go toward danger instead of her typical behavior to run the other way. She couldn't let herself shut down or run away, otherwise nothing would change and she would once again be alone.

Her fingernails dug into her palm when the tall man - no zombie - rounded the building like he was taking a stroll. Immune to the sounds of battle, overwhelming stench, and violence around him, his gaze immediately locked on her. He remembered she'd run past him? But only the fast zombies seemed to have any sort of memory, although it wasn't anything substantial from what she'd learned over the years. If someone evaded them long enough, they would forget or be distracted by fresh prey.

Mark screamed. Renee lost her balance and stumbled. More gunfire and then Tom cried out. Her conscience told her to turn and try to help, but logic said they were already dead and even though she disliked Mark, no one ever deserved what happened when a group of undead got a hold of someone.

They're all dead... again.

Dead.

I'm alone.

Renee took in her surroundings as her heart threatened to beat itself out of her chest. Had to move, but exhaustion made her lethargic and her movements even more sluggish. The group around the tall zombie had reduced its speed to a shuffle as the smaller horde moved in her direction. Her brain couldn't process the information; what was happening didn't make sense because some of them had been the fast zombies, they never approached their prey slowly, and she couldn't make sense of where they all came from so suddenly.

Her head snapped to where Mark and Tom had been. She forced the acidic lump in her throat down. She knew they were dead, but... they had been reduced to pieces that the undead fought over, paying her no attention.

She veered to the left, focused on the double doors when she heard a guttural cry from behind her and feet slapping the pavement.

Run! Her brother's voice called out.

Broken out of her panic, she felt energized and took off toward the hotel. Just as she lifted her foot to clear the curb, she slipped and fell against it, cracking the left side of her head against the concrete. She cried out but only caught the beginning of her shriek because the sound cut out, signaling that she'd damaged her last implant.

Chapter 5

Renee's eyes opened, and she saw the morning sky. The sounds of animals disturbed her sleep. She couldn't remember where her group was, but it sounded and smelled like an animal enclosure. She pushed herself up and almost gagged.

All around her were hundreds, perhaps thousands, of zombies feasting on carcasses and tearing pieces of people or large animals. Her eyes darted around. She had to get out of wherever she was before they realized she wasn't dead. Her throat tightened, because her entire group was dead... again. The hazy memory of Mark and Tom... and that meant Iris was gone too. The last thing she remembered clearly was running and hitting her head, then she entered a hotel and hid. Maybe that hadn't happened. Maybe she'd been out on the street the entire time.

There were feral growls and grunts all around her as the horde fought and shoved one another for meat. How long had she been there? As she peered around, she realized they were eating any human remains they could sink their decaying teeth into. They'd run out of prey. Shit. She *had* to get out of there. No way could she outrun them all.

In the distance, a thunderous growl echoed off the buildings. The sheer volume of it sent vibrations through her chest. All the undead stopped and became silent as attention turned to the city square. With sure, almost graceful strides the tall, dark-haired zombie she'd seen chasing her walked toward the center of the horde. The rest of the undead appeared to be bowing as he neared.

What the hell?

There was a zombie king?

Renee was certain humans weren't aware because if they had been, then they might have changed their tactics.

A willowy blonde woman trailed behind him. She was definitely a zombie. A part of her shoulder was missing, yet she seemed to be taking in her surroundings, observing the comings and goings of the horde around her. Renee swallowed when the female zombie's bloodshot, pale blue irises locked on her. The woman might be a zombie, but she knew Renee wasn't dead from the intelligence shining in those terrifying eyes.

Crap. No choice but to run. With a quick scan around her, she found one alley clear. Some dead littered the ground, but it was a straight shot. If she made it up the fence before they got to her, she might live for another day. Renee jumped to her feet and used the element of surprise to bolt. Pure luck made her steps confident and sure, enabling her to jump over several of the dead. The speed and agility with which she ran shocked Renee, she never realized she possessed such skill. She'd cleared the horde and was down the alley, lacing her fingers into the chain-link fence as she scrambled up. She was going to make it!

Rough hands seized her from behind and slammed her onto the pavement. Her eyes widened when she peered into the face of the zombie king, his bloodshot, amber irises lit with fury. Now seeing him close up the veins and arteries stood out even more against the deathly pallor of his skin. So dead. She was so dead. He bared his teeth at her before he growled and turned away. The hell?

"Why would you do that?" The blonde zombie appeared in Renee's view.

"What?"

"He doesn't like when we run. Get up. Don't do that again." Fear filled the zombie's pale eyes as she put her hand out to Renee.

Hesitantly, Renee accepted her hand. Was a zombie helping her? Wait. A zombie talked to her? Her lips were ruby red. At first, Renee thought it was blood but then she realized the blonde, willowy zombie was wearing lipstick.

"You *don't* want to be punished," she whispered to Renee, as she wrapped her fingers around Renee's arm, and led her back to the horde.

Renee shook her head and tried to pull away.

"*Stop*. Stay with me and do what I tell you if you want to survive." She hissed at Renee.

She stopped fighting and let the zombie with the red lipstick lead them toward the horde. Renee was surprised she had no trouble hearing the quieter words the female had spoken. The horde was on the move now. The more zombies that passed, the sicker Renee felt. She'd underestimated their numbers. Was all of humanity zombies now? Zombies walked by in all stages of decay. Those who led the horde, she found it difficult to tell if they were dead at all. Some, like the female zombie who had a hold of Renee, had only one visible injury, the rest of their body in seemingly pristine condition. As those who walked by her grew in number, the damage to their bodies worsened. They stood waiting for what seemed like hours. Finally, when the zombies seemed like nothing more than dried-up bags of decay that slowly shuffled by, only then did the blonde let up on the pressure on her arm but didn't let go.

"Follow me."

They joined the ranks and padded along keeping pace. Renee was thirsty and wanted to ask for water but knew she was lucky to be alive, so she opted to say nothing. They walked for hours in the sun, away from Baltimore. She thought maybe they were headed north because the air seemed slightly cooler but it was hard to tell with the sun beating down. Occasionally, one of the rotting zombies would fall, but the horde kept moving.

"Why did you help me?" Renee whispered.

"I didn't help you. I'm doing what I was told," she snapped with annoyance.

"Are you like them?"

The blonde's head turned in her direction, her brow furrowed.

"I just meant... because," Renee pointed to her shoulder, where a chunk had been torn off and left an uneven indentation. The blue floral printed off-the-shoulder dress contrasted with her stark skin.

The blonde scowled and stared ahead. "I guess. My boyfriend did that to me. Now, this is my life."

"But you aren't the same as the others. You seem... I don't know - alive?" Renee didn't want to make her angry, yet everything since she'd woken up didn't seem to make any sense.

"Do I look like I'm alive? Would I be here if I was alive?" The bitterness in her tone wasn't lost on Renee.

"Okay, but how can you talk when they can't?"

The blonde rolled her eyes. "You're just full of questions, aren't you?" She flipped her pretty, clean-looking hair behind her.

Renee shrugged and noticed a twinge of pain in her neck. She picked up a dirty lock of her own brown hair and wondered how a zombie could be cleaner than her. The fact she couldn't remember the last time she bathed wasn't a good sign.

"Just do what you're told, and you might survive this existence."

"Can I ask one more thing? I swear it will be my last question for a while." Renee was thrilled to not only have someone to speak with but also, she recognized she didn't have to stare at their lips the entire time to understand what they were saying.

Her face tightened with annoyance. "What?"

"What's your name?"

They stopped. The blonde seemed surprised by her question.

"You want to know my name?"

"Yeah, why wouldn't I?"

"You'd think you would want to know..." She let out a long breath. "It's Brie."

"Thanks for saving me, Brie."

Brie's lips pinched together like she wanted to say something, but then her head snapped toward the horde, and she stared for a long time. "We need to catch up to the chosen."

"The who?"

"You said no more questions," Brie reminded her. "Hold my hand, so I don't lose you in the horde."

Renee's mouth dropped open. "You actually call them 'the horde'?"

Brie didn't answer. Instead, she tugged Renee's arm until they were speeding through the mass of the undead. Renee didn't know how Brie navigated them so easily or why it was so easy to keep up with her. Almost proud of herself until the sight in front of her made her double over and puke.

It was the fast zombies. They'd attacked a small encampment of people ahead of the slower horde members. The screams rippled through her. She considered tearing out her cochlear implants to make them stop. Brie's hand clutched hers. Renee flicked her eyes at Brie and stopped breathing. The hunger she must have felt in that moment made her face sharp. Renee plucked her hand from Brie's as a low, menacing sound came from her. Brie flashed her teeth and glanced to the right.

The zombie king stood alone, perched on a roof, surveying the madness. His stance was powerful and proud. It disgusted her. He declined his head, and Brie took off into the massacre. Renee didn't know what to do. She wanted to run again, but where would she go? The horde approached from behind. Renee was surrounded by undead, but for unknown reasons, they hadn't attacked her or tried to eat her.

She sensed the king's gaze. It made her entire body tingle and her stomach uneasy. When Brie tore off a man's arms, Renee turned and glared at the bastard who watched his mindless monsters devouring another group of victims. To hell with it. Maybe she'd die a horrible death, but at least she'd try to take him down with her.

Renee stalked toward the building he was on and climbed the fire escape. When she reached the top, his hand waited for hers, she let go of the fire escape and almost fell. Why would he help a human who he must have known wanted to kill him? Instead, he hauled her up to the roof. Panting, she glared at him again. A thousand things ran through her mind. The most paramount was how stupid she'd been racing there without a weapon.

"Does this mean you're done running?" His deep voice made her flush.

She hadn't expected him to have such a sensual and appealing voice. It made sense he'd be able to talk like Brie and she'd be able to understand him. After all, he seemed to be the horde's king, but a rich, sexy voice? No.

"You're a monster." Her own voice sounded different to her now. It was more… natural? It was hard to tell, she didn't have much of a reference of what was "normal." Renee couldn't quite put her finger on it but reflecting on her conversation with Brie, it was almost like she could perceive tonal shifts easier. Was something wrong with her last implant?

He tilted his head to the side with a smirk. Even with his gaunt cheeks he was still attractive.

"You're horrible. I came here to kill you!" Sweet Jesus, what was wrong with her? Everything she'd said made her sound like the biggest idiot.

"You have no weapons. Do you mean to strangle me?" Zombies weren't supposed to have voices that made your heart speed up. She wasn't sure if it was because it sounded so smooth, like silk brushing against skin, or because it was baritone. Which was easier for her to *feel* his voice. Typically to pick up on subtle vocal shifts, Renee relied on body language to give her hints. But she hadn't missed the almost teasing tone in his words.

He also seemed to have some level of logical cognition. How did this zombie make sense of her plan of attack, or rather, lack thereof?

Renee planted her feet and attempted to appear fierce. "If I have to."

He stepped back and opened his arms in invitation. Covered from head to toe in black, which made sense since he was basically death incarnate if he and his horde showed up in your town. The black t-shirt he wore clung to his muscular torso and distracted her.

Shit. Would she really do this? Could she? It didn't matter, she had to try. She leapt at him and wrapped her hands around his throat. He grinned at her antics. It wasn't until seconds later that she realized her legs were around his waist. That wasn't right. He should've fallen over and been gasping. She squeezed. He smiled. Shit. The undead weren't supposed to have inviting smiles.

She squeezed harder. He laughed. He actually fucking laughed in her face. Crestfallen, she relaxed her hands. The vibrations from his laughter reverberated against her and tickled. It was at that moment she realized one of his arms was around her waist, and the other was under her ass, supporting her weight. Blood made her neck and face hot. She wanted to crawl inside of herself. This sonofabitch was literally the reason all the people below were dying, and she was wrapped around him like a lover. She yanked herself off him.

Stumbling to stay upright, she scanned the rooftop for something to use as a weapon. Nothing. Why hadn't he tried to kill her? Why hadn't any of them? Why had she really gone up to the roof, with no weapon, no plan?

"Why am I here?" she asked, trying to avoid glancing at him.

"I thought you meant to kill me."

"No!" She took a breath. "With you. Why am I with you? With zombies? Why haven't they attacked me?"

He stared at her a long time before he turned to the massacre down below. "They won't harm you."

That explained nothing. Renee wondered if she had a death wish because when common sense told her to shut it and not pester monsters, she only pushed until they answered her.

"Why?"

His face was impassive. "Because I told them not to."

"And they listen to you because you're their king?"

"King?" He glanced at her.

The breeze carried the sickening scent of death to her nostrils. Her mouth was so dry, she really needed a drink. Renee watched as the dark tendrils of his long hair lifted with the breeze. Why did he have such pretty hair? Another scream and the awful sound of the remaining portion of the horde reaching the settlement rushed her senses. She clasped her hands over her ears. Her entire life, all Renee wanted was to hear like ordinary people. Now in the midst of the apocalypse, she just wanted blissful silence.

She shut her eyes. She was such a coward. If she was a decent person, she'd fight him or jump down and try to save some lives. Probably pointless, but better than doing nothing. Cold hands suddenly clasped hers. The touch seemed familiar, comforting.

This was all a bad dream. She was still asleep outside the city, in her group's encampment, she would have the chance to convince the others not to go into Baltimore. She'd make them listen to her. Explain the sense of dread she had felt since they'd come within a few miles of the large metropolitan city.

Her eyes fluttered open. Bright, bloodshot, amber irises were inches from her. He was so close he could kiss her. Instead, his hands lifted hers off her ears. She couldn't hear anything anymore except her own heartbeat. His fingers slid into her hair near her ears before she felt a tug on her left side.

An odd sensation, akin to pain, of something being pulled out of her head made her stiffen, but she didn't move. After a few seconds, it hurt, almost burned, but it wasn't like any other pain she'd experienced before, and she was too terrified to react. The sharp pain faded as she stared, transfixed by his sharp attractive features.

"You don't need this anymore," he said in a low voice.

Her eyes flicked to his hands. It was her cochlear implant. Not only the transmitter but also the receiver, antenna, and electrode array that had been implanted. The external parts were severely damaged, probably from when she hit her head.

"Why would you do that? I can't hear without..." Her brows pinched because she'd heard every word, she herself had just said. "How?"

He put the cochlear implant in her hand and turned to the side of the building she'd climbed up and stood at the edge of the roof. A heartbeat later, he was gone.

She ran to the edge. He'd jumped down like it was nothing and barked orders at the horde. They all cowered in front of him. She slid the implant into her pocket and climbed down via the fire escape, more confused than she'd already been. Still paranoid, she eyed the horde as she maneuvered through them, but followed the king to see what was happening.

Renee covered her mouth and nose as she approached the slaughtered encampment. Unlike when she'd woken up, the beasts weren't fighting over the scraps. They seemed scared and huddled together. Once she reached the clearing, she understood why.

Brie stood next to the king as two of the zombies were dragged forward. Renee could tell by the captives' fluid movements they were recently made, they moved like the swift zombies she'd seen around. Other fast zombies held them. The king stalked toward the prisoners and their guards, making gestures that made no sense to her along with weird guttural noises. The mass twitched around her.

The king roared before pulling the first captive zombie up and out of the others' hands, ripping it in half above his head. The monster's entrails poured over him and onto the ground like rain. Renee covered her mouth and chewed back her vomit. More animalistic sounds were heard before he threw one half to the horde where they snatched it without delay.

Renee's eyes widened when she understood it wasn't actually dead yet. He'd kept the top half, and the head hissed at him in defiance. Wasting no time, he ripped the head off and tossed the torso to the horde. She stumbled back from all the gore and violence she witnessed.

He motioned for the other zombie to be brought forward and showed it the head. Weirdly, it seemed to bother the captured creature. Was it like Brie and had the ability to talk as well? Renee speculated if the creatures knew each other. The king handed the head to Brie. She held it up proudly, and the horde cheered. Well, it sounded like a distorted cheer. The quick zombies dragged the remaining prisoner elsewhere.

Any remaining humans were screwed. Totally screwed. Renee didn't know what the hell that display was, but somehow, since the original zombies showed up, they had evolved and become intelligent or smart enough, anyway. There was some crazy, barbaric shit going on, and she was smack dab in the middle of it.

As disgusting as it was, they'd set up camp in the small makeshift town that'd been there before the horde decimated it. The shamblers were somewhere on the outskirts, along with the creepy yet nimble zombies that seemed to be on patrol. The swift dexterous zombies that appeared more like monsters than animated corpses were highly feared. Unlike the shamblers, the slower zombies of the group, the quick ones seemed to understand humans - at least their movements - and hunted people down like rabid animals chasing their prey.

In the center of the horde was a mix of creatures. Some seemed more alert and thoughtful, while others were not. Some zombies moved with purpose, gathering items of use or starting fires. Renee's situation was awful but she couldn't help but be fascinated. All kinds of subtle forms of communication surrounded her. She swore they talked to each other, just not using words. Before she got her implants, she'd used American sign language, so she would have recognized it. But they weren't using signs to communicate. It was actually a series of facial expressions, hand gestures, and guttural sounds.

She used the time she was left alone to search for water. When she found a case of it, she sat and drank at least four bottles before propping herself against a wall. She was so tired. Maybe she could sleep. He'd said they wouldn't hurt her because he told them not to, but why? It didn't matter. Nothing made sense anymore. Until she figured out a way to escape, she'd have to play along.

On the rooftop, she was convinced she was useless and a coward, but now she had a purpose. Renee was positive that none of the human survivors had a clue about how the undead actually operated. If she gathered enough information, then the surviving humans could finally turn the tables on the monsters that had devoured most of the world.

His high cheekbones, amber eyes with long lashes, and dark hair filled her mind. She hated him. He led the army of the undead, and they were terrified of him. So, he called the shots, which meant he was responsible for the mayhem and death that'd ruined her life and everyone else's. Lucky for her, he didn't seem interested in eating her or letting anyone else do it, either. Not sure why, but she would definitely use his "no Renee buffet" mentality to get close to him. She would get more info, or possibly kill him herself, as long as she wasn't so dumb in her next attempt. Her eyes slid closed, still thinking about the king.

Chapter 6

"Get up. You can't sleep here. It's not safe." Brie's voice cut into her dream; she was eating ice cream by the ocean.

"What?" Renee straightened and peered around, still alone in the shed she'd claimed for herself. She frowned at Brie's bloody hands that clutched her arm. Renee smacked Brie's arm aside and frowned at the smears of blood that stained the fabric of her sleeve now. "I'm fine."

"I wasn't asking." Brie hauled her up.

"Wait. I want to take some water." She loaded her arms with bottles.

Brie peered at her like she was crazy. Her lipstick was back on, and there wasn't any blood on her face. She'd changed clothes, too. Now she wore a pretty dress that hung to her knees covered in roses. So weird.

"Yeah, I get it. You don't get dehydrated, but I do."

Brie huffed and led her outside. It was still night, and the undead roamed everywhere. Brie led her through the denser part of the sea of monsters until they arrived at a set of three buildings and the faster zombies milled around. Brie shoved her forward. Renee gave her the stink eye but trudged to the front of what appeared to be a tiny house.

"Go. He wants to talk to you. I can't believe you pissed him off twice in one day. It's like you want to actually die."

Renee was about to open her mouth when Brie marched past her and opened the door. Biting her tongue, Renee entered the candlelit room behind Brie. The bastard sat in an old wingback chair like the king he was and glanced at Brie.

"She was asleep in one of the buildings," Brie explained.

"Do better tomorrow. Get out."

Brie shot her a warning look and closed the door. Renee peered around the room. No windows. It appeared to be built after the uprising. There was a door to the right that probably led to another tiny room. She straightened her back and put her bottles of water on the one table in the room, and refused to look at him. Nervous about being trapped with him, she opened the water and chugged it.

"What's your name?"

His question caught her off guard. From the way Brie acted, she didn't think anyone had names in the horde. Her first thought was to lie, but what did it matter?

"Renee. Why?"

"Renee."

Her stomach fluttered at the sound of her name on his lips. "Yeah, why do you want to know my name?"

"Do you remember what happened to you?"

She turned toward him. Such a weird question, and she wasn't sure what he meant by it. Perhaps he meant after she'd fallen and hit her head, but she'd been stuck with his horde the entire time. He was still dressed in black, but the clothes seemed newer because they weren't covered in bits and pieces of flesh and gore.

"Is Brie your queen?"

"What?" He was the one to seem surprised this time.

"You gave her the zombie's head, and she held it up. She keeps showing up and keeping tabs on me."

"What is your obsession with court titles?"

She tried to resist staring at his lips when he spoke but, old habits. Lip reading was how she got by before and during the apocalypse. Sure, her cochlear implants were helpful, but she'd take advantage of whatever was visible to her to help piece together context and tone. His lips were smooth, not chapped like hers or most of the other humans she'd been around.

"It's not an obsession. There's a very obvious hierarchy here. Is it more of a tribe thing? Are you a chief?"

"No. That's nonsense."

"So is Brie your queen?"

His eyes narrowed. "Would it bother you if she was?"

Renee straightened. "No. I don't care. I'm trying to understand my situation."

He raised an eyebrow.

She threw her hands up in frustration. "I don't know what you want. I don't know why I'm here or why you don't want them to eat me. I'm not any different from anyone else that used to live in this small town your horde just wiped off the map." She swallowed hard. "I'm not stupid enough to think I can get away. There are too many of you, and I'm trying to figure out how to handle things."

He stood and appeared in front of her so quickly she stumbled back. His hand circled her waist, preventing her from falling. When their eyes locked, it was like everything around them faded except for the sounds of their heartbeats. Her eyes widened. His heart thundered against hers. Zombies were dead. They didn't have heartbeats. She was questioning her own sanity.

Renee studied his handsome face. Thin, almost emaciated, with sharp cheekbones and a strong jawline. His skin was so pale it was almost translucent, and his blue and purple veins prominently stood out against the alabaster white tone of skin. The shadows under his eyes accented the bright goldish color. His long, dark hair fell around his face and hung past his shoulders. It took all of her willpower not to reach out and trace his jaw or brush his hair back.

"You can't escape. You're only safe with me." His voice caressed her, making her lightheaded.

"Why do you want me safe?"

"I..." His face twisted before he frowned, releasing her as he sank back into the chair.

Renee put her hands on the wooden table to steady herself. She couldn't let him get that close again. An odd keening noise drifted from the door to the right, causing the king's eyes to flick to the door then back to her.

"Don't move," he commanded, and went into the room.

Renee considered leaving but remembered the creature he'd ripped in half, so she drank another bottle of water to occupy her mind. Damn, she was getting hungry too. She hadn't eaten in days and water could only sustain a person for so long before food was necessary.

Whimpering sounds and what could only be described as begging came from behind the door. She padded closer and listened to what was more growling and begging. What twisted shit was happening in there? Heavy footsteps neared the other side of the door. Renee dashed back to the table right before the king walked out and sat in his chair again.

"Um, so I need to eat something. It's been a few days, and if you want me to keep marching with everyone else, I have to eat."

"You need to eat?"

"That's what I said. Can I go search for food? It's not like anyone else is gonna want what I do."

He remained silent and stared at her before grumbling and stomping to the door and leaving. *Unbelievable.* She was his prisoner, for some reason he wouldn't tell her, and now he was irritated because she needed food, unlike the rest of his minions. Renee pulled out the rickety wooden chair at the table and sank down.

Minutes passed and more whimpering seeped into the room. She should sit and wait. She probably didn't want to know what was in the next room, however curiosity got the better of her, and she ended up tiptoeing to the door. Her fingers wrapped around the knob and she tried turning it. Unlocked. *Last chance,* she told herself.

Renny, you don't want to see that. Her brother's ghostly voice warned her.

No. She had to see. It could be a secret that would help humanity get an edge over the monsters.

She turned the knob and pushed open the creaking door. Oh shit. The zombie that'd been dragged off from the public display of violence was in the room. All of its limbs were gone, and it floundered around on the floor, trying to get to the other head the king had ripped off, the one Brie had held up. Shit. Shit. She shouldn't have opened the door. The blood rushing in her ears masked all sounds.

Renee backed up and hit something solid and cold behind her. Damn it. His arm wrapped around her waist before reaching out and slamming the door in her face. He spun her around and bared his teeth. She swore his irises glowed brighter, causing her to shrink back. He was terrifying like that, and looked every bit the monster he was.

"I told you not to move," he said through gritted teeth. "You don't listen."

"I'm not a part of your mindless horde. You don't control me!"

He laughed in her face. A genuine laugh, and it made him even more handsome than he already was which pissed her off. She shoved against him. His fingers threaded in her hair before he yanked her head back as his gaze sharpened.

"I *own* you. You want to know why you're here? Because you're *mine*."

"What the hell are you talking about?"

"You're mine, and you'll do as you're told, or I'll make you."

She shoved him harder, making him laugh again at her attempts.

"I hate you!"

"Do you plan to kill me again? When I brought you food? And something to sleep on?" His voice was filled with mirth.

"Screw you. I'll starve."

"Then you'll die. You don't want to die," he said confidently.

"Fuck you. I'd rather die than be owned by *you*."

He bared his teeth at her again. Good, she was glad she pissed him off. He brought his face closer to hers, so close their lips almost touched.

"You need to eat." His tone was gentle again. "Then sleep. You're safe with me."

Her stomach tightened at the timbre of his voice and his words. How could she be safe with a zombie king who'd just told her he owned her? He let her go and returned to the chair but didn't take his eyes off her. On the table was more water and what seemed like raw meat. Eww. Near the table on the floor were pillows, a sleeping bag, and a blanket.

Renee stared at the meat. "What is this?"

"Dog."

Once again chewing back vomit, she glared at him.

"It's the best I could do under the circumstances. Eat or starve."

She slumped into the chair. "You could've cooked it."

As horrendous as the idea of eating a dog was, it wouldn't be the first time. Things had been bad the last couple of years, sometimes it came down to eat or die. However, when she had eaten dog before, it was at least cooked.

"You know, if you were going to take someone captive who wasn't accustomed to living like your horde, you should've planned better. I don't eat raw meat."

"It's not raw. Touch it."

Renee grimaced but touched it. It was warm, almost hot. Okay, extremely rare meat was also gross. But what did a zombie know, right? Her stomach grumbled. She sighed and picked it up. The scent of the almost raw meat made her stomach growl. She'd get through it tonight, and then they were going to have a talk. Trapped by an insane zombie king who claimed she was his, how in the hell was she going to get out of this?

Chapter 7

Sometime later, though it was impossible to tell without windows, Renee stirred and woke to the pitiful sounds coming from the room with the dismembered torso. She propped up on her elbows and peered around the space in the darkness. Weird there weren't any candles lit, and she saw everything. Her night vision hadn't been great before. She could see better than most in her most recent group, but she figured it was because her other senses compensated for her loss of hearing during most of her early childhood.

She sat up and pulled her knees to her chest, unable to tune out the whimpers now. Renee rubbed her dry eyes and reached for a bottle of water, emptying it down her throat. She must've been way more dehydrated than she thought. Why would the king mutilate one of his own kind? The faster zombies seemed to be more like him than the slower, decaying shamblers.

Her eyes darted to the wingback chair, and she inhaled sharply. In the darkness, his odd irises glowed. Before, outside, she thought it was a trick of the light, or perhaps because she was slightly delirious. But in the pitch-black room, there was no denying it. His fucking goldish eyes glowed and were locked on her.

Although Brie showed emotion, it had only been anger or irritation. He often showed anger, yet mixed in laughter or sarcasm. No other zombies behaved like him. When he assured Renee of her safety, his tone reminded her of a love interest from her books. Renee flattened her lips and stood.

"Whatever you're thinking, don't. Just go back to bed." His posture was still proud, but his voice was weary.

"Why don't you sleep?"

"So, you can try to escape?"

She crossed her arms across her chest. "That's not what I meant. But yeah, if I woke up, and you were asleep, I'd try to run."

"Where would you go that I wouldn't find you?"

She swore his voice sounded almost playful, but she ignored it. No way would she actually tell him her plans, but Renee wasn't a good liar either. She decided to keep it vague and somewhat truthful but with no details. "I don't know. I guess I'd try to find a stronghold or some military base. Help gather enough weapons to take as many of you out as we could."

Her mind drifted to every military group she had been near or observed. As safe from the zombies as she might be with soldiers, there was a tradeoff. Instead of fearing zombies would tear her apart, she would be paranoid that the other humans would recognize she was useless and use her as bait or toss her out of the group or safe haven. Many of the people who still survived were hardened, distorted versions of themselves. They were almost as terrifying as the zombies.

He sighed. "Your world is dead. This is all there is now. Stop trying to escape, it will not be like you want or remember."

"Because you and your horde destroyed it! You think I don't know that things are shit?" She stomped over to him. "Why are you so different?"

He cocked his head to the side. "Different?"

"Are you their king because you can talk? Think? Have glowing eyes?"

"I'm not as different from the others as you believe."

"Prove it."

He stood and pressed his body against hers. She squared her shoulders, not allowing him to keep bullying her. For whatever insane reason, he wanted her around, so that meant he wouldn't kill her - yet. His fingers dug into her arm before he dragged her to the tiny house's door and opened it.

Renee's mouth dropped open when she gazed outside. The horde stared at their king and his captive expectantly. So many of them had glowing irises like him, including Brie. Brie's expression hardened the longer she stared at them in the doorway.

The king leaned down and whispered in Renee's ear, "Our eyes glow when we've fed. The reason humans can't see us in the dark is because I send in the starving first. By the time my stronger creatures reach them, it's already too late."

Renee pushed against him for all the good it did. She hated his words. His logic. He was too strategic for a zombie. She detested how her heart skipped a beat with his mouth so close to her ear. More than that, she hated the realization that came from his words. Without fully understanding that night... she felt it was her fault. She had accidentally killed them all – again. Even though she'd tried to save them, she'd pushed them towards their deaths. In front of her was the fabled sea of stars, only now it was ruined and ugly.

"I hate you," she bit out.

He yanked her back inside. Another door slammed in her face. He held her against him. The coldness of him against her back strangely heated her skin.

His voice was rough when he spoke. "We are the monsters humans fear the most because they created us. We *are* them."

"You're nothing like me. You'll always be a monster," Renee's voice sounded confident, even though inside she was terrified and something else she couldn't quite identify. The tendrils of heat crept up her body and made her face hot.

He growled and shoved her to the floor on top of her sleeping bag. "You need to sleep."

"I can't sleep with that noise." She motioned toward the other room.

"Then I will silence the traitor."

Before Renee could ask what, he meant, he was in the room. The sounds of tearing flesh, sounds of moisture... and then the whimpering stopped. She closed her eyes and placed her hands over her ears. How could she hear without her implants? She rocked back and forth, her face on top of her knees, her arms wrapped around her shins, trying to think of something, anything that would calm her. Find her happy place. The problem was every happy place she'd ever had was gone. If she'd been alone, at least Liam would've comforted her but with the king around, she was on her own.

A soft touch against her back signaled it would be okay. Fingers grazed the side of her head and brushed her hair back. She exhaled. The memory was fuzzy, like most memories from before the downfall. Maybe it'd been her brother who touched her with such protectiveness before. Didn't really matter. Just remembering the gentleness, the love in their touch, was enough. Renee stopped rocking and opened her eyes.

The bastard wasn't on his throne. He crouched in front of her, studying her. She put her hands down and slid back.

"Death bothers you that much?"

She blinked. Was he being serious? Considering he killed people every day, he probably was. "Yeah. I'm not a murderer like you."

"I don't murder."

"What?" The audacity of his words floored her.

"It's survival, there's a difference. We're the superior species."

"You can't be serious."

"It's obvious. We've destroyed a better part of your world in only seven years."

"You've been around as a zombie the whole time?"

"Does it matter?"

"No. Yes. Maybe." Renee pinched her lips. Not sure why she'd asked that. "Fine, for argument's sake, you're a new-ish species who eat people. You're still a murderer because you lead them. You go from place to place and tell them what to do, who to kill. You're their king, and they follow you."

He flashed his teeth at her. It was hard not to notice how clean and perfectly white his teeth were, not decayed or gross. "I'm not their king. Stop calling me that. They follow me because I'm the strongest of us all."

Renee's back hit the wall. "Well, I don't know your name, and they follow you, so unless you tell me who you are, you're their king. That's what I will continue to call you."

"Have you ever considered how quickly we spread? How we dominated the globe before the military could form a response?" His voice was laced with bitterness.

Renee hadn't thought about any of that. When shit hit the fan, she was still in high school. At first, she and her few friends thought it was a big joke. A silly social media prank. From the rumors she heard over the years as she went from group to group, it had been a virus or sickness spread through contact. If you were bitten, you were toast. If they scratched you, you might make it, but you'd lose a limb. The way he made it sound; it couldn't just be that.

"Fools, all of them. They brought this hell upon themselves, and we'll reap the benefits. They will either submit or die." He stood and stalked to his wing backed throne.

She was so screwed. He hated humans and thought the blood-thirsty mob he led was superior and every human deserved to die. She wanted to cry but wouldn't give him the satisfaction, so she slid into the sleeping bag and turned away from him.

Chapter 8

"Get up." Brie's annoyed tone was like a sweet greeting compared to that asshole's voice.

Renee cracked her eyes open. Brie stood over her and glared, irises still glowing. Renee sat up and reached for another bottle of water.

"I said get up. You don't need that. We need to go. We're already moving."

"Okay. Okay," Renee said and stood. On the table was a beat-up backpack that wasn't there before next to her water with a few extras' bottles added. She loaded the remaining water into the backpack and strapped it on. The sun was still low, but the light hurt her eyes as she lifted her hand to shield them.

Brie huffed beside her and pressed a pair of sunglasses into her palm. "Put these on, they'll help."

"Thanks." Renee slid them on and instant relief spread through her. She didn't want to admit, as they began walking with the horde, that she looked for him. It appeared they were right in the middle of the group, but it was hard to tell, neck-deep in zombies.

Today seemed different. The horde trudged along, like yesterday, but seemed more animated. She stared when a couple of the undead actually traded shirts they'd found. They communicated with a series of gestures, grunts, and guttural noises. Yet the strangest part was she didn't feel threatened in the slightest. It was like she wasn't even there - just another day in the horde.

Renee had drunk most of her water by the time they stopped as the sun set. She should have rationed it out better. Brie hadn't said one word to her all day. Renee sensed her sour mood and knew asking the questions burning in her skull wasn't a good idea. She had to stay focused. Observe and remember everything, then figure out a way to escape. She'd yet to uncover any valuable information that would change the war with the undead, but she would keep trying.

"Come with me," Brie said and veered to the left as the rest of the horde continued forward. Her pretty rose dress flowed with her graceful steps.

Renee followed without question as they approached an old work van that only had windows in the front. The rest of the horde wandered around, appearing busy. Curious, she watched them.

"What are you doing? Get in." Brie motioned to the back door.

"In the van?"

"No, the boat. Yes, the van. This is ridiculous," Brie complained.

"I agree," Renee replied, opened the door, and stopped. *He* was in the van and took up most of it with his size. She stepped back and bumped into Brie.

"This is where you sleep tonight." Brie shoved her through the opening.

Renee almost fell into the van but stopped just in time. She shot a dirty look at Brie and climbed in. The anger in Brie's eyes as she closed the doors was unmistakable. Renee pinched her lips. This wasn't fair. She'd made a point of not asking questions so that she wouldn't annoy Brie, and she was still upset with her. Perhaps being a zombie made them moody. She sat in a tiny spot against the van doors, not bothering to look at him.

"Why am I here?"

"You need to sleep."

She jutted her chin out. "I could sleep out there with them."

"No. You can't." His words sounded like another order.

"Why?" she asked, staring at her dirty shoes.

"I already told you."

She turned her face to him. "I am *not* doing this every night."

"You'll do whatever I tell you to do. Stop acting like a child. I have more water for you." He motioned to half a case shrouded in shadow next to him.

Screw him and his water. But she *was* thirsty. She eyed it with interest.

"If you want the water, it's right there." He gestured beside him.

That would mean she'd have to move closer to him. Nope. She'd just be thirsty. Stubbornly, she turned aside. They sat like that for a long time before she yawned.

He sighed. "Are you always so stubborn?"

"Are you always a monster?"

"You're the one who reminded me you need water and food. If you don't want it, I won't bother to have it scavenged for you."

She turned to face him. *That* interested her, and it might change everything. "You had someone get it for you?"

"No, I had someone get it for *you*."

Fighting with herself, she had wanted to continue defying him because it made him angry. If he was mad at her, she had a reason to continually avoid him. However, she had reasons for going along with this insanity that could hopefully help save her fellow humans. Zombies controlled by a king were one thing. The possibility they communicated on their own meant so much more, but if what he told her was true...

Renee scooted toward the middle of the empty van just across from him. She picked up the bottles of water and put all but one of them in her backpack. She downed the one she'd left out, then shifted her attention to what was soft under her. It was the sleeping bag she'd slept in the night before.

"You told them to find water, and they did?"

"According to you, they do anything I tell them because I'm their king."

"I didn't know zombies could scavenge for things like people," she said honestly.

"Not all of them can. Some are more useful than others."

Useful. Renee had to push back the urge to berate him for his choice of words. Maybe they were mindless murdering machines, but he was their king and shouldn't talk about them like that. Well, no, she wasn't entirely positive they were mindless. At least a good portion of them weren't. But either way, he was being a dick.

"Do you hunger?"

That was a weird way to ask her if she wanted to eat. She shook her head, even though she was starving, she couldn't do another replay of last night. Not yet, anyway.

"You need to sleep. We have many miles to cover tomorrow."

"Where are we going?"

"To eat more humans." His cold, glowing irises fixed on hers.

"No."

"The horde hungers and must consume. If it doesn't consume humans, it will consume itself."

Did he mean they'd eat each other? If so, that could be exactly what she needed. "Eww. They'll start eating each other?"

"They won't have a choice. It must consume." His tone was haunting. A familiar expression of loneliness covered his face. He'd been such a shit since she got into the van, but right now, he seemed to hurt as he spoke those words. It was like he wasn't talking about the horde anymore, he was talking about himself, and unlike last night, it didn't make him feel superior. It made him a monster he didn't seem to want to be.

"But if you keep traveling and eating all the humans, there won't be any left. You'll all die."

He locked those harrowing eyes on hers. "Yes."

She shook her head. Too much. They wouldn't stop until everyone was dead. The entire plan was to eat until they died. Her eyes burned, and she turned around wiggling into the sleeping bag, keeping her back to him. Why would he tell her that? She just had to hang on long enough until she could escape.

Chapter 9

"Wake up, princess." Brie's acidic words yanked her from her dream.

Renee couldn't remember exactly what she'd been dreaming about, but it was better than reality. In her dream, someone had held her while kissing her neck. It made her feel cherished. In real life, she'd never felt that way. Her fingers fumbled for the sunglasses. She slipped them on her face, sat up and drank a bottle of water.

Renee was *so* excited to walk in silence with someone who didn't like her for miles and miles, then witness another massacre. And to top off her evening, she was sure she would have another horrible encounter with the king of the undead. Yeah, she was *real* motivated to get her day started.

"Get out of the van, now," Brie said as she slipped her red lipstick into the top of her bra. Good idea, considering she didn't carry a bag or anything.

"Okay. Okay. I'm coming. Can I please talk to you today?"

"No." Brie led them into the horde.

"I'm really trying, Brie. I don't want you to hate me. I get it, you're mad because your king is making you babysit me, but you don't have to. I won't run. You can go be with him and do whatever your queenly duties are."

Brie stopped and stared at her like she was crazy. The horde shuffled past, unfazed by how they'd stopped.

"What the fuck did you just say?"

"I said you don't need to babysit me and-"

"Stop. It was rhetorical. I can't believe this."

Brie's raised voice only caused a few glances from the more coordinated zombies that shuffled by.

"Are you blind, deaf, or just stupid?"

Renee straightened her shoulders. Perhaps it was her childhood trauma, but when someone said crap like that, it hit a little too close to home. "I am *not* blind or stupid!"

Brie's brow crinkled, and she flicked her eyes to the front. "I have to monitor you during the day."

"But I won't run. I said I wouldn't, and I won't."

"You wouldn't make it far, but it doesn't matter. If you try, I'm dead." Brie grabbed her forearm. "Come on, we need to catch up."

"Wait, why would you be dead? Did the king tell you that?"

"Why are you calling him that?"

"Because he's your leader."

"We don't have a title for him," Brie said dismissively. She narrowed her eyes. "Why did you call me his queen?"

"Because you're important, almost like his second in command. And you're pretty like a queen. Dressed better than the others." Renee shrugged and peeked at her own filthy clothes. The only zombies who seemed like they'd bathed in all the years she'd seen the undead were the king and Brie.

"That's because you haven't been around the other chosen." As soon as the words left her mouth, Brie's eyes widened, and she squeezed Renee's arm until it hurt. "Do not repeat that to anyone," she said in a hushed tone.

Renee covered Brie's hand with hers. "I want to be your friend, Brie. I won't say anything, I promise. I haven't had any friends in a long time."

"You only want to be my friend because there isn't anyone else." A vulnerable expression crept over Brie's face.

"No. It just makes you befriending me potentially easier, for both of us. I was never the cool or pretty girl, but I can tell you were. Before all this, I know how things would've been. You'd be popular and make fun of cringy girls like me. It sucks, but now we're on even ground. I have a chance for a girl like you to actually see me and maybe, like me. It could be good for you too, unless I'm totally off base when I say that most of your friends weren't real friends, and I would be. You could be who you really are around me."

"Hate to disappoint, but there wasn't much to me before and now..." She shook her head. "I'm a fucking zombie. Even less interesting. Good looks no longer matter, and being pretty was all I ever had to offer."

"Maybe that's true, and it sucks, but this is also a second chance."

"How in the fuck can you say that and be so positive? Look around you."

"Because I haven't given up, and you shouldn't either."

"You can't get away. There's no escape, especially for me. I have to..." She averted her eyes.

"I know you have to keep eating people or other... things, or you'll die, right?"

Brie nodded but didn't look at Renee.

"From what I've seen, the horde eats the live prey first, preferably humans. Then they finish the scraps." Renee swallowed. "If they can't find humans, that's when they go after animals, right?"

"Yeah."

Becoming Brie's friend might speed up her plan to get all the info she needed. "Well, if there weren't so many of you, it wouldn't be such a problem. I mean, if you and I got free, we'd need to make sure there were big animals for you. Sounds tough, but it wouldn't be, not if you are hunting only for yourself."

"Are you batshit crazy? Why would you even suggest that? I'd probably end up eating you. It doesn't matter, he won't let me leave." Brie tugged on Renee's arm and started walking.

"Because you're his and have to do what he says?" Renee whispered.

Iris' words from before they entered the city crept back into her mind. *Evil leads that one. A demon controls it, demanding nothing remains but bones.* As much of an ass as the king was, she didn't believe he was evil. Arrogant and ruthless, sure, but evil? When he said they were the superior species... but last night he seemed to hate all the words that came out of his mouth.

"Something like that. He calls the shots. If you do what he says, he won't lord over you. You keep fighting him, he'll never let go."

Renee thought about her words. Perhaps Brie was trapped by him because she'd fought against him, so he kept her on a tight leash. Brie wasn't his queen as much as a prisoner, same as her. Except she was dead and Renee was still alive, for now. She considered changing tactics with the king. If she didn't push him so hard, perhaps he'd lose interest, and she could get a little more freedom, allowing her more time to plan her escape.

Chapter 10

Renee glanced around her as she tried to hide. They had found a large group of wild deer and stopped to *grab a bite*, barf. Now it was night, which meant quality time with the king.

"Come on. He's waiting." Brie had changed again. Now she was in a black skirt and floral blouse. Her long locks were braided on each side, giving her a fierce warrior look, even though no blood marred her delicate features.

Shit, not again. Begrudgingly, Renee got to her feet. Yesterday she'd been confident in her plan, but when they'd stopped in a collection of cars for yet another night, she couldn't act as if they were on friendly terms just to get more information. After a brief bout of heated words, she turned away from him, while sequestered in the same vehicle, and slept, refusing food again. Her stomach hurt from lack of food. She cracked her back and trudged after Brie. No idea what time it was, Renee noted stars lit up the sky. They'd attacked the herd of deer right after sunset. The eating, gnashing and slurping seemed to go on for hours.

"She was hiding in a building," Brie told the king as they approached him. He stood outside a tiny ramshackle of a building.

"Leave. Eat," he told her without turning around.

Brie gritted her teeth before stomping off in a huff. Renee noticed a small fire beside him. Reminding herself to be pleasant, she stepped toward him but was distracted by the smell of meat cooking in the fire. God, she was hungry. *Please, please let that be dinner.* She crept closer to the fire.

"Sit." He gestured to a log near the fire.

She plopped down, her eyes still glued to whatever was being cooked and her mouth watered. She had to stop being so stubborn when he tried to give her something, at least food-wise.

"Those are for you."

Her view drifted down and she saw bottles of water against the log. "Thanks, is that?" She glanced at the fire.

"Yes, I remembered you liked your food cooked." He moved to the fire, lifted the meat off it, and sat beside her. "Will you eat? Or are you going to be stubborn and starve?"

Her stomach growled. Damn it, her body betrayed her. "I'll eat."

With a smirk, he handed her the cooked meat. Without hesitation, she tore into it and devoured all of it in an unladylike and grossly disturbing way. She even licked her fingers like a caveman. It wasn't until she finished, she realized what she'd done and wanted to hide.

"What was that? Did I eat dog again?"

"Horse."

Shit. Not happy about that, either. She'd only eaten horse once out of desperation and vowed never to do it again because she liked horses and worried the undead would eat them all out of existence. Renee also didn't want to admit how much better she already felt. Starving herself to spite him wasn't exactly helping her.

"Your eyes are still glowing, but you're not bloody. It's like you bathed. How do you stay so clean?"

"Why can't I bathe?"

"Why would you? You're dead and -" She stopped when he seemed offended. "You bathe?"

"Your perception of what we are and what we do is very skewed."

"Sorry, it's not like humans have had time to learn about your culture." She tried to keep the sarcasm from her tone.

He glanced at the dark sky above them. "I guess that's true. Some choose to bathe."

Renee drank another water and thought about what he said. They chose to bathe, which meant at least some of them were aware of hygiene or cared about their appearance, which didn't make any sense. Other than Brie, she'd seen very few clean undead in his horde. Perhaps it was the chosen Brie mentioned. She had to keep him talking.

"So, this is it?"

"What?"

"We just walk from place to place and eat everything until there's nothing left and then turn on each other?"

He leveled his gaze at her. "We?"

"Well, like you said, I can't get away because," she cleared her throat, hating the words. "I'm yours, so that means, I guess I'm along for the ride."

"I guess it does." He almost smiled at her.

"And you're gonna keep getting me food and water? Making me sleep with you?" After the words left her mouth, she wished she hadn't said them. He never slept, as far as she knew. And when she slept, at some point in the night, he'd leave. So, she'd wake up with Brie barking at her instead.

"Sleep with me?" A wolfish grin played on his lips, making it hard for her to breathe.

"I meant... Damn it. I hate you. I can't ever say things right around you." She averted her eyes.

His icy fingers touched her chin and turned her face toward him. She meant to look elsewhere, but once her eyes locked on his, everything else blurred.

"Why do you think that is?" his voice sounded husky, and god, it was sexy.

"Probably because I'm afraid of you."

"You should fear me, but you don't." His grin turned into a smile.

Her heart skipped at his larger-than-life smile. "Of course, I do. You're the king of the dead."

"You still believe that?" He slid his hand to her neck and tugged her closer. "Do you remember what happened to you?"

"Happened to me?" Again, with this. He obviously didn't understand head injuries.

He put his forehead against hers. "Renee, I need you to stop fighting me. Accept this life. Accept me."

She tensed and didn't know how to respond. Accept it as her life forever? Accept him - a freaking undead king? She couldn't decide if he was crazy, or she'd lost it and just hadn't gotten the message yet.

"I'm not fighting you. I didn't run," she whispered.

"Yes, you are; you fight me every day. You're disgusted by everything around you and you wait for a time to run. The world outside won't be like what you expect. You're safe with me." His words traveled through the vibrations from his hand that still clasped her neck, making her lightheaded.

Her breaths were coming faster, making her dizzy. What mental games was he playing with her? How could a zombie even illicit this type of reaction from her? Shit. *Shit.* She might be in over her head.

"You're monsters who want to kill all of humanity. I can't accept that." For an unknown reason, she felt guilty about her words.

He released her and gnashed his teeth. "Is it destroying humanity? They were on their way out long before we started consuming them. Most were weak and served no purpose, other than sustenance. Others were chosen and found a new existence in death."

Renee perched forward when he used the word chosen. Brie said chosen, too. Maybe those were the nimble zombies, the ones who scavenged water for her. Her gut told her that was the information that could change things around. The chosen. If she wanted answers, she'd have to play the game and find out what they actually were. It scared Brie just mentioning them and the king avoided actually answering her questions, providing only vague explanations for the way things were.

Once again, Renee was resolute in her choice. She would befriend Brie, and the king, too. She was anxious, he seemed to want more than friendship with her, but she'd have to deal with it. One way or another, she'd get the answers she needed.

Chapter 11

Renee was hiding in a patch of trees, trying to ignore what was happening all around her. It was hard, but she'd managed not to assume the fetal position every time the zombies attacked. Instead, she'd go within viewing distance of Brie and hunker down. She'd cover her ears and either stare at the ground or close her eyes.

It made sense the king was so cold. How could anyone maintain any traces of humanity when all they did was rip people or animals apart? Today was no different, except she'd found a better place to hide. Before she entered the overgrown brush, she locked eyes with Brie so she wouldn't get yelled at.

With her ears covered, she rocked in place and shut her eyes, wondering when the nightmare would end. At least this nightmare. The rest of it... being a captive to the undead king... that was going to go on until she escaped or her luck ran out and she died.

Something brushed against her leg and trembled. Terrified, she cracked her eyes open and found a rabbit. From the size, it appeared to be full grown. It peeked up at her and froze. It was such a crazy thing that both she and a rabbit hid in fear of the mass of monsters outside the overgrown foliage. Its white fur was a stark contrast to her filthy jeans and shoes.

Everything in Renee wanted to reach down and pet it, but it was wild and would run and then she might be the reason a zombie caught and ate it. They stared at each other for a long time. They stared long enough, the din of the massacre lessened and with extremely slow movements, she lowered her hands from her ears.

The bunny didn't move and had stopped trembling, squeezing itself against her. Renee's lips trembled as she tried to hold back tears. Animals. Renee felt they always understood her, even when no one else did. She drew in a long breath to calm her nerves before she reached down to stroke its soft fur. To her delight, it rubbed its face on her leg.

She no longer cared that tears slid down her cheeks and dropped from her chin to her jeans. This tiny creature had brought her more happiness in a few quick seconds than she had experienced in years. Renee continued to pet the small animal and almost exclaimed in delight when it clamored into her lap. She tried to stop the thoughts of asking the king, begging if she had to, to keep this creature. The rabbit's presence made everything else more tolerable.

Before the end of everything, she never had a pet, despite her efforts. No amount of begging or proving that she was capable of caring for an animal convinced her parents. They had a strict no-pet policy in their house, and it stayed that way until the day they died. Renee had always believed her house wouldn't have seemed so much like a prison if they had let her have a companion.

It would have been a true friend. One that could have possibly still been with her now. She sighed. Her parents never cared what she wanted. The only time they were more than tolerant of her was when there was company. Then they'd put on a show like they loved her, that they didn't believe she was broken and shouldn't have lived.

Shh... Renny, don't listen to them. They're the stupid ones, not you. You're perfect. One day everyone is going to see it too. Her brother's ghostly words filled her mind.

He'd told her things like that all the time. Renee's chest tightened as the memories of him tried to invade her conscious thoughts. Nope. Nope. She couldn't let herself remember. It would break her, shatter what was left of her of her resolve. She *had* to survive her time with the king. Find out the zombies' secrets and tell the other survivors. End all the monsters.

The leaves from the bushes rustled. The bunny pressed itself into her and hid its face, trembling again. Brie's face appeared with a frown. She opened her mouth but caught the tiny movements of the rabbit as it panicked.

"What in the fuck?" Her eyes flicked from the rabbit to Renee's face and back to the rabbit.

"Don't hurt it. I want to keep it for a pet." Renee stumbled through her words and chastised herself for just blurting things out, once again making herself sound dumb.

"You can't keep a… get the fuck out of the bushes." Brie blew out a long breath and let go of the branches.

Renee made cooing noises at the rabbit before she whispered in its ear. "It's going to be okay. I'll convince him to let me keep you. You'll be safe with me."

Awkwardly, she crawled out of the brush, still cuddling the rabbit. The knees of her jeans were already worn and her scooting on them made the fabric more threadbare. Renee of course, had unfortunate timing because the majority of the horde was milling around searching for scraps when she emerged. All their hungry eyes turned to her.

Shit. *Shit.* They stared at her like she was lunch. Her backpack was still strapped to her. Her eyes darted around, looking for a path, any space she could run to get free as they closed in around her. The rabbit panicked and tried to escape, but she had to save it. But could she save the innocent animal and herself?

One of the more vicious-looking zombies with sharp teeth, opened its mouth and made odd, guttural, barking noises. Renee's knees smacked together. She didn't exactly know what those sounds meant, but at the same time, she did. It meant she was a goner. So much for the protection of the king. They were going to rip her apart like they wanted to weeks ago.

Another of the undead made barking noises and clicks. Her heart slammed into her ribcage. Screw this. There was a tiny opening to her right. She took it and ran her ass off. Behind her, chaos broke out. The horrible sounds of the horde chasing their prey filled her ears as she clutched the bunny and pounded her feet against the earth.

Ahead, she saw a clearing with only shamblers. Bingo! She picked up the pace. She'd wanted to learn more information, but she had to get away.

Renee picked up her foot, so she didn't stumble over a root that poked out of the ground when she fell forward and screamed. Just as she'd slammed into the dirt, her arms locked to absorb the hit so the rabbit wouldn't be squashed. She didn't care that she smacked her face into the dirt. The rabbit was still in her arms. No. Please god, no. But there wasn't time to find out if her attempts had worked because they rolled her on her back as several zombies surrounded her. Many hands reached for her.

Wait. Not her - the rabbit. Shocked they weren't grabbing her, she screamed as her furry friend was torn from her arms. The pink eyes locked on hers, mirroring her own terror before they ripped it into pieces in front of her.

Renee pushed up on her knees and screamed. Screamed for losing the only good thing she'd had since the beginning of all this. Screamed for everything she'd lost. Screamed because nothing she did ever mattered.

Alone.

The zombies froze in place and stared at her. If she had to guess, she would've said they were shocked, but that made no sense. She crumpled and sobbed. When the roar she remembered well signaled he was coming, she couldn't even muster the energy to pull it together so he wouldn't see her sobbing like a child.

His heavy footsteps made her look up. Once again, the entire horde had their heads bowed. His fierce expression spelled disaster for someone. That someone probably being her, for causing problems. The king scanned the area before he peered at Renee. Brie pointed to the small group that had stopped fighting over the rabbit and twitched where they stood.

Without words, he crouched in front of her and tilted his head to the side. Renee swore she glimpsed compassion in the depths of his eyes, but that was wishful thinking. Still, it made her look elsewhere. She didn't want to look at her dead friend, but she couldn't help it. Fresh tears welled up in her eyes. There was no way to unsee the white fur now covered in red.

The king stood and turned to the horde before he zeroed in on the small cluster that held the pieces of her rabbit. Without a word, he grabbed the one in the middle and tore its head off. The others that still clutched pieces of the rabbit shook. Renee wanted to call out and stop him, but couldn't make her mouth open.

The king snatched the one to the left and yanked it forward. In the background, a few quiet clicks from the herd signaled they wouldn't interfere with their king's punishment. He picked up the zombie by its throat, spun, and threw it into a tree. The display of strength awed Renee as the zombie bent backwards around the tree. The sickening crack meant its back had broken.

The king sidestepped and tore off the other zombie's arms as easily as he'd done everything else. The pieces of her friend, what was left of the bunny, hit the ground when the zombie's arms did. The zombie fell to its knees and made pitiful sounds.

Renee wanted the king to stop, but still couldn't make a sound, caught between horror and fascination. The king eyed the crowd and barked orders at them. She watched as the others closed in around the wounded one that lay prone in front of the tree, the armless one, and the body with no head. Her hand flew up to her mouth as soon as she realized what was about to happen and she snapped her eyes shut.

Rough hands seized her and yanked her up. She expected to find the king but was met with icy blue eyes. Brie dragged her away as the horde descended upon their former members. The king hadn't moved but stared at her as Brie led her away with the oddest expression, one she didn't understand. As brutal as what she'd witnessed was, something about his face didn't make sense. He seemed torn, almost sad, but not because of his actions. What she thought might be compassion earlier had infiltrated his eyes again, and he almost seemed... human.

Chapter 12

Renee settled into her sleeping bag and tried to mentally prepare herself for whatever the interaction would be with the king tonight. Impossible to predict his moods or what affected them, she was making her best attempt not to talk to him. She was still upset about her rabbit friend. At least he kept his distance when they were alone. It bothered her he didn't sleep and, from what she could tell, stared at her all night. It would have been uncomfortable, but she figured it was because he didn't want her to run and didn't trust any of the others to monitor her.

"If you had escaped, where would you have gone?" His voice made her stomach flutter, which annoyed her even more.

"Why are you asking about that again? You made it crystal clear it couldn't happen," she grumbled.

He lifted a shoulder. "It won't, but I'm curious."

"Why would I tell you? It will just make it easier to find me." Renee straightened her shoulders to seem less intimidated.

"There is nowhere you could go that I wouldn't find you. Nowhere. I *own* you." He leveled his gaze at her. "Now tell me," he ordered.

Condescending prick. He didn't own her. Just because he captured, and kept her prisoner, didn't mean he *owned* her. People didn't own people anymore. Of course, he wasn't a person. Shit. Why would an undead creature care about owning anything?

"I already told you I'd find a military base." She muttered and moved her view away from him.

"You don't know where they are."

His self-assured tone made her want to slap him. Probably because what he said was true. She *had* known of several places years ago that were run by the military and safe, but they were gone now. The zombies were a plague that ate or destroyed everything in their path, including secure military facilities. It wasn't hard to take down an established safe place made by humans. Infect one of two people, and it was only a matter of time.

The king leaned forward, his amber irises brightening at his words. "Even if you did make it to some sort of military installation, the soldiers are no threat to us. We are too many and they are too few. The pitiful humans who are hiding on those bases barely understand how to use the weapons they are surrounded by."

She frowned. "You don't know that."

The corner of his lips ticked up before it turned into a smirk. She tried to ignore how much more attractive he appeared at that tiny movement reshaping his features. "Can you use a gun? Or even melee weapons?"

"I'm not a soldier, of course I don't." She snapped.

"Not even after all these years?" His smirk grew into an unsettling smile.

Great. He was picking on her too, for not being a badass like almost every person she'd met in the last seven years. In the beginning, many more people like her were lucky and somehow survived the initial assault of the zombies. But because they were "soft," lacking any real survival skills, they didn't last. Luck only got someone so far. How she still existed was almost miraculous.

"I don't like violence or death. You know that." Her words were barely above a whisper.

"I understand, but you aren't weak and you don't like when others are hurt. Wouldn't it make more sense to learn to use a weapon to defend others, or at least yourself?"

Her eyes flicked back to him so see if he continued to mock her, but his expression was serious. He didn't think she was weak? Her brother was the only other person she recalled who didn't believe she was pathetic.

He leaned even further forward, his gaze sharpening as he spoke. "You are a survivor."

She blinked. Any human alive was a survivor. Except when he said it to her, something inside of her clicked, made her sit straighter, almost convinced her she wasn't weak. How dumb was she to be flattered by her enemy, telling her she was brave when he was subjugating her? It was his fault everything was horrible.

Renee sighed. Okay, it wasn't *his* fault. The king might be the king of this horde, but he wasn't patient zero that started the zombie apocalypse. As fucked up as it was, technically, all zombies were victims of other undead who turned them. Shit. Did that mean her vengeance was pointless?

No. The current undead might not be the ones who started everything, but if the humans didn't stop them, nothing would be left and he'd already told her that was his plan. Logically, it was likely the plan of all zombies. Of course, she hadn't met any other zombies that seemed to have any agenda other than eating what was in front of them.

She grit her teeth. This was why she hated nights with him. Every conversation was worse than the last because it confused her or made her question things. Sometimes she even questioned herself.

"I'm just lucky." She shrugged. "It sucks for all the groups I've traveled with, because apparently that luck doesn't extend to anyone else. They're all... gone." She turned her head away as her eyes burned.

"They weren't chosen, you were. You're meant to be here, with me."

Renee was worried she gave herself whiplash with how fast she turned her head back to him. The confidence of his tone, the absolute lack of doubt in his features, astonished her. Chosen to be his prisoner? Is that what he was saying? It didn't make any sense.

She shook her head. "They used weapons and could fight. Sometimes they even had important skills, like medical or teaching. I just... I'm here."

Damn it. It wasn't what she'd planned to say and as she reflected on the words, she wished she'd said nothing.

The king rose from the floor and approached her. Her stomach tightened, unsure if it was from fear or something she didn't want to consider. Bending over to take her chin in his chilly fingers, raising her head until their eyes locked.

"You cannot see what I see." His bloodshot eyes traced her face. "I assure you; you are not what you believe. You are more." His thumb stroked the side of her face.

Shit. Shit. Her heart raced in her chest from his stupid praise, making her miserable as her body tingled from his words. He wasn't lying, but she couldn't understand why he thought that way. His touch was still foreign, but she couldn't deny how much she craved contact with another person, even if that person was dead. How much she wanted hugs or gentle touches that showed affection. Something she couldn't achieve with her own parents, much less any others she'd come into contact with.

Her mind screamed at her to tell him to stop, to move away. But her body begged her to let him stay, let him give her any small amount of kindness because who knew how long it would be before someone else would gaze at her like this? He was part of the reason the world was hell, but at that moment, she was the closest to heaven she'd ever been, and she prayed it wouldn't end.

"I am?" Her hushed words crossed her lips.

"Yes, and one day you will see it, too." His irises shifted and, although still bright, deepened in color. It reminded her of a setting sun. It was breathtaking. His grip tightened on her flesh and his expression hardened. "So, stop trying to escape. Accept this life."

She pulled out of his grip even though it hurt. "I'll never accept this! I'll never accept being trapped by you!"

He straightened and loomed above her, showing his teeth like the monster he was, before he schooled his expression. "You are trapped by your past, your mind. Your world is dead. *This* is your world now - you have no choice."

"There is always a choice." She told him through gritted teeth.

He laughed and moved away. "Not for you. Go to sleep."

Renee fought the urge to jump up and hit him. He continued to insist she was safe with him, but she was so irritated she wanted to test that theory. If she attacked him, what would he do? Her lips pinched when she recalled the roof. He'd laughed at her. Angry with herself, she grumbled and turned away from him.

Chapter 13

The next day was more of the same, marching for what seemed like endless hours. Renee worried they would encounter what the horde viewed as food, but thankfully it was a long boring day. She couldn't wait to get inside because it had started to drizzle, and she didn't want to march in the rain.

Renee huddled against the decaying wooden wall. She was grateful she was under a roof because it was raining, but this tiny shed was even more decrepit than the last one she and the king had been in overnight. Brie led Renee to the entry door and nudged her inside. To Renee's surprise the king wasn't already waiting like he usually was.

She shifted on the sleeping bag and unzipped it, planning to slip inside to escape the chill in the air. Renee considered peeling off her top shirt because it was dusty and worn but currently had no other clothing and removing it would only make her colder.

Renee wiggled into the worn, but in decent condition, sleeping bag, and yawned. She wanted to sleep but couldn't turn off the awful echo of noises in her mind that she had experienced as the horde ransacked the small town they had traveled through. When the zombies first arrived and she saw a local bookstore, she made a beeline to it hoping to find new books.

She flattened her lips, reliving the memory. That was until Brie yanked her back and told Renee she couldn't go. Seconds later the screaming started and her intentions faded as she ripped herself away from Brie to run and cower as far from the horde as she could. By the time she had her wits about her Brie was dragging her up and out of the town.

Once again, frustrated with herself, Renee pulled the bag up, wanting to cover her head - at least she could still hide from the world that way. But moments later the door creaked open, and the king entered. Renee turned her face away. The door closed softly and his heavy steps moved across the loose boards. She pinched her brows but refused to look at him but it sounded like he was coming toward her.

"Renee."

Goosebumps covered her skin just from the sound of his voice. Damn it, why did her body react like that when he spoke to her? She felt like her body was betraying her. She took a breath before she replied, not wanting him to know how he affected her.

"What?" She asked but stared at the rotting wall.

"Sit up."

Renee fought the urge to debate with him or refuse his request. She was supposed to be gaining his trust. She unclenched her jaw and slid the sleeping bag down, sat up, and faced him.

He had crouched beside her, his amber eyes held a dim glow and he smelled fresh again, like he'd recently bathed. She zeroed in on his hair and it still appeared damp but she was unsure if that was from the rain or a wash.

"You don't sleep well, most of the time." He stated as fact.

She frowned at his words. Of course she didn't. She was surrounded by a vicious horde of zombies with an asshole king that claimed he owned her. Playing it safe, she chose vague words. "Most humans don't."

"They shouldn't, but they are inconsequential." He paused and flicked his eyes toward the door and took a quick breath before turning his attention back to her. "But you need to get more sleep."

"I do?" Renee scrunched up at his words because she didn't understand why it would make any difference to him, she was his captive.

"Yes." He swallowed and cleared his throat. "I have something for you."

Renee's eyebrows shot up. Had something for her? What did that mean? The king reached down and picked up something wrapped in a dirty cloth. She focused on his deathly pale hands and fingers as they unwrapped the rectangular object. He hadn't even finished uncovering it and she knew exactly what it was.

Her heart raced in her chest and an urge to hug him almost overcame her. Once it was uncovered, she saw the title and squealed in delight causing him to recoil a bit. Her palm slapped over her mouth as heat rose in her cheeks.

The king held the book in front of her to take. Her fingers trembled as she touched it. Part of her wasn't quite sure if any of this was real or if she had fallen asleep and was dreaming. The king gifted her a book. And not just any book. It was the second installment in one of her favorite series. She hadn't seen a copy since before the world had been dominated by zombies.

She tugged it from him and shrunk back. He raised eyebrows and stood. Renee was pretty sure she needed to say something but wasn't quite certain what she wanted to say. In a typical scenario she would have thanked someone profusely but considering the situation it didn't seem appropriate. Of course, she was also trying to befriend him, and friends were typically nice to one another.

The king backed away and sat across from her, staring at her. She wondered if he was waiting for kind words.

"Where did you find it?" she asked instead.

"The bookstore we passed."

"I wanted..." her words died away. She bit her lip debating on whether she should ask him how he knew she wanted to go to the book shop. Brie.

Renee realized that it had to have been Brie that said something because how else would he have known? Of course she hadn't told Brie the name of her favorite series, just a few of the titles. At the time, it didn't seem like Brie had committed them to memory but even if she had, why would she have told the king? More than that, why would he bother to have his zombies search for a book? Renee shook her head. That didn't add up.

"You wanted what?" the king prompted.

"I wanted to gather supplies in the town but Brie wouldn't let me." That was also a true statement.

"We weren't meant to stop there but the horde hungers and there were humans," the king said with a shrug.

Renee closed her eyes and tried not to think about his statement too much. "Will we have to march in the rain?"

"Why would the rain make a difference?"

Her eyes snapped open. "Because not all of us are undead! I can get sick if I'm out in the cold rain all day."

The silence stretched out in the tiny space as he continued to stare at her. He titled his head up and viewed the roof, fixing his eyes on one of the corners near the front of the building, there was a small hole that dripped with water.

"I hadn't considered that." He finally said.

"Figures." Renee grumbled and scooted down into the sleeping bag, book in hand. She wasn't going to tell him but she was sleeping with it like someone would a stuffed animal because for her it brought the same kind of comfort.

"I'll have the scouts find somewhere to stay if needed, but we can't remain here. I doubt this roof will hold up." He said, still looking at the steady drip from the rain.

Renee almost sat back up. Had he just agreed to not make her march in the rain all day? Because she told him she would get sick? A twisted desire to pacify him, make him happy because he had shown concern for her lack of sleep, gifted her something she valued and also wanted to shield her from the elements, made the words tumble from her mouth before she could stop them.

"If you can somehow get me a raincoat or umbrella - maybe both, I'll be okay."

The king turned his face toward her again. In the dim light she barely noticed his sickly pale skin tone and how dark the circles under his eyes were. Her mind was trying to trick her into thinking he was alive when she knew he wasn't.

"So, if I find these items, the horde can continue?"

Renee pressed her lips together to keep herself from saying something even dumber, instead she nodded.

The king perched forward. "On one condition. You sleep soundly tonight."

"You just want me to sleep?" Renee couldn't figure out why her resting was so important to him, especially considering his horde was outside in the rain and wind.

The king got up and strode over to her side. Renee forced herself not to move, not to flinch as he drew near. He once again crouched down and reached for her cheek. She clenched her jaw. His eyes roved over her face and his expression softened.

"Sleep. Now." He commanded.

Renee sensed her entire body relax. Her eyelids grew heavy and slipped closed. It was unnatural how quickly exhaustion took her. The last thing she felt were the king's fingers brushing her hair back.

Chapter 14

Days turned into weeks. It was difficult to keep track, but Renee figured she'd been traveling with the horde for roughly a month. The routine was always the same. Brie woke her up every day, then Renee would try to get her to talk and engage in conversation. Sometimes it worked, and sometimes it didn't. They would walk for hours and if she had angered the king the night before, she and Brie would walk with the shamblers at the rear of the procession. The shamblers didn't communicate and stunk. Now that she ate every night, it made her nauseous to be with them first thing in the mornings.

Every few days, the horde would find, and decimate a group of people or a pack of wild animals. Renee continued to hide or go as far as she was allowed from the mess. Sometimes the king would be involved, and sometimes not. Brie would never divulge where he was all day, yet Renee knew he was always at the front leading the group of undead. Anytime Renee asked Brie something she didn't want to answer, she'd stare forward and stop talking for the rest of the day or simply change the subject.

Renee was pretty sure that the chosen were at the front with their king. They were probably like his knights, the ones he sent in first to clear a path. Maybe the nameless king had been right. She was pretty fixated on the whole royal hierarchy concept. As much as she tried, she couldn't keep her mind from drifting back to what happened with the rabbit. Brie refused to talk about that specific incident or what the king had done.

She wanted to mark off the brutal interaction as another display of strength and brutality from him, but it seemed like more. She'd tried to bring it up a few times with him, but hadn't mustered up the strength yet. When Renee told Brie about her desire to clear the air with the king about what happened with the rabbit, Brie snapped at her and told her not to bring it up again. Renee assumed Brie was short with her because Renee had tried to run Brie had got in trouble with the king. He'd told her not to run, and Renee had tried, not for the reasons he probably thought, but it didn't change her actions.

If she tried to ask about his odd expression, the almost kindness in his eyes - what would happen? Was he angry because she tried to escape? If she brought it up, would he punish her? Or would he be decent and talk to her? It was a gamble, and she wasn't sure if she had what it took to test her luck with him.

Nothing had changed; she was only playing along to gain any information that would help the humans, but the longer she traveled with them, the more things blurred in her mind. As upset as she was to lose her rabbit friend, she also understood that the horde almost couldn't control themselves. Whether it was animals or humans. Being around them as they ate their way up the east coast had traumatized her, but she had learned that once they were worked up into a frenzy, the only thing that seemed to stop them was their king.

Renee glanced at Brie who strolled beside her. It was weird sometimes, when she was comfortable, Brie talked a lot, but if Renee didn't engage her, she'd stay silent, staring ahead. Renee could tell she was always thinking. About what, she had no clue, but if Brie was in a mood, it was almost impossible to get her to talk.

"Brie... I was thinking about talking to him about what happened with the rabbit. So, he knows I wasn't trying to run away." Renee dared to open the topic again.

Brie slowed her pace and gave her a hard look. "You really don't know when to let something go, do you? I get that it was probably traumatizing to you but it's nothing to us."

Renee swallowed because her words hurt, even if they were true. It seemed like a pattern. Nothing she valued seemed important to anyone else, even before the end of normalcy.

"It doesn't matter why you ran. I *told* you the first day you were with us and you did it, anyway." Her tone was so cold it made Renee shiver.

"I was trying to save my friend-"

Brie stopped and put her hands on her hips. "Your *friend*? Are you fucking kidding me?"

Renee stopped and looked at the dirt beneath her feet. "I don't have any friends. I want to be friends with you, even though you don't want to talk to me most of the time. If companionship from a rabbit was all I'll get it, I'll take it."

"That's not - it's not like that. Okay, it is but not for the reasons you think." Brie stumbled through her words. Normally, whenever she spoke it was with confidence. Brie's body language remained proud and didn't display the stress lines in her face. Her mouth thinned out with a grimace. "It's complicated but I don't hate you, Renee."

"But we can't be friends," Renee whispered, dropping her view back to her feet.

"Fuck me. I didn't say that. You're so goddamn relentless," Brie breathed and adjusted her stance.

She flicked her eyes back to Brie's face, which was still tense but also seemed more... open? Renee blinked because she wondered if she was only seeing what she wanted to see, but it looked like Brie wasn't staring at her with the usual annoyance.

Brie threw her hands into the air in front of her. "Okay. Okay, we can fucking talk until we reach where we're going. But trust me, *don't* bring up the rabbit. You *ran*. If you were anyone else, he would've... it doesn't matter. Be smart and don't draw attention to the fact that he treats you differently. You do, it's your funeral."

Renee bounced on her feet. "Can I pick what we talk about?"

Brie rolled her eyes but then gave her a small smile. "Yes, you can pick. However, please don't pick those damn vampire movies again. Sparkling vampires make no sense."

"But the second half of the last book was never released in cinema!" Renee protested.

"And you already told me you read all the books so you know what happened. Romance books are ridiculous, anyway. Why would a vampire be interested in a high school student? It's fucking creepy." Brie's face twisted in contemplation.

"Says the zombie," Renee shot back and then laughed.

Brie pushed her forward so they'd start marching with the others but then laughed too. Renee grinned as she launched into the difference between the books and the movies. Although Brie protested and acted like she hated it, she listened to *every* word and had many questions.

Renee's plan was to eventually work her way to her favorite romantasy book series. Brie may not have recognized that she herself was interacting and seemingly interested in what Renee was saying, but she was, so Renee kept on talking. Perhaps it was simply because there hadn't been any entertainment in a long time, but Renee hoped it was because Brie secretly liked the stories as much as she did.

Renee, lacking in most useful skills, had a stellar memory of the various stories and characters. She could easily recall the important details of plots and the different, made-up worlds, and she'd talk about the stories that she'd coveted and had helped her through the worst times. Renee's hope was that the stories might help Brie too.

Nights were the hardest. It didn't matter where they were. He'd always find some enclosed place for shelter and she would be forced inside with only him. Sometimes he was a chatty, condescending prick, and they would bicker, which meant she and Brie would be with the shamblers the next day. She could deal with the arguing, but it was when he was almost kind and spoke to her like a person that confused her.

It had only been a few nights since he gave her the book she was reading. Embarrassed when she squealed at the title. It was one of her favorite romantasy books from before the world ended. He'd just raised his eyebrows at her and walked away. When he wasn't looking, she hugged the book because it was the closest thing she had to a friend at that moment. The last few nights, she had less trouble going to sleep because she read until she passed out.

Cuddled in her sleeping bag, she yawned as she opened her book. She was using a ripped wrapper from a water bottle as a bookmark. She missed beds but was grateful to have pillows. She briefly wondered, who carried her pillows all day while they traveled?

"You seem to enjoy that book." His voice caused goosebumps to rise on her skin.

"Yeah, it's really good." She smiled and started to read, but then stopped and stared at him. "How did you know I liked to read?"

He shrugged. "I guessed. You seem the type."

She frowned. "What's that supposed to mean?"

He smirked before he answered. "I didn't think you cared about my opinion of you."

"I don't," she insisted.

His smirk turned into a grin.

"I *don't*."

"Those books are pointless, anyway. Filled with unrealistic nonsense." His tone sounded bored, but the grin remained plastered on his face.

Renee stuck the wrapper in between the pages to mark where she left off and closed the book. "What?"

"People don't act like that."

She wiggled her torso out of her sleeping bag and sat up, keeping her lower half cocooned. "Don't act like what?"

She had a sneaking suspicion the king had at least glanced at her romance book and if that was the case, it was the funniest thing she could imagine. The horrific, terrifying king of the undead reading a romance book about elves and fae. Just the image of him bent over any book almost made her laugh.

His grin disappeared. "Those books existed before. I knew people who read them."

"Oh." Damn. There went any fun she might've had. She slid back into her sleeping bag, intending to read.

"I meant you seem the type to read because people who like to learn tend to be curious... and read. Regardless of what they read."

Renee turned her head toward him to see if he was mocking her, but he wasn't. It was almost a compliment, even though he'd basically just made fun of her book.

"I do like to read. It's just hard to find books. Most of them were destroyed; having been exposed to the elements... it's sad."

"There are probably still libraries that are untouched. It's not as though many of my kind would be interested in them unless there was food in the libraries."

She swallowed. He was right. Once again, she felt dumb because she hadn't thought of things that way. She could've been hiding in an old library this entire time while they ate the rest of the country. No. She'd promised herself she would help destroy the zombies, not hide until it was all over.

"Could... could you read, if you wanted to?" she asked tentatively.

He sighed. "Yes. There's no point, but yes, if I wanted to, I could. Read your book. It relaxes you."

She pinched her lips, not happy that he'd closed the conversation or that he figured out that reading helped her sleep.

Chapter 15

Back in another van with the king, she slumped against the metal door. Trying to get Brie to be an active participant in their friendship was proving to be more challenging than she thought. Renee couldn't figure out what it was about her that most annoyed Brie. It could be her constant talking, her inability to deal with violence, or just her general and somewhat bubbly personality, despite the circumstances. Popular people never changed. Girls like them were always so confident and posed. While girls like Renee were awkward and usually shy. Shit. Maybe Renee *was* being a judgy bitch and their personalities just weren't compatible.

"You're not going to read?" his voice filled the tiny space and pulled her from her thoughts.

"Yeah, I am. I was just thinking."

"About what?"

Damn it. She never knew when he would try to have a regular conversation with her versus baiting her into some sort of argument. Other than Brie, he was the moodiest person - monster - she'd ever spent time with.

"The bunny." The words slipped from her lips before she could stop them. She bit her lip. Not at all what she intended to say. She hadn't worked out how she was going to bring the rabbit up yet, but she hadn't intended to blurt it out. Shit. Shit. She always screwed up when she tried to talk to him.

His jaw tightened. "You were very upset."

"I wanted to keep it," she whispered.

His glowing eyes widened at her words. "Keep it?"

"Yeah, as a pet. It liked me and I thought…" Renee stared at her lap.

"Liked you?" His tone sounded almost strangled.

"It knew I wasn't going to hurt it."

His jaw worked as he frowned. "You cannot keep an animal with the horde. The same thing will happen every time. Animals are food. Humans are food. Nothing more."

For reasons she didn't understand, his words hurt. They hurt a lot. Why in the hell was he keeping her trapped with him if she wasn't anything other than food? No one wanted to hang out with their lunch or dinner for as long as he had with her.

"If I'm just food, then just get it over with!" She raised her voice. "Why are you forcing me to stay with you if you're just going to eat me? Do it already!" She picked up her book and threw it at him.

Before she could utter another nasty word, he had her pinned against the metal door. The entire van rocked from his quick movement. His fingers dug into her shoulders, his face only inches from hers.

"Don't."

His one word of warning should have shut her up. Anyone who wasn't crazy would understand their life was at stake, but he'd more or less told her she had no future anyway, so what did it matter?

"Don't what? Speed up the process? Are you trying to fatten me up first? Is that why someone feeds me every night? So, I'm good and juicy for when you finally decide to devour me?"

He showed his teeth, and her stomach tightened. She might've gone too far, said too much and ended her own life. However, as she stared at him, his expression morphed into something that was unmistakably like… desire.

"If I chose to devour you…" He released her shoulders and slid his hands up to cup her face. "You wouldn't want me to stop."

His breath mingled with hers and made her lightheaded. His words couldn't mean what they sounded like. Surely, he was threatening her - right? He bent his head to hers. His lips were so close to hers they almost touched when he spoke.

"Do you want me to stop?" he whispered.

She couldn't speak. If she did, she'd betray herself and every other human still breathing, since her honest answer was that she didn't want him to stop. Renee balled her hands at her sides because she wanted to touch him so badly it was like trying to stay afloat on a raft in a storm at sea. Every beat of her heart, a wave that crashed against her, urging her to reach out and trace his jawline and tangle her fingers in his hair. He seemed, in some ways, so human. It was clear, given his translucent skin, the visible veins and arteries beneath it, that he was a zombie. And she couldn't forget his eyes that glowed, the ones that seemed to be undressing her as he had her pinned inside the van. With no visible, fatal injury, her mind constantly ping-ponged about whether it was right or wrong to be attracted to someone who, for all intents and purposes was dead, but didn't look, or act like he was.

Renee tried to move her head and caused her lips to brush against his for a second. The brief, tiny touch sent tingles down her limbs and made his expression heat. She froze. Not what she intended. She had to get away from him before she did something else equally as reckless.

"I should... I should read," she mumbled.

Disappointment made the glow in his irises dim as he backed up. He tilted his head and stared at the ceiling.

Renee grabbed her book and pretended to read with her back to him, she berated herself for allowing him to get so close to her, again.

Chapter 16

Still trying to recover from her encounter with the king, Renee was subdued during the morning's march with Brie. Renee tried to start conversations with her because if she didn't, Brie would notice something was off and she couldn't handle it if Brie asked why. Generally, Brie didn't ask many questions, but every once in a while, something Renee said would catch her interest and get her talking or wanting to know more.

It always surprised Renee what the topics were that Brie brought up because it was never any of the ones, she'd thought a popular girl would want to talk about. She hadn't learned much about zombies from Brie but she had learned that Brie liked kickboxing, had taken several self-defense classes, could and *had* literally run a marathon, and had just started some type of martial art Renee had never heard of just before everything collapsed.

Most popular girls Renee knew talked about things like hair, make-up, fashion, and other superficial topics. They were all about taking selfies in exclusive locations, proving how their looks would gain them access to almost anywhere. Renee glanced at her almost-friend.

Although it was apparent Brie knew all about those things, she had so much more to her. Not only that, but there were characteristics Brie embodied that didn't match the preconceived ideas Renee had, making her consider she'd been just as judgmental as she believed others to be. She had assumed popular girls were all the same, which was a terrible, childish mistake.

"I was going to learn to use a sword, in a traditional sense, like fencing, but then..." Brie gestured around her.

"But you've used weapons, I've seen you." Renee countered.

"Yeah, but I make that shit up on the fly. I guess I'm better at it now than when I was first like... this." She shrugged.

"It seems like you enjoyed dangerous hobbies and experiences before." Renee grinned at her.

Brie tried to keep her face neutral but also grinned. "Yeah, that's true enough. I guess I was a bit of an adrenaline junkie. Or would've been, if the world hadn't turned into this."

"Yet somehow, even though you're a zombie badass, you still look great." Again, Renee was feeling like a mess in comparison, and she was human, the only one in the horde. Shouldn't she feel special, or above all her insecurities in some way? It wasn't fair. She had always been a train wreck and struggled with routine her whole life. Her mind was always daydreaming or escaping reality because even before the uprising, she wanted to escape. Only then, it was for different reasons.

Renee's distracted daydreaming led her to be perpetually late for most things, always showing up in the wrong clothes or forgetting things. Her grades in school had been a rollercoaster. When she kept it together, she would get straight A's. Her report card fooled a few of her teachers into thinking she was gifted. But if she couldn't focus or got lost in another fantasy world, sometimes in the form of a book, she would flake out on just about everything for weeks at a time.

"True, for a zombie, I am hot." Brie actually broke out in laughter.

It made her entire face light up. Renee stumbled because Brie was always pretty but when she smiled – holy crap – she could've been a model. Her missteps drew Brie's attention and her laughter fell away as well as her smile.

"None of that matters now, anyway. Why do you insist on asking me about things before? It's annoying. Don't do it again." Brie snapped and shifted her view to the front of the horde.

Damn. She'd screwed up again. Every time she thought she made progress, it seemed to piss off Brie, one step forward, two steps back. The rest of the march was silent as Renee racked her brain, trying to think of new ways to reach and connect with Brie. If she couldn't get the king or Brie to trust her, open up to her, at least a little, she'd never be able to uncover the secrets that made them seem more like people and less like zombies.

Chapter 17

They'd attacked another small settlement. She meant to search for water during the zombies' feast, but the brutality of the attack unnerved her, and she hid in an empty building and curled into a ball. Why didn't she try to save someone? Even one person? *Coward,* her mind screamed at her. Her conscience demanded action even as logic told her it would've been pointless.

You can't keep hiding. Her brother's voice drifted in between her hands that were clasped over her ears.

Damn it. No escape from hearing him because he wasn't really there, but god she wished he was. The hole in her heart would never heal from his loss.

"I'm not hiding," she snapped.

So, you're in that position, under a shelf, in a building because... his voice drifted off.

"You're supposed to support me. Not pick on me."

I'm your brother, that's what we do. He chuckled.

She pinched her lips in annoyance. "Not you. You were always nice to me."

That's not true. Stop putting me on a pedestal. No one is perfect.

Her ghost-brother was a lot more annoying than the real one.

"Maybe you did pick on me, but you loved me, and right now I need you to love me. Not make fun of me. I'm fucking scared, Liam."

Sorry, princess. I guess death has made me snarkier.

"It's okay. Staying alive in this crap has made me more bitchy." She wanted to open her eyes but understood if she did, he would be gone again. The idea of being alone was agonizing.

You don't have to do this.

Her brow furrowed. "Do what?"

You're not built for vengeance. Let go of it. A good queen doesn't get lost in vengeance.

"Are you kidding me? There is *no way* I'm letting this go. This is the closest I've ever come to actually being able to *do* something to stop them. I promised."

I know, but I don't want to lose you, Renny.

"Lose me? I don't care if destroying the zombies costs my life. Think of all the human survivors I could help. You know how hard it's been for them – for me. If they knew there was a king, or that zombies could talk... I'm still trying to figure out who the chosen are, but it's the first time I've really believed things could be different – better."

I'm not talking about your life.

Renee stopped breathing when she felt a slight pressure on her shoulder; it was so similar to when her brother would touch her shoulder to calm her. It almost made her open her eyes. As fearful as sensing his touch made her, it also thrilled Renee because it was almost like Liam was there with her instead of only in her mind.

Things are changing. Open your eyes. His voice drifted off.

Her lips trembled because she understood when he sounded like that, it meant he was leaving again. Nothing she had tried in the past kept him with her. Perhaps the trade was any sanity she had left. She was tempted to let the horror of the world tear her mind apart just to be with her brother again. It wouldn't be real, but she wasn't sure if that mattered long-term.

No. She couldn't let go of her self-imposed purpose, not yet. Not until she discovered the thing that would change the tide in the war for survival with the zombies. The sound of Brie's voice signaled for Renee to uncurl from her fetal position and climb out of the abandoned building.

Chapter 18

They had been heading north for days, which Renee wasn't thrilled about. Unlike the ranks of the undead, she still breathed, and it was getting colder as they traveled. It pained her to admit, even to herself, but she was relieved when the king found an enclosed shelter of some sort. She kept meaning to ask Brie if they traveled when it snowed and what that was like but kept forgetting.

Renee glanced at the king. He'd appeared forlorn while outside, staring at the sky most of the time, Renee had been eating and glancing in his direction every so often. Tonight was going to be one of those nights. It was moments like these, when he seemed depressed and lonely or when he was thoughtful and cooked her meat the way she liked, that made her doubtful about her plan. He was too... human.

After they entered the small shack, she thought about climbing into the sleeping bag and calling it a night. But his despair filled the tiny space and felt like a weight on her chest. His back was against a wall, one knee bent, and the other leg stretched out. His right hand rested on his knee. Renee tried not to notice, but he'd changed clothes and smelled clean again. The king's hygiene practices seemed to also be more frequent.

"You, okay?" she asked in the dimly lit room.

"Does it matter?"

"Yeah, of course, it does. You're protecting me. If something's wrong, that's bad for me, right?"

He stared at her for a long time before he answered, "We are about to enter a long span of travel with no available food."

"Oh." Did that mean they would eat each other? If so, it could be the opportunity she'd been waiting for. She'd hoped to at least see the chosen or get more information about them, but there might not be another opportunity for a while.

"Do you understand what that means?"

"Umm... everyone is going to get hungry, and I guess turn on each other?"

"Yes, but that's not my concern. It's time for a culling, anyway. The strong will remain, they always do."

For a king, he was a bastard who didn't give a crap about his horde.

Renee ran her fingers over the worn cover of her book. "Okay, well then, what's the problem?"

"You."

"Me?" The heat left her as the meaning of his words sunk in. Shit, they were going to eat her. "I'm screwed. There are too many of them." Her mind flashed back to what they'd done to her rabbit, making her stomach uneasy.

"You will not die," he said resolutely.

He needed to let her go if he wanted her to live. Is that why he was upset? She still didn't really understand why she was there, anyway. Their discussions or arguments, depending on the night, couldn't be that interesting to him that he wanted to keep her around.

"You have to let me go. You can't stop all of them."

His jaw ticked. "I am their *king*, as you've pointed out. They obey me."

She shouldn't have been so insistent on the title. It was going to his head. How did a zombie's brain even work, anyway? *Not the time*, she reminded herself.

"Then, I don't understand."

He stood and moved until he was hovering over her. His fingers wrapped around her shoulders before hauling her up. "Every time we eat another group, even animals, you run in fear."

"Because I don't like it."

"You can't escape this. You can't escape me."

His words made her lips tremble as warmth crept over her skin. "I'm not trying to run."

"When the horde turns on one another, there will be nowhere to run, nowhere to hide."

Her stomach tightened. "But you said they wouldn't hurt me."

"They won't." He released her shoulders. His fingers drifted up to touch the side of her face. "I didn't know it would be like this. That you would be like this."

"I don't understand." She didn't understand anything anymore. His body was so close to hers, there was actual fear evident in his eyes. Her mind wandered to that moment in the van when she thought he might be threatening her, but his voice sounded like it did now.

His fingers threaded into her hair as his other hand slid around her neck. "I won't lose you. You're *mine*."

Renee tried not to let his words affect her, but not one person in her life had ever said anything as romantic. This was so screwed up. All those characters in her books were beautiful creatures saying things like that and she got a crazy zombie king. He only meant it in the way someone owned property or an object, but still, it made her heart speed up.

"I'm not going anywhere." It was a lie, but at the moment, it was the absolute truth.

"Mine," he whispered as he lowered his mouth to hers.

She expected to be disgusted and push him away. Instead, she leaned into his hungry kiss. It was frosty, like the first chill of winter, yet so gentle and feathery. He kissed her like she was precious. She sighed and wrapped her arms around his torso, delighted by the hard lines of muscle under his shirt. His mouth moved over hers more fervently. She opened her mouth to him and moaned when his tongue slicked against hers.

Her hands roamed over his chest and stomach as their kiss heated. He broke their kiss and moved his lips to her chin and then her neck. She felt like she was floating as they shifted to the floor on her sleeping bag. Every kiss, every touch, grew more frenzied. His fingers snaked inside her shirt, briefly skimming over her scar before moving up and sliding over her bra. She moaned again as he captured her lips and slowed his movements.

Reluctantly, he broke their kiss and gazed at her. She reached for his hair and ran her fingers through it. God, it was as glorious as she'd thought it would be. He turned his head and kissed her fingers. He was a wizard, for somehow, he'd cast a spell on her, and she was entranced. How could a zombie be so coordinated? Interested in something so emotional? Renee had to be missing something, but at the moment, she didn't want to keep questioning why things were the way they were, she only wanted to lean into her feelings, and into his safety, affection and protection.

"Will you let me help you?" he asked quietly.

She was pretty sure she'd agree to just about anything if he kept kissing her. She nodded.

His gaze slid back to her. "Do you trust me?"

Crap. She didn't want to lie, but she also didn't want him to stop. It wasn't a lie, not completely. She *did* trust that he wanted her alive and would protect her, so she nodded.

"Then you'll listen to me until we reach more food?" He kissed her fingers again.

He was making it hard to focus. Her fingers traced his lips as she nodded.

"Promise me."

She pinched her eyebrows, unsure if she could promise that. At her hesitation, he leaned over and brushed his lips against hers. She tugged him closer and slipped her tongue into his mouth. He tasted so good. Such an unlikely paradox, but it was the truth, like fresh citrus. She couldn't get enough. He gently nipped her lip and pulled back. Damn, that was hot.

"Promise me."

It was like she'd regressed into a horny teenager and was starved for sex. She'd had sex a few times, but the way things were, it was risky and not worth it, in her opinion. She would willingly trade those experiences for his kisses any day.

"Okay. I promise. I'll listen to you." Renee tried to pull his mouth back to hers.

"Without a fight?"

"Yes, okay. Without a fight."

He finally brought his lips to hers. Renee kissed him like it was the last thing she'd ever do, because maybe it was. A tiny voice in the recesses of her mind condemned her even as she clutched him. She had to make the self-hatred worth it. Too soon though, he ended the kiss.

"You need to sleep."

To hell with sleep. "Later. Just a little longer." She put her mouth against his.

"Only if you behave," he said against her lips.

"What?" She pulled back.

"If you keep your promise to me, then I'll give you almost anything you want." His eyes moved over her face like he was trying to memorize it.

She nodded like an idiot. Pretty sure she'd just made a deal with the devil because she was horny. No, not the devil, with the king of the dead. When she went to Hell, she'd deserve it for sure.

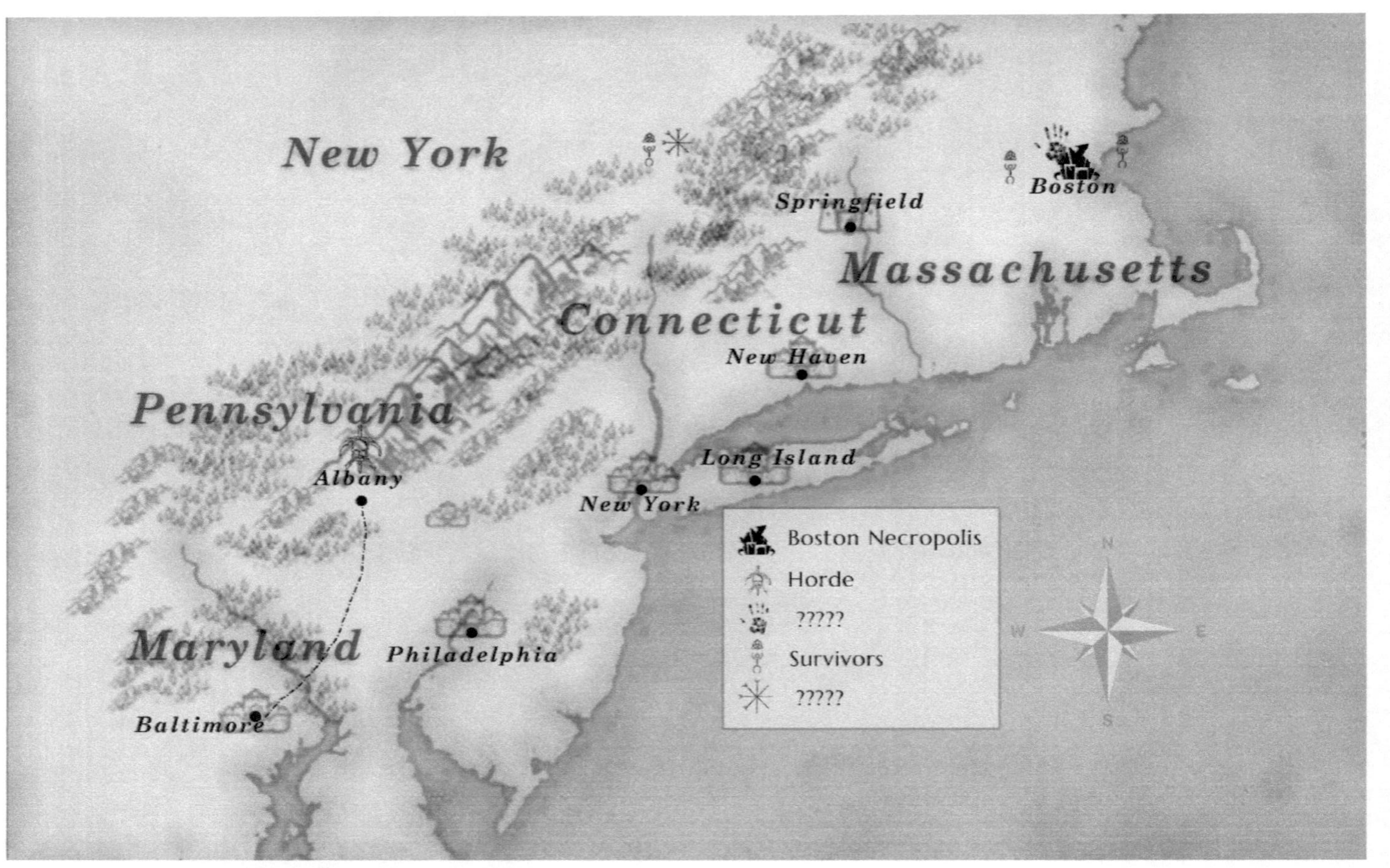
New York
Springfield
Boston
Massachusetts
Connecticut
New Haven
Pennsylvania
Albany
Long Island
New York
Maryland
Philadelphia
Baltimore
Boston Necropolis
Horde
?????
Survivors
?????
N
E
S
W

Chapter 19

The next morning was identical to all the others only Renee was the irritable one. Damn him. He had kissed her one more time last night and then made her go to bed. She'd agreed because she didn't want to look like a sex-starved freak. Disappointed when he moved away from her, she had to force herself not to be pathetic and ask him to cuddle. How sad was she that she'd wanted a zombie to cuddle with her? Her self-hatred was in full swing from the moment she woke.

She tried to rationalize that she was only doing what she had to so the king would trust and confide in her. But the nagging voice inside her told her she was only fooling herself if she believed that.

After slipping her sunglasses on, she drank a bottle of water. Her head hurt again. Shit. She'd been waking up with a headache for over a week now. It usually disappeared after a couple of hours, but it annoyed her. It could be because she only ate once a day.

She yawned and stretched before standing. Renee wanted, no needed, a bath even though it was hard to tell from the general stink of the horde. But it'd been weeks since she bathed. She brushed off her dirty clothes and noticed Brie staring at her with an odd expression.

"What?" Had Brie somehow guessed and knew she was a horrible person who'd made out with the king of the undead? Her slightly swollen lips reminded her of how many times they kissed before she finally let him slip away.

"We're going to leave soon."

"Right, big endless march for hours. It's what we do every day." Renee chuckled at her bad joke.

"Yeah, but before we leave, you need to bathe."

Wow, her stench was so bad Brie wanted her to wash, or she was a mind reader, which Renee doubted. She followed Brie and wondered why today of all days, she was supposed to bathe but then stopped, embarrassed. That was probably why the king didn't want to do anything other than kiss her. Somehow, he was cleaner than she was.

"Move," Brie barked at her.

They went into another tiny shack not far from the one she woke in; this new one had a large metal tub. It may not have been initially a tub, but it was being used as one now. Steam rose from the water.

"Is that... is the water warm?" Renee asked in shock.

"Yeah, princess. You're so fucking special that you get a warm bath. Enjoy it." Brie slammed the door behind her.

Renee approached the tub with excitement. She remembered hot showers as a teenager, but since the zombies arrived, there weren't working showers, and when you could bathe, the best you could get was room temperature or cold water. Stripping her clothes off quickly, she got in and almost moaned. Best day ever. Okay, not true, but since this screwed-up situation started, it was a top-five highlight.

When the water cooled, she used the soap beside the tub and scrubbed herself till her skin hurt. Her hair took the longest because it had grown out almost to the length it was in high school. Once everyone started dying or turning into zombies, she'd chopped off her hair and worn it short for years. It made it harder for the zombies to grab you. Then she traveled with a group where one woman used to cut hair for a living. Renee grew it out just long enough to need a trim. They had almost been friends, but after she died, Renee didn't bother anymore and always tied it back.

Now, it fell to the middle of her back, and she needed to cut it. Although, she wasn't in a hurry. Guess having the zombie king protecting you had some benefits. Didn't have to worry about the undead clawing at you all the time. When she finally climbed out of the tub, the water told a really gross tale of how nasty she'd actually been. She felt like a new person.

Renee was tempted to peer at her reflection, but ultimately didn't since she hadn't seen herself in years. She'd made the mistake many times earlier on, which freaked her out. Gone was the shy but attractive teenager with bright, green eyes who tried to hide she was different with her long dark hair intentionally styled to cover her ears. In her former reflection's place was a weary, broken haunted-looking adult who somehow survived a zombie apocalypse. It was like her outside appearance reflected who she was on the inside and she never needed to see that again.

Renee reached for her old clothes but saw her name on a piece of paper on a pile of clothes not too far off from her discarded ones. Moving the paper with her name aside, she examined the clothes and was surprised to find they were all the right sizes. Used but fresh jeans, a shirt, several underwear, and a new bra. It was like hitting the lottery. She ignored the fact that the clothes were probably from someone they'd murdered and ultimately eaten. She put the spare bra and extra panties in her backpack. It'd been months since she had backup clothes.

Brie stood outside the door, waiting. "You took long enough. We have to catch up now." She slipped a small mirror and lipstick into the pocket of her flowing dark blue skirt. Why did she always wear skirts? It didn't seem practical.

They jogged past the shamblers and into the mass of the horde. Renee was stupidly confident that she'd be okay, but was worried about Brie surviving the culling. Was Brie one of the strong ones? Would she lose the only other person she could talk to?

"I don't want to make you mad, but how long have you been... um..."

"How long have I been a zombie?"

"Yeah."

"Always with the questions. Time doesn't seem the same anymore, so I'm only guessing, but years?" Brie used an elastic band to arrange a small bun from the braids she'd done up the day before, at the rear of her head, on top of her loose strands.

"Wow, years?!"

"I look good, right?" Brie laughed. It was genuine and beautiful. "What?" she asked when she caught Renee staring.

"I keep forgetting how awesome and pretty you are."

"Renee, you're the silliest friend I've ever had. I was always awesome. Empty inside, but still awesome. I was gorgeous. I'm just *okay* now."

She liked Brie, even if she was still planning on running as soon as she could. Sure, Brie was grouchy in the morning, but who wasn't? Knowing how lonely Renee was, Brie consciously used her name and tried to make an effort to be nice for over a week, even when she was clearly irritated. And today, she used the word friend. Maybe they were friends.

Renee smiled her genuine smile. Brie called her a friend. Despite her frustrated mood, Brie's words warmed her like the sun on a winter's day. She didn't care if Brie thought she was silly. As long as she was her friend, the rest didn't matter.

"I didn't know you before, but you're not empty now. When you feel like talking, you have a lot of interesting stories. And you're funny. And," Renee paused because the guilt nagged her. "You're pretty badass when you go all zombie. But don't tell anyone I said that."

Brie laughed again. "Your secret is safe with me. I won't snitch to the humans."

Renee's words haunted her for the rest of the day; the dissonance she experienced left her feeling off kilter. Even so, it was oddly comforting to know Brie would probably survive the culling, as the king called it. When night fell, they entered a wooded area where Brie led her away from the horde.

"Where are we going?"

"You know where we're going," Brie replied. "Listen, I know what's coming. Most of the chosen are already prepared. Don't come out of the cabin. I mean it, Renee. You're not ready."

"The cabin? Am I going to be locked in?"

"Probably, and it's necessary." Brie put her hands on her shoulders. "I'm serious. Please, as a favor to me. Don't run, okay?"

"I'm not going to run."

"Whatever. Just don't for the next couple of days, for me." Her frilly, floral-printed sleeves lifted with the breeze.

"Okay. Okay. I'll stay locked in. Is it that bad?"

"It's bad enough. It's going to be intense with a lot of death. You can't run..." Brie paused. "I have to go."

The cabin door opened. Brie walked away as Renee shuffled toward the cabin, feeling conflicted. Her plan had been to try to run during the chaos, but Brie seemed concerned for her, and the king had seemed almost afraid.

The king's eyes darted around before he ushered her inside the cabin. As soon as the door closed, he pressed her against it and captured her mouth. Wow, what a way to greet someone. Her arms snaked around his neck. After all, she had to sell it, right?

Chapter 20

She wiped her hands off on an old, discarded towel she found in the kitchen, feeling content now that she'd eaten. Probably wouldn't eat again until after the horde was finished eating each other. A shiver ran down her spine at the thought. She wasn't even sure she'd be brave enough to run. She glanced at the plywood that covered a window. The cabin must've been built before the downfall of man.

She padded out of the kitchen area and wondered when he'd leave and lock her in. Her fingers touched her lips, remembering how he'd greeted her. Her chest tightened at how he was the one who'd made them stop and told her to eat. Renee retrieved a bottle of water but made herself drink it slowly. He had more water waiting when she got there, but because things were going to be crazy, she figured it was better to ration it out.

Frustrated, and a bit repelled by her own reaction to him, she maintained her distance and plopped down on the couch. He watched her from the one armchair in the room. Did he like sitting in those because it made him feel more like a king?

"How old are you?"

Renee was startled at the sound of his voice. Not because she was scared, but because it made a twinge of excitement shoot through her. "Twenty-two, or three. It's hard to keep track. Why? How old are you?"

"That isn't an easy question to answer."

Mesmerized again watching his lips as he spoke. She blinked to break the trance. "Why?"

He rubbed his jaw and averted his eyes. After a painfully long period of silence, he spoke, "Around twenty-eight, give or take."

The king of the dead wasn't even thirty. She peered at his face. He appeared young. Didn't have the weather-worn skin like everyone else did that aged them so much. Well, humans, anyway. Despite the fact that he was dead, his face was wrinkle-free and smooth. It appeared soft. Who would've thought being dead would make you more attractive than people with heartbeats? But that wasn't right, anyway. He had a heartbeat. She felt it every time he pressed against her. Not sure if Brie had one or not. She should check. Did zombies have heartbeats? Did their hearts somehow change into something decrepit and evil at the core? Renee continued to find her mind spinning with curiosity, confusion and fatigue.

"You should rest tonight. Tomorrow, it might be hard to sleep through the noise."

"Is tomorrow the start of the culling?"

"Yes. I'll begin it at dawn."

"You start it?"

"Not always, but I will this time."

"Why?" She pitched forward.

"Because of you." He stood and approached the couch putting out his hand.

Hesitantly, she closed her fingers around his and stood. He led her to the loft and motioned for her to climb the ladder. When she got to the top, she was thrilled to find a proper bed, and it wasn't rotten. She fell back with her arms spread and closed her eyes. If she weren't with an army of zombies, it would have been blissful.

Renee stiffened when the nameless king climbed in beside her. Shit. He probably thought that was an invitation. She cracked her eyes open and found he was on his side, gazing at her. When he caught her looking at him, he lifted his hand and smoothed down her hair before his fingers traced her lips. Her chest moved up and down with rapid breaths as his hand slid to her neck and then down her chest, between her breasts, to her stomach near her scar, and stopped. The palm of his hand rested over the scar.

"Why am I yours?" she whispered.

"Because I chose you. Because," he stopped and positioned his body next to hers. He was almost on top of her. "Renee," he said her name like it was both a prayer and a torment all at once before slanting his mouth over hers.

She had wanted to push him away, but she didn't. Renee suspected she might never be able to push him away again. Their kiss ignited, and they devoured each other's lips. He rolled on top of her, and she discovered something else she hadn't known about the undead. The length of him pressed against her heated center and made her breathless. Aside from his skin, irises, gait, and clear dominion over the horde of zombies, he felt... human.

Her hands drifted into his hair as desire clouded her thoughts. He tried to pull back, but she wouldn't let him go, couldn't. She'd gone too far now. She would truly hate herself after, so she had to make it worth it. He tried to lift his hips from hers, but she wrapped her legs around his waist and yanked him to her, making him groan into her mouth.

His mouth moved to her chin and neck before it dipped down to her breasts. She unlocked her legs from his waist as he lifted her shirt for access and tugged her bra aside from her breasts. She arched her back as he licked and sucked on her nipples, wanting him to continue even though she knew she shouldn't. Maybe if he continued, she would stay in that perfect moment where nothing existed but them. She'd have no reason to run if they could stay in intimate bliss forever.

Suddenly, he stopped and cleared his throat before he moved off her. She pinched her brows. He appeared pained as he drew several ragged breaths.

"I'm sorry, I didn't mean..." His eyes flicked to her breasts, still on display. His tongue darted out, licking his lips.

God, that was sexy. Her nipples pebbled. "It's fine. You said you'd give me what I want if I listened to you."

His eyebrows lifted. "You don't want me to stop?"

"If I did, I would've said something." She rolled closer to him.

His eyes shifted and were almost loving. "Zane."

"What?"

"You asked my name."

"Zane," she repeated, trying it out. Her fingers touched his chest as her eyes roamed over his face. Dead things weren't supposed to be so gorgeous. "I like it. Kiss me, Zane." She brought her mouth to his, determined to keep up her charade.

He growled and kissed her until she thought she'd die without air. When they pulled apart, gasping for breath, he looked feral. His features caught between the monster he kept on display and the sweet, human-like side he only showed her. It was intoxicating.

"Touch me, Zane, and make me forget about everything but you," she breathed.

He leapt on her and almost ripped off her clothes. Renee wasn't sure when he shed his own clothing, but they were both naked, exploring each other before she knew it. In the midst of his hands and lips roving her body, she tried to glance some sort of injury on his body, to prove to her mind that he was in fact, one of the undead. Zane kept switching between ravaging her and touching her like she was the most cherished thing in the world. It shattered her defenses and made her feel vulnerable in a way she didn't know she was capable of.

Several times, she attempted to rush to get him inside her, but he would simply distract her or move just out of her reach. There was no going back after this and she had to know what it would be like with him. Fooling around with the king was positively the most intense experience of her life. She wasn't trading her soul for anything less than the whole package.

"Renee, my heart, there's no reason to rush," he said and peeled her fingers off his shaft.

She froze. *My heart.*

The lump in her throat made her eyes moisten as she averted them. It had gone too far. The deception. She was only doing this so he wouldn't suspect when she snuck out later - right? He couldn't say things like that. It ruined everything. He was the zombie king and the murderous bastard who thought his horde was better than any human. Shit. What was she doing?

"What's wrong?" his tone shifted, suspicious.

She couldn't tell him the truth, but she doubted she could pull off a lie either. "I'm nervous." That was partially true. He had been too sweet and made it too real. They were supposed to have really sinful, hot sex, and he'd made it weird.

His fingers traced the side of her body. "I won't hurt you."

Shit. Did he have any idea how much worse he'd made it? The uncaring, undead king who found his horde *useful* tried to reassure her.

"Won't your queen be pissed off you're doing this? Or can you screw anyone because you're the king?" It was a cheap shot, but she couldn't take any more of his kindness. It was paining her in ways she might not recover from.

He stopped touching her and moved aside. "Why would you say that?"

Zane sounded hurt. That was stupid. No way could she hurt the king's feelings. "Because I don't want Brie to attack me when she finds out. She's the queen, right?"

His jaw tightened. "Again, with the titles!"

Renee scooted away from him and searched for her discarded clothes. The realization of her actions was seeping in swiftly. She had to make him leave before she lost it. She tugged her underwear toward her. The underwear he had his creatures get for her. So messed up. His fingers wrapped around her wrist and stopped her from pulling them on. When she turned to face him, she was not surprised to find anger brightening his irises.

"She is *not* my queen. Don't say that again."

"Let go of my wrist."

He narrowed his eyes and yanked her body to his. She pushed on his chest while his other hand grabbed the back of her neck and he slammed his mouth on hers. She meant to bite him or fight him, but ended up melting further against him. When her back touched the bed, she lifted her hips, aching to be filled. His manhood brushed her core, but he didn't enter. Growling in frustration, she reached for him again to line them up herself. Zane inhaled when she gripped him but shifted his body to the side to keep him from her entrance.

"Are you so eager for me? Didn't you want me to touch you?" he teased, sliding his fingers over her slick folds.

Her eyes rolled back in her head as he continued stroking her. Why hadn't anyone else touched her like that before? When she had sex previously, it'd been mostly bent over something and rushed. She couldn't risk getting attacked in the middle of the night and didn't want an audience, either. Sure, men had touched her, but not like this, not so perfectly. It was like Zane somehow knew exactly where and how to move. She couldn't catch her breath given how well he worked her body.

Panting, she realized she wasn't touching him, and she was supposed to be the one in charge. Everywhere tingled. Goosebumps covered her skin, and flashes of pleasure and heat kept flaring up between her legs. She tried to focus, to move her hand.

"My sweet, Renee. Come for me."

She moaned at his words. Never in her life had she been so turned on, or felt like this. It was surreal and dreamlike, it reminded her of a scene from one of her books. Too magical to be real.

Something was wrong. Her legs trembled, and her face was too hot. Something was building inside her and threatened to tear her apart. Her fingers dug into his skin. He had to stop before it was too late. He was going to kill her. A scream tore from her lips as her core clenched his fingers over and over.

She tried to speak but only managed his name, "Zane."

His lips brushed hers, then her cheek, and then her temple. Her legs kept twitching.

"You're so beautiful," he whispered in her ear.

No. He couldn't be like this. It had to stop.

"You need to sleep now."

"No," she mumbled but didn't open her eyes.

"Let me help you. You told me you wouldn't fight me." His tongue traced the shell of her ear. "Sleep so I can make you come again."

Renee wanted to ask if that's what had happened but drifted off in Zane's arms.

Chapter 21

Her head hurt again. Out of habit, she covered her eyes and reached for her sunglasses, only to find she was still naked. Still in the bed with *him*. Actually, they were both still naked. Renee snapped her eyes shut as the night replayed itself in her mind. His words. Shit. *Shit.* His hand caressed her breast in a lazy, possessive way.

She clenched her jaw, feeling relieved at not looking at herself in the mirror anymore, she would never be able to stomach her face now. She was literally sleeping with the enemy. Why couldn't he have been like every other man she'd ever been intimate with? He hadn't even had sex with her, but she knew he wanted to. It was all backwards and made her stomach roll.

Slowly, she opened her eyes. Her mouth dropped open. He was sleeping? Next to her was the undead king, Zane, with his eyes closed and a peaceful expression on his face. Like that, he seemed almost human. Had he always slept and switched shifts with Brie before she woke up? Her brain screamed at her dumb heart to remember that he does in fact, sleep. Has left himself vulnerable. It could be important later if she avoided being distracted by his sharp beauty or the way he'd made her feel.

Should she try to run now? It was quiet outside. She'd promised Zane and Brie she wouldn't. However, if she didn't, it made her the worst example of a human possible. But the things he'd said, the way he'd touched her, cherished her, he couldn't be evil. Not entirely. Her idiotic heart rallied for her to stay, to solve the mystery of why he seemed a cold-hearted prick one minute and switched to a gentle, considerate, loving creature the next.

Almost as if he had read her mind, his hand slid from her breast and covered her heart. With the pulse quickening, his eyes opened. Renee's breath caught in her throat. The adoration in his eyes made hers watery. All her thoughts of running evaporated as Zane's hand slid down to her stomach and over her scar, then rested there.

"Renee." Her stomach fluttered at the sound of her name on his lips. He moved until he hovered over her. "Mine." He brought his lips to hers.

She swooned. Fucking swooned while lying down in a bed, being kissed by a zombie that tasted like citrus and sunshine. It was almost better than anything she'd ever read in her books. Too soon, he broke their kiss.

"I have to leave." Zane's words seemed to distress him.

"Okay. When will you be back?" She wanted more of his kisses. Wanted him to touch her again. If that'd been an orgasm, then she wanted more, many more.

"I'm not sure."

Her brow furrowed. She licked her lips, needing water. His eyes flicked to her lips.

"I don't... I don't want to leave." He sounded sincere and looked distraught at the idea of leaving.

"Then don't." Her fingers trailed down his muscled chest to his taut stomach until they reached his shaft.

He made a sound that resembled pain and put his forehead on hers. "I don't have a choice. It won't let me stay. It must consume."

Her brow wrinkled with worry. He'd said that before. It was almost like he didn't want to eat people. Perhaps he didn't, but he had said zombies were the superior species, so that didn't make sense. She removed her hands from his sex and cupped his face.

"But you'll come back?"

"Yes." He kissed her. "Yes. You're mine." Another kiss. "I'll always come back to you."

Her heart slammed against her ribs.

"Always?" Why had she asked that? Stupid, stupid heart. Shut up.

"There's nothing that will keep me from you, my heart."

He sealed his promise with a kiss that shattered her. Destroyed her. She didn't need to be torn apart by the undead because he'd done it with words instead. She was utterly and wholly screwed because she wanted him to return to her. Zane, her king of the dead.

Chapter 22

Propped up against a piece of wood that covered the window in the loft, she opened a book she'd found downstairs. She hadn't really enjoyed reading anything but fantasy before the downfall, yet discovered recently she liked reading just about anything. Because of how things were, Renee didn't have any complex preferences for the type of books she read, except that they were fiction, just not horror. She may not have learned anything practical from fiction, but it was one of the few escapes left to her.

Her previous favorites were always sweeping romances with magical creatures, but not scary ones. Beautiful ones, with fae or elves that existed in another realm. A realm that might have its own problems but had magic and beauty that Earth could never touch. Everyone in her stories wore elegant clothes in gorgeous colors and had elaborate hairdos. Even if the female characters were warriors, they were stunning like Brie, and also like Brie, usually had other talents. And there were always crucial, elaborate scenes in idyllic locations where everything was perfect, often including the female in their most luxurious clothing. Sometimes there would be parties or galas where the main male character would dance with the main female character, trying to hide his desire or occasionally flirt with her.

Her view strayed to the fantasy book Zane had gifted her, and she ran her teeth over her lip, reflecting on what the men would say to their potential mate, it reminded her of how Zane sometimes said things, like how he claimed ownership of her. He brooded a lot like the characters in her books. She shook her head to clear her mind, this wasn't a fucking fairy tale. She shouldn't compare him to her books, it was dangerous and would only confuse her more.

After he made her come again the other night. She finally understood what the big deal was about sex. Well, good sex. All she thought about was him returning, and it happening again and again. Zane refused to let her do anything to him, saying he only wanted to learn her body. They hadn't even had sex, not real sex, but she couldn't wait. It would be the best thing she ever experienced in her life.

She drank another bottle of water and tried to ignore her empty stomach. If she'd been allowed scavenge before when they were in a town, she probably would've found some dried goods to shove in her backpack. She'd looked in the kitchen downstairs, but it was barren.

The first guttural scream came about an hour later. Then another scream and another and another. She couldn't keep reading after hearing that anymore. She slapped her hands over her ears. Sounds of fighting and agony surrounded the cabin. She tried to block it out, but it seemed like the melee was in the cabin with her. She hurried away from the window. Perhaps the sound was coming through the glass, so she climbed down the ladder and checked for a closet.

After searching the entire cabin, she found a utility closet with an old water heater, climbed in beside it, and covered her ears again. It muffled the sounds but didn't block them entirely. It sounded like a pack of wild animals fighting, like vicious animals clashing until one cried out, and then there was silence. She hated it so much. Her stomach had been rumbling all this time with hunger. She was thirsty too, but wasn't leaving the closet for any reason. Not until he returned.

The sounds got louder and louder. The volume of it all convinced her they were right outside the door. Zane really wanted his army to go through this to get rid of the weak? He was horrible. This was awful. Even worse, she'd been making out with him and wanted to do more of it. What was wrong with her? Weak. And he knew exactly what to say to her, how to touch her, and how to make her forget what he was. Who he was.

Her stomach protested and disrupted her self-degradation. Staring at the surrounding blackness, she thought about how committed she'd been to her plan. A traitor to her own kind, sitting in a closet, cowering because she didn't want to be apart from him. Her heart squeezed, remembering his soft, full lips on hers. No. This time she wouldn't let her heart make the choices.

"I told you, princess, it was my job to protect you. It's okay. Let me go."

Renee's body shook as she tried to drive out the memory of her brother's last words to her. How she had vowed to him not only that she would keep going, surviving for him, but also, destroy any zombie she could for taking the only person she'd ever loved. The only person who'd ever truly loved her in return.

Her fingers grabbed at her hair as she gasped for breath. She couldn't do this. She wouldn't survive the memory of losing him again. Liam had been everything to her, the one constant in her life. He'd always put her first. Forgave her when she was a brat. Always included and considered her thoughts and feelings, something her own parents couldn't manage.

He'd been there for her entire recovery after she'd been attacked, stayed with her in the hospital until she was strong enough to go home. He drove her to all her doctor appointments and therapy sessions.

The day when everything fell apart, he'd raced home to protect her because he was her self-proclaimed knight commander and swore to protect her until his last breath. Renee's breath hitched. He had kept his word. Traded his life for hers. So, she could go on. No one had ever loved her like that. No one would ever love her like that.

Liam was the kindest, most perfect person she'd ever known. He was honorable in a way people only were in books. Devoted in a way that didn't exist anymore. Perhaps never existed. If she stayed, she wasn't just betraying her own kind, she was betraying Liam's memory, all the sacrifices he'd made for her.

She forced her fingers from her hair and smacked her head against the wooden wall to drive her flawless brother from her mind. With a deep breath, she let herself think, really think and remember a time before the end of the world. It hadn't always been great, but it wasn't a horror movie every day like it was now.

Renee opened the closet and crept out. Zane was right; that world was gone. It was in ashes now. She stood. But that didn't mean it was over for all humans. She could keep her promise and give them all a chance against the creatures destroying what was left of the world.

Renee climbed up the loft's ladder to retrieve her backpack, loading the last of the water into it along with her books. Light from a corner of the plywood against the window created a line on the wall. Daylight. The fighting continued. The time of day wouldn't change anything, apparently. Her fingers traced the edge of the sheet of plywood and pulled it. The sheet of plywood easily separated from the wall. Owners probably thought they were safe in the loft and didn't reinforce it. She tugged at it and smiled when it slipped off the window. The sun shone outside and made her feel hopeful.

Renee popped her shades on. She'd wanted to learn more, but that moment was an opportune chance to get free. Zane's face flashed in her mind and almost made her put down her backpack as her breath hitched. But that was the exact reason she had to go. As impossible as it was, she liked him, and if she stayed, she was afraid of what it might mean.

The window opened and didn't have a screen. It would be a tight squeeze, but she could manage. Thankfully, there was a tree close to the cabin Renee could shimmy down without falling. Her eyes flicked to the bed, and she hesitated. She'd promised. He wouldn't trust her now. It didn't matter, she wouldn't see him again.

Renee climbed out the window and clambered into the tree. It was sturdy, but the branches were thin where she clung, so she moved lower until she saw it. Her eyes snapped shut. They were right outside, as she'd guessed - so many zombies. Peeking below, she blanched at the scattered pieces, and the quick zombies bent over, eating the others. Somehow, as she watched them devour their own kind, suddenly, what they did to the humans seemed less despicable.

She wasn't able to see very far out due to the trees, but from the noise, it seemed like most of the action was taking place at the front of the cabin, not the back. She waited until the two undead feeding below the tree she was perched in heard something around the side of the cabin and took off. As quickly as she could, she lowered herself until she jumped the rest of the distance from the tree to the bloody ground.

Renee dashed as quietly as possible into the trees behind the cabin. Not sure where to go except away. She glanced behind her, even though she knew it wouldn't do any good if the faster zombies came for her.

Shit. She shouldn't have even been thinking about them. Their approach sounded like thunder. She didn't bother to turn around to see how many chased her. She was going to die the way she thought she would weeks ago in the city.

The guttural, animalistic noises terrified her. She was fast, but nothing could outrun fast zombies because nothing stopped them. If one got hurt, the rest just kept coming, not worrying about their downed companion as they raced toward their target. Renee was slammed into the dirt and leaves on the ground. Her face pressed into the earth as something crashed onto her back.

"This her?" the creature grunted.

"Don't care, need meat." A different gurgling voice responded.

A terrible growl reverberated through her from the zombie on her back. A heartbeat later, she was driven further into the dirt when the zombie on her back used her to launch itself onto another zombie.

Renee put her hands into the soil to push up when suddenly her head was yanked up by her hair. A deformed face made noises at her before it bellowed. Behind her, a female responded with noises Renee recognized as communication. The one holding her hair bared its teeth and dove at her throat. She smacked at the zombie, trying to yank herself free. The zombie snapped at her face. Shit. Shit. Renee shoved, but it did nothing. Black blood exploded in her face.

She wiped her eyes and saw Brie's icy ones glaring at her, ringed with blood and muck. Her clothes were covered in guts, but her bright red lips remained. Was it lipstick or blood?

Renee coughed and spat out the tarry blood. "Brie, you saved me."

"Of course I did. You're my friend, you idiot. Get up." Brie's eyes darted everywhere.

The two that attacked Renee ripped into one another a few feet from them. Brie grabbed her arm and dragged her to the side of the cabin. She yanked a piece of plywood near the ground and exposed a hole.

"Get in. Go forward five feet and reach up. There's a trapdoor. Go now and don't argue with me."

"But-"

"Don't. I'm this close to letting you die out here for lying to me." Brie pushed Renee to the ground near the hole. "You can't escape."

Renee climbed down, under the cabin. It was really nasty, and she didn't waste time searching for the trapdoor. It took a minute to get into the cabin with the wood of the trapdoor having warped over time, and it was tough to pry open. Once it was vertical, she wriggled into the kitchen and closed the door. She wanted to weep at her failed attempt but couldn't.

Like everything else in her life, her attempt at running was another failure. She'd continually written off the missteps of her "normal" life before the world fell apart. Renee had tried so many different things in an effort to be helpful to humans' survival and was never quite good enough at anything. Unable to keep anyone alive and lacking any real friends, she also never had any badass skills that made her wanted in any surviving human group.

She wanted to blame her disability because it was an easy out, but it was a lie. It'd made her shy and apprehensive as a kid, but once she mostly passed for normal, things could've been different. She could've done *something*.

Once the beginning of the end started, she could've stepped up and risen like a phoenix from the ashes. Been someone awesome or made herself into a fighter. Perhaps read more stuff that made her wiser, or learned an essential skill that would've helped rebuild society one day—hell, even being good at caring for others. She'd seen so many others do it.

Become awesome.

Not her. She just *was*.

She kept surviving, like a cockroach, even though she shouldn't. How screwed up was it that the very things that killed everything were the only ones who truly *saw* her? Somehow, Brie and Zane had become convinced she was worth protecting. Even going as far as wanting her around. She put her face on her dirty knees. Except her intention was to kill them. Her friends? And all the others. Was it wrong that she felt guilty about it?

Chapter 23

Renee made herself sit there as she listened to death as it surrounded her. It could've been hours or days; it was impossible to tell. Yet, she forced herself because she was a coward. Not only for failing humanity but also for failing herself. Her stomach repeatedly reminded her she was hungry, but she ignored it.

When the door opened, and she heard his heavy footfalls, she didn't look up at him. She knew he'd be furious at her and was positive Brie had told him everything. He lifted her up, but she continued keeping her eyes on her feet. His bloody hand touched her cheek.

"Renee."

The way he said her name gutted her. The tears that threatened to fall for hours finally did. She cried because she despised herself. Because she made Brie angry. Because she'd hurt him, and because she wasn't sure if she was going to keep trying to run from him.

She didn't protest when he pulled her to his chest, even though it was covered in black blood and fragments of *something*. She ugly cried on him until she sounded like a five-year-old who was spent yet couldn't stop. Zane kept smoothing her hair over and over. Why wasn't he yelling at her? It made everything so much worse.

"Come, you need to clean up."

He led her to the small bathroom, where she stood in the dark until he returned with a candle and a bucket of water. She twisted aside before she caught her reflection. Never had she wanted to avoid it so much. With a cloth, he wiped her face, which made her sob.

"Why aren't you yelling at me?" she choked out. He said nothing and kept washing her face. "Aren't you mad at me?"

"I'm furious. You lied to me." He paused. "You betrayed me."

"You should just let me go. Send me out there to die because I'm a traitor." He'd called that other zombie a traitor, and she wasn't any different. She'd meant to find humans and return to kill him.

He struck the mirror behind her. It shattered, causing her to flinch.

"I would never do that. I would never hurt you deliberately."

She tilted her chin up. "Why? I don't understand."

His hands cupped her face. "Yes, you do."

His irises were so bright in the darkness. He'd eaten his own kind.

"Is it over?"

"No." His jaw worked. "I came to check on you." His eyes moved over her face. Zane tugged her out of the bathroom to the table and pushed her into a chair. "You need to eat. We'll finish this later."

Renee stared at the cooked meat on the table. "What is that?" She was wary because he'd said there wasn't any food which meant that was… one of the horde? A random animal?

"You promised me you would let me help you and that you wouldn't fight me." He reminded her.

"Obviously, my word doesn't mean anything." She stared at the floor.

His fingers snatched her face up by her chin. "That's your choice. It can mean something if you choose to keep your word. You told me you trusted me. Prove it. Eat."

Her eyes drifted to the meat. God, she was hungry. Only what if it was one of them? She'd never eaten a former-human, but would she really know? She had to decide if she trusted Zane or not. Decide if he would trick her into eating zombies. Her mind wandered to before he left, his sincere words. She picked up the meat and took a bite. It was a deer. The flavor was immediately recognizable.

"Thank you," she muttered and ate.

While she did, he reattached the wood over the window and checked the other windows. At some point, he washed the yuck from his hands and disappeared outside for a while. She drank a bottle of water and put her head on the table. So stupid, always so stupid about everything. It was no wonder why she'd spent so much time alone after the zombies rose up.

Zane went in and out of the cabin a few more times. She caught sight of Brie closing the door behind him when he carried a large barrel in. Shit, that looked heavy.

"Come with me." He held out his hand and led her into the bathroom.

The tub was half-filled with water. Her eyes snapped to him. "Why? I don't deserve…" She paused when he put his finger over her lips.

"No, you don't, but I don't want you to ruin the bed. We'll be here another night before we leave." Zane lifted her shirt over her head and tossed it to the floor before unhooking her bra and placing it on the closed toilet. "You're lucky there are clothes here. You didn't have any other shirts."

She nodded and undid her jeans. He helped her out of them and slid her panties down. As mad as he was, she didn't miss how desire made his eyes heat.

"Do you have to go again?" She stepped into the cold water.

"Soon. I shouldn't be here now."

"You don't have to stay. I really won't run now, I swear." She choked back her tears as she scrubbed.

"I want to believe you." He leaned against the door frame.

Zane was so handsome, casually standing there. Even with blood and guts all over him. Even with the sounds of his horde killing each other. Somehow, with him near her, Renee's fear and anxiety wasn't as powerful. When she got to her hair, he helped wash her scalp; damn, it felt good. She dipped under the water to rinse. When she emerged, he caught her lips and kissed her with such passion it made her light-headed.

Wrapped in a towel and nothing else, he made her climb the ladder to the loft. Her backpack was slung over his shoulder as she eased into bed. It was so surreal. Although she felt relaxed, she kept waiting for the other shoe to drop. No way would she be able to run away, she had finally accepted she wouldn't succeed. Brie had warned her more than once.

Zane kissed her again. Forgetting he'd recently eaten; she opened her mouth to his and was amazed he still tasted like citrus. How the hell was that possible? His fingers glided down her torso and then down her leg. Renee nibbled on his lip, lost in him, until something cold wrapped around her ankle. A distinct metal click made her eyes fly open.

"Like I said, I want to believe you, but I can't risk losing you, and I can't stay."

Renee stared at the metal cuff as her mouth dropped open. There was a chain from it to the loft's railing. "You can't…"

"I'll come back to you. If you pull the rail down, it will make a lot of noise."

"Zane! You can't chain me up like an animal!"

"I told you not to run!" His teeth flashed. He was back to making threats. "You're lucky I'm not doing something more drastic."

"Oh, right, I forgot because you're the asshole king. Maybe I should grovel and beg for your mercy!"

He advanced until he was hovering over her, teeth still bared. Renee had grown more aware of the blood and flesh stuck on him now. His hand grabbed her throat as he held her in place. Not squeezing, even though she could tell he wanted to.

"You should seek my forgiveness because you lied to me," he said through gritted teeth.

"You should seek my forgiveness because you've made me a prisoner!"

"You didn't act like a prisoner when you practically begged me to fuck you."

Renee's eyes burned, although she wouldn't break down in front of him or allow him to see he'd hurt her. "You know nothing about me. Maybe that's why I decided to run, because you wouldn't follow through. You just teased me." She instantly regretted every word that came out of her mouth but couldn't stop herself. Renee wanted Zane to hurt, too.

He let her go and stepped back. "I let you see a part of me I thought was dead, and it meant nothing to you." He turned and continued to the ladder.

Shit. She'd really made a mess of things. "Zane, no, I didn't mean it. I didn't mean any of it. Please, don't go."

Except it was too late. He was already down the ladder. The cabin door closed softer than she thought it would while she remained naked and chained to the bed. It sounded like a weird porno from before the end of the world.

Chapter 24

Renee woke and scooted closer to Zane's large frame. He smelled good, clean, like soap. Her eyes flew open and found Zane wrapped around her. Even their legs were entwined. She peeked and found the leg cuff was still attached. When had he returned? Why was he cuddling with her? He was pissed off when he left. Okay, perhaps he was more hurt because she'd been a bitch. Still, he was back with her like he'd promised.

Not one person had ever been so devoted to her and kept their word, even if she'd screwed up or they were upset. She blinked. Everything was so confusing. Nothing made sense anymore. The simple lines between hating the undead and wanting to save humanity blurred as each day passed. She had to get away from him before she actually was a traitor to her own kind.

Her fingers brushed his soft hair back as she studied his handsome face. His eyes opened, and he peered at her, the ache still present in his gaze. It was her fault he looked like that. They stared at each other for a long time and touched each other lightly.

"I'm sorry, Zane. I really am." Renee's voice cracked. "Not just because I tried to run, but for the awful things I said to you. I didn't mean them. I swear I didn't."

"My sweet Renee, please stop. It's alright. Shh." He kissed her cheeks.

"It's not. I was a bitch because I wanted to hurt you and because what you said upset me and-"

His lips covered hers. Their mouths met over and over before he spoke against her lips, "I shouldn't have said the things I said to you, either. I'm not used to anyone disagreeing with me. They always follow orders."

She pulled back. "I'm not like them."

"No, you're not." He gazed at her in wonder.

"Are we leaving now?" She tried to mask her misery because she liked being there with him. Sleeping with him. It made everything else more bearable.

"Soon."

"Because you don't have a choice."

"No. It must consume." His voice held that odd, detached sound again when he spoke. Whenever those words left his lips, he seemed more upset.

"Is the culling over?"

"Almost. We're stronger now."

"And that's good, even though you have less of an army?"

"Army?"

"Horde. Whatever. You know what I mean."

"Less in number but stronger. More capable. It's the nature of evolution."

"Will we ever be able to be like this again?"

"I promise we will. If you stay with me."

"I will," she vowed and meant it. "Besides, you already told me I can't get away because you'll always come back to me because... I'm yours."

"Mine," he whispered, then reminded her body twice, that it was also his.

Renee tried to catch her breath as he gazed at her and bent to kiss her stomach and scar. Part of her wanted him to keep going until he devoured her the way he mentioned in the van, eat her, in a different, less threatening way.

"Why won't you let me touch you?"

"Soon enough, but I can't let you yet." He laid his head on her stomach and sighed.

"But why?" She felt so selfish because she was the only one getting anything out of their interactions.

"I won't be able to control myself. I barely can now. You're intoxicating." His fingers trailed down to her thighs.

Tiny sparks traveled up to her heated center from his ministrations.

"I don't want to leave," he whispered. It sounded like it had before the culling, only more desperate.

"Then we should stay here a little longer," she replied as she ran her fingers through his locks.

His fingers clutched her leg. "I want to, but we can't." His voice was rough, like it was difficult for him to get the words out.

"We have to leave." His tone now resigned as he sat up and undid her ankle cuff.

She wanted to debate it with him even though she knew there wasn't a point. So, she let it go, her heart heavy as she packed her things. As she strapped the backpack to her, she couldn't shake the feeling like their reprieve had ushered in something so much worse.

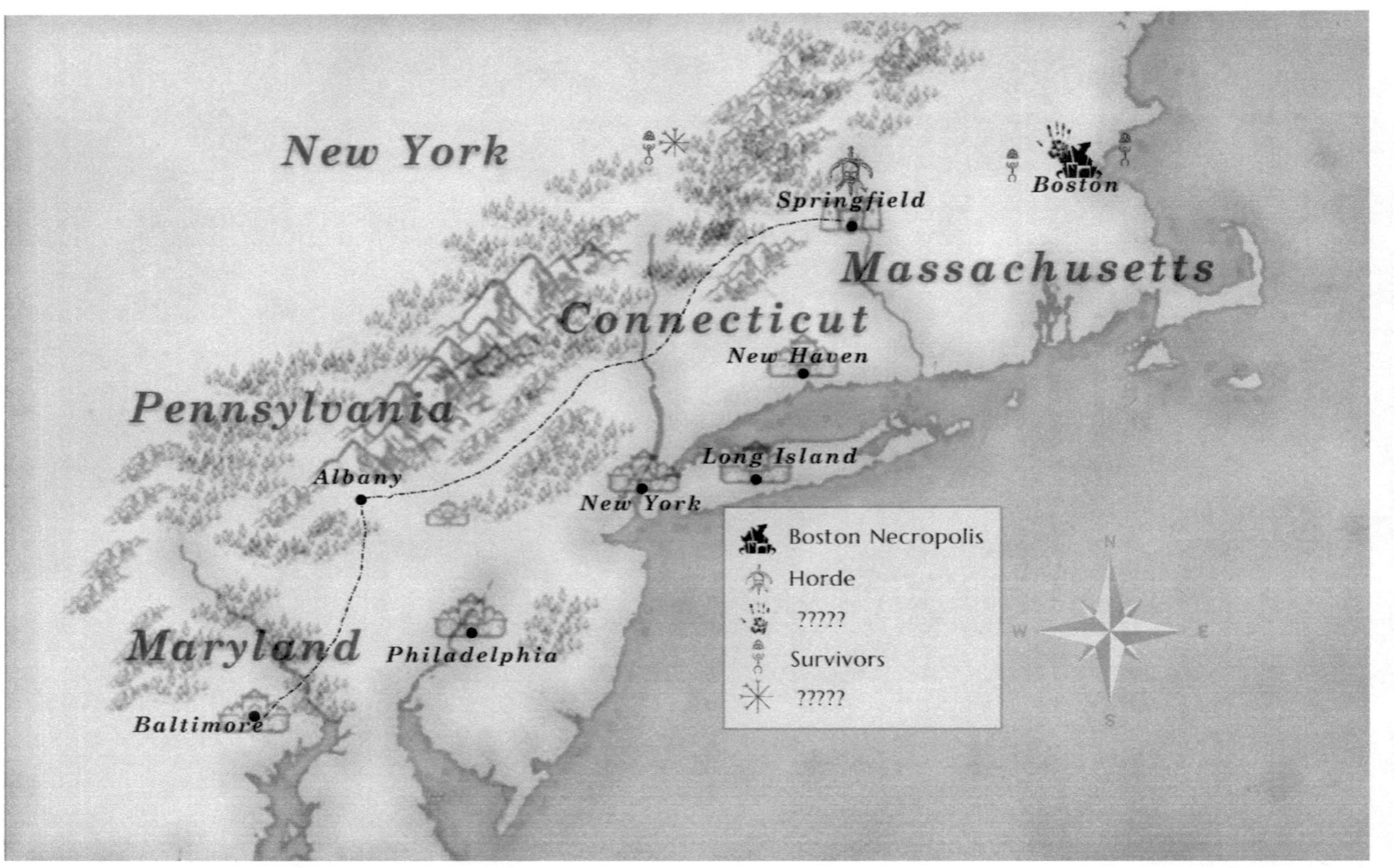
New York
Boston
Springfield
Massachusetts
Connecticut
New Haven
Pennsylvania
Long Island
Albany
New York
Maryland
Philadelphia
Baltimore
Boston Necropolis
Horde
?????
Survivors
?????
N
W
E
S

Chapter 25

Brie had been subdued for the last three days. She kept her hair in a bun or in a simple French braid, which meant she didn't want to fuss with it. Her clothes and face were still immaculate, but something wasn't right. Renee tried to get her to talk, but she wouldn't. If she had to guess, she'd say she was depressed but Renee didn't know why.

The first two days after the culling were decent, just endless walking followed by snuggling with Zane at night. No death. Everyone was stuffed from eating their former horde members during the culling. *Barf.* Zane made sure Renee had something cooked to eat for dinner each night.

He hadn't slept since they left the cabin, which kinda creeped her out because it meant he spent the last two nights staring at her while she slept. They had bickered the first night, after they'd been on their feet all day walking, when he suggested cuffing her feet together. Why did he even have handcuffs? Renee wasn't sure she'd ever regain his trust.

Finally, she persuaded him to lay with her and make out. He promised when they had proper shelter, he'd make her tremble again. She was desperate to arrive at their next destination until on the third day, she realized the horde approached another metropolitan city. Shit.

Zane barked orders at the horde when the broken skyline came into view and everyone shifted to different positions. Brie dragged Renee off to the side. A fierce look made Brie's face tighten.

"What's going on? It seems like he's getting the units organized," Renee whispered.

"Units?" Brie, tying her hair in a high ponytail, glanced at Renee. Shit, Brie meant business and didn't want any carnage in her hair.

"Yeah. The horde is his army, right?"

Brie rolled her eyes. "He's sending in the... ground *troops*."

Renee grinned at her words.

"It's dangerous to enter a city. He always sends in the shamblers first. It doesn't matter if they die."

Humans were always nervous about entering a city too, worried they'd be attacked. Apparently, large cities were treacherous for everyone. Renee paused at the word "everyone" as she realized she thought about both humans, and zombies.

She flattened her lips before she spoke. "Why is entering the city dangerous for the horde?"

"Because humans hide in them. They gather supplies and weapons. We always lose a lot of us in cities."

Well, damn, that's exactly what every human she'd ever spent time with thought too. Except, surviving humans didn't understand this horde, whether or not it was true for other hordes, went into cities intentionally. Everyone Renee had traveled with believed the undead didn't do anything strategically, especially plan how to enter a city.

"But you said the shamblers don't matter."

"They don't. They're not like us, they're just animated corpses. They don't feel pain or have any feelings."

Woah. Renee's mouth dropped open, and she stared at Brie, shocked at her words. That meant the other zombies felt pain and had... feelings? In all the time humans had spent fighting them, it seemed like nothing stopped them. They could have their limbs torn off or giant holes in their bodies, and they still kept coming. Her mind wandered to the zombie head that wasn't dead even after being detached thanks to Zane's rage. Nothing stopped them. Renee considered the amount of agony the zombies endured and she felt strange.

She glanced around her at the waiting zombies. The members of the surrounding horde were nervous. Renee wasn't sure why or how she could sense it.

"I thought the horde was just the horde."

"It is. But we work as a team for survival. We'll always die, lose numbers, but the chosen must survive. The humans want to destroy us. We have to fight." Brie's eyes darted around, observing the horde.

Renee's brow furrowed. Brie made it sound like they were at war, that somehow, they were the ones fighting just to exist. It was so backwards. Humans were the ones fighting to live. It was the zombies that were hell-bent on devouring them until there was nothing left. Zane had said as much.

"You already lied to me," Brie began, flicking her ice-blue irises to her.

Renee averted her eyes. She'd been waiting for Brie to chew her out about her actions for days.

"You seem pretty cozy with him now. I doubt you'll be as stupid again."

Renee's cheeks heated at her words.

"Are you really my friend?" Brie seemed to squeak out the question.

Something in her tone made Renee peer at her. She was being sincere, so Renee reached for her hand.

"Yes. I'm sorry. I shouldn't have lied to you. And sometimes, I wasn't lying, I had no intention of running that night, and then, well, the opportunity presented itself." She wouldn't apologize for trying to run, but she could tell her she was sorry she'd lied.

Brie huffed. "If you're sorry, prove it. Don't be a dumbass and get yourself killed today. Stay *with* me and do what I tell you so I can protect you. You may think your humans will help you, but they won't. You're with us. They can't tell the difference between enemies and friends."

Renee studied her. There was more than what Brie was letting on. She wasn't sure exactly what it was, but there was something personal about how she'd said that. Had Brie tried to help humans before?

The horde eventually split up and scattered around the outside of the city. Renee tried to find Zane. If she could catch a glimpse of him, she wouldn't be so scared. Odd that she was with the enemy and was as terrified as she'd always been going into a city.

"Why is the horde dividing up?" Renee whispered.

"Because we enter the city from multiple areas and meet in the center. At least, that's the plan with this city. He always tries to figure out the best way in and out of a location based on geographical features, city street layouts and any other information he's gathered, so we don't lose too many."

None of Renee's groups ever figured that out. It seemed like the undead were nowhere and then, suddenly everywhere, now it made sense why. He tried to figure out the best way so the horde wouldn't lose as many of them? When Zane talked about it, he hadn't cared at all. Or at least it seemed that way.

"It's going to get messy today. You're going to have to decide if you're with us now. Or if you're going to run. Because if you run this time," she paused and averted her eyes. "Then you need to be gone. Don't come back."

"Brie," Renee clasped her hand again. "I shouldn't have lied. I know you don't have any reason to believe me, but I won't put you in danger again because I'm being selfish."

Brie cocked her head to the side. "You finally get that?"

"I get bad things will happen if I try to leave. I understand you're supposed to protect me, even if it puts you in danger." Renee stared at the ground. "I didn't know at first. I was a selfish friend, but I won't be anymore."

"It won't just hurt *me*, Renee, or just put *me* in danger. If you run," she paused as her face tightened with anger. "You would put the entire horde in danger. You'd destroy *everyone*."

The gravity of Brie's words struck Renee in the chest. She was too anxious to ask why. She didn't want to know. "I won't run. I promise," she whispered.

Brie grimaced and averted her gaze. "Your humans will be here."

"I know. I... don't want to see them right now," Renee said because it was true. She was too mixed up, and being around others like her would only further confuse her. Perhaps the next city. Besides, she still didn't know who the chosen were, and she should have that information before she ultimately left Zane's horde.

"It's time. We have to move. Stay behind me."

Renee trembled as she ducked down and silently followed Brie. They only had to get through today. Everything would be okay as long as they didn't run into any people. She couldn't trust herself if she saw other humans because then she would be betraying her only friend and Zane.

Chapter 26

They'd been crouched and hiding for what seemed like ages. She'd tried to ask Brie what they were waiting for, but Brie's glare shut her up. The shamblers had entered the city hours ago. A chill set in after the sun left the sky. Renee was hungry and tired from all the miles they'd marched. Brie's fingers squeezed Renee's arm as her eyes flicked over the pile of debris they hid behind.

Humans. Militant ones who worked as a unit cleared out the remaining shamblers. Random gunfire had been going off since they arrived, but it was their first time seeing a group of living people. Seconds later, Brie made some clicks and guttural noises. The fast zombies leaped from their hiding places and attacked.

"No!" Renee cried out, but it didn't have the desired effect. One human saw her and then aimed his gun directly at her. Shit! The fast zombie to his right tore into him as Renee was knocked on her ass.

"Stupid!" Brie snarled at her.

Renee didn't argue. Shouting out like that had been stupid.

Brie bellowed and moved her hands, issuing orders to the pack. She yanked Renee up and thrust her into the open. The zombies feasted on the dead humans; two fought over the intestines of a fallen soldier. Renee bit her lip and looked elsewhere. She'd never be okay with this. Never get used to it.

She felt worse as they quietly dashed through the city. Tears obscured her vision, and she knew it would only infuriate Brie more. More gunfire. Brie yanked her behind some cars and waited.

"Go around wide. Report." Brie told the pack that followed them.

Several minutes later, some odd clicking and grunting above told them another group was just ahead. Renee pinched her brows. Another group? She wanted to avoid people, and it seemed like they ran into them everywhere they went.

"Go ahead. Call for help." Brie said and signaled back before she turned and leveled her gaze at Renee. "Are you going to be stupid again?" she asked in her normal voice.

"No." Renee's stomach rolled, not just because she was starving and not because the gore was making her nauseous. It was because she didn't know what she would do when they encountered the other group. She *had* to help the humans, she was one of them, but... she didn't want Brie or Zane to get hurt.

They advanced closer to the sounds of fighting. Cries for help filled the air. Horrible, scared voices who didn't want to die. Both she and Brie hurried to the scene. She had to do something, but who would she help? The humans who howled in misery? Or the horde?

When they reached the fight, Renee froze. Her breaths were shallow as she tried to understand what she viewed before her. Brie, beautiful, brave Brie, charged in to save her group. The screams and the cries hadn't been the humans. It had been the zombies. Had they always screamed in pain? Did humans even realize how much agony they were in? Renee's heart beat so hard it threatened to break free from her chest.

Brie moved around the humans like a dancer, fluid and deadly. Her expression was so cold as she tore out a man's throat while evading a machete beside her. She twisted and knocked his feet out from under him and used the machete he'd threatened her with to impale him. Her fancy sunflower shirt was ruined.

"Brie!" Renee called out when another human raised his gun at her friend's head.

Brie spun to the side and jumped in the air. The man turned and aimed his rifle at Renee. Shit. Her own people were going to kill her. It'd be her own fault. She didn't want Brie to die. He squeezed the trigger, but Brie knocked the rifle up, smacking him in his face, dazing him. A heartbeat later, she ripped his head off.

Renee stumbled back. Too much.

All of it.

She couldn't stay there. Brie's eyes widened, and she shook her head.

"I'm sorry. So sorry."

Renee turned on her heel and ran. She ran unthinkingly down an alley and then pivoted and ran down another. No sense of direction on where she'd gone. She had tried, and wanted to be a good friend, Renee especially didn't want to hurt Zane. She didn't want to hurt anyone. How she truly hated this life. Everything since the end had been all about death and blood.

Renny, stop running.

Her brother's voice echoed off the buildings' walls, but she ignored it and pounded her feet against the street. Renee wasn't cut out for any of this, which was why no one ever wanted her around.

Only out of desperation, would others let her travel with them. Most of the time, her only duties were to stay awake, make food, and warn them if zombies were headed in their direction. Sometimes they wanted her to search for supplies in the most dangerous areas because they didn't care if she made it back or not.

She was useless because she couldn't deal with the harsh realities of life. At least this one. She never liked horror, avoiding all the scary stories or movies. Now, everything was a horror movie. She tried to keep her vision clear by wiping away the tears, but they kept coming. Cries of pain echoed off the walls of the buildings she darted past. She couldn't tell anymore if they were human or zombie.

Renee stopped and slumped down a wall. Alone. Always alone. She couldn't make it with the humans and wouldn't make it with the undead. No point. There wasn't any point anymore. Her eyes slid shut. Just find the happy place. Find the happy place to remind herself why she kept fighting.

Shit. Ice cream on a beach wasn't doing it.

The hand slid up her back. She let out a breath. There it was. Cool fingers brushed her hair away, causing tingles on her neck. It kinda reminded her of the tingles she felt when Zane touched her. Nope, she couldn't think about him now. Held. She'd been held, cherished. Zane made her feel that way. *Stop it*. She was not thinking about him.

Crap. Noise. Her eyes flew open and scanned the alleyway, almost expecting to hear her brother's voice in her ear, warning her to get moving. Someone was getting closer and fast. There was nowhere to hide and she would have to jump to her feet to run.

Zane barreled around the corner, painted in blood, and appeared okay yet furious. He was in front of her in seconds. She shrunk against the wall.

"Renee." He crouched down in front of her.

Her lips quivered. He'd hate her now. She loathed herself.

"Renee." His tone was gentle as he smoothed down her hair.

She broke down and bawled like a baby. How could he dismantle her with only her name? Zane pulled her to his chest, where his heart thumped so rapidly, she was worried it might explode. A loud bang sounded, and his body rocked against hers. The vibrations from the bullet rippled through his body to her ear and were almost deafening. Directly beside her face was a hole in his chest. Another shot. Zane picked her up and ran at dizzying speed, rounding a corner.

Shouts, gunfire, and growls surrounded them as he ran. She caught glimpses of the chaos. There were weapons, fire, and teeth everywhere. They ended up in an old store when he finally put her down, and his eyes raked over her.

"I'm fine, but you're hurt." Her eyes were fixed on his shirt, which had a hole in his chest and splattering of blood all over.

"It's nothing. I need you to stay here. There were more humans than expected. I need to know you're safe."

"You can't keep fighting. You're hurt." Her shaking fingers traced his multiple wounds.

"There's no choice. We fight, or we die." His irises dimmed with his words.

"Monster!" a woman's voice said.

In Renee's peripheral, the woman advanced with a gun pointed at Zane. Without thinking, Renee spun and jerked the gun from the woman's hand. It went off, but she ignored it and leapt on her.

A terrifying growl filled the store and almost paused her assault, but all Renee saw was red. No one - *no one* would take Zane from her.

Strong hands lifted her into the air. Renee screamed in frustration and swung her arms. Her fists were covered in red. What?

"Renee, my heart, shhh." Zane held her, even when she shoved at him.

She wanted him to let her go but couldn't get her hands free. She nipped at his chest. He inhaled sharply but didn't let her go.

Muffled voices in the background filtered in over the sounds of blood rushing in her ears. Brie. One of the voices was Brie.

"That was her?" Brie asked.

Zane kept Renee locked in his arms, immobile. "Yes, I need you to finish the sweep. We'll meet you soon. Make sure the others keep watch. The city's almost cleaned out."

Brie huffed. "Because of you. You decimated them to get to her. There will barely be enough now to feed the herd."

"There is another settlement a day from here. They use the supplies in the city to sustain themselves."

"Fine," Brie snapped.

The only remaining sound was Renee's own breathing and Zane's heart. No longer struggling to escape, she trembled in his arms.

"Renee?"

She shook her head, keeping her face buried in his chest. Her mouth tasted like blood. It was... his blood. Her fingers touched her lips. Her tongue darted out and licked them. Not his. Odd that she immediately knew the difference. But his blood tasted like him, fresh and with a hint of citrus. The blood on her fingers was more metallic. It tasted delicious.

Lifting her head, she peered at the wounds showing from his torn shirt. His blood wasn't black like the others. It was red. Not a typical human red, but still a shade of red.

Her eyes lifted to his face, and she stepped out of his arms, turning to the dead woman on the floor. Her hand flew up over her mouth in disgust.

She was shredded to pieces. Renee stumbled backwards and rammed into a counter behind her.

"Renee." His voice sounded so vulnerable.

She gazed at his handsome face. Better. So much better to look at him. Even though he was covered in death, his mouth and chin were bloody. He must've done that to the woman. But then she'd tried to kill him. Maybe it was okay.

Her hands shook when she pointed to his chest wounds. "You're hurt."

"I'll be fine."

"No." Renee shook her head. Her voice was distorted and didn't sound right. "You're a zombie. Zombies don't heal, they die. You can't die." She crumpled to the floor. He couldn't leave her now, not like this. Nothing was right.

"I won't." He crouched down, leveling his gaze on her. "I promise, I won't leave you. It won't let me die."

"You can't die?"

"No."

His voice sounded so despondent when he said it. Shouldn't that make him happy? Who wouldn't want to be immortal? That's why he was their king. But then, who would want to be a zombie king?

His hands cupped her face. "Stay with me, please." His voice trembled the way her body was.

It was like they'd traveled back in time, and Zane wasn't the king of the undead, he was just Zane. A younger Zane, who was scared she was going to leave him. Where would she go? He already told her he'd always come back, always find her, and that she was his. She wanted to be his.

"Do you remember what happened to you?"

Renee didn't know what he meant, so she just stared at him. After a moment, he lifted her up into his arms and carried her out of the store. She closed her eyes and leaned her cheek against his bleeding chest.

Chapter 27

Renee opened her eyes, surprised by her surroundings. She propped herself up on her elbows and surveyed the room. It was a lovely, clean bedroom full of neutral colors and a big, comfy bed she realized she lain on.

Naked.

She was naked on a soft mattress with fresh sheets. No sign of her clothes or anyone else. She sat up and swung her legs over the side of the bed.

Tiptoeing to what she assumed was the bedroom door, she opened it and found a walk-in closet full of clothes. Nice. Whoever had lived there seemed to enjoy a variety of colors and styles. It was like walking into a store before desperate and destitute ransacked it. There were some places that still had more clothing than others, but they were always in heavily concentrated zombie areas. Places Renee didn't dare to go, not for clothes anyway.

Her fingertips brushed against some of the fabrics as a small grin tugged at her lips. For the first time in years, she might be able to find clothes that fit properly. Almost all the clothes in the past seven years, save the ones Zane got her, hadn't fit right.

During the initial panic of the downfall, many places were destroyed or scavenged until almost nothing useful was left, including clothing items. Or maybe she wore the same size as everyone else. Renee touched a soft green blouse with long flowy sleeves. Not practical, but it was so soft. She'd have to check before she left if there was anything that would fit her.

Her eyes flicked over to the other two doors. One had to be a door that allowed her to leave the room. As her fingers closed on the knob to the middle door, it turned, and she jumped back like a rabbit. Zane's eyes widened as he stepped into the room.

Shit. His shirt was off, and he looked clean. Renee pinched her eyebrows. Her memories were hazy, but she swore he had been shot. Slowly, she raised her eyes to his glowing ones. He'd eaten recently. They were super bright. Her fingers traced over where she thought they hurt him, but it was smooth skin. Perhaps she was confused since she'd been terrified in the moment.

His fingers wrapped around her hand and held them to his heart. "Are you thirsty?"

Renee thought about it, but for the first time since she'd traveled with the horde, she wasn't. She shook her head. "What happened?"

"We took the city."

All the humans were dead. Like every other place they'd traveled to. Her stomach sank. She berated herself for being cheeky about shopping for clothes only moments before in the closet. A foggy memory crept into her thoughts and her eyes widened, recalling the woman who tried to shoot Zane. She yanked her hand away and stepped back, grabbing her head.

She had wounded someone, another human, to protect him. Too far, she'd crossed the line and was a traitor. The woman's screams and Renee's own fear that Zane would die enveloped her. He stepped forward, but she backed up.

"Get away from me."

Traitor repeated in her mind. She shook her head.

His tone was calm as he spoke. "Don't say that. We need to talk."

"No, we don't. Get out." The worst human, she'd betrayed her own kind.

"I can't. I'm sorry, Renee, but it can't wait anymore. Too much has happened."

"Stop! I know what I did." Renee let go of her head, taking rapid breaths. "I hurt that woman. I'm a traitor."

"You're not a traitor. Please listen-"

"No! I hurt people to protect you! Do you have any idea how screwed up that is? I hurt someone because... because I can't lose you. What's wrong with me?" Her knees went slack, but Zane caught her before she crumpled to the floor.

"Nothing's wrong with you. You're perfect. You always have been."

Her brow pinched. That didn't make any sense. "No. I've always been a screw-up. I hate myself."

"Please don't say that."

"I'd do it again. I'd hurt anyone who tried to kill you. I don't care who they are." Renee sobbed at her admission because the horrible truth leaving her lips sealed her fate. She'd never return to her people, because she no longer had people. Somehow this undead creature had made her feel alive in ways she didn't understand.

Zane led them to the bed where they sat on the edge. He drew her into his arms and held her, whispering sweet nothings in her ear. How was it possible the kindest person she'd ever met wasn't even a person? She clung to him until tears no longer fell.

After taking a shaky breath, she asked, "Why am I naked?"

"Because your clothes were ruined."

"Did you bathe me?"

"Yes." His hand ran up and down her spine.

"Why don't I remember that?"

He tucked her hair behind her ear. "Could be a lot of reasons. Probably shock."

That checked out. After all, she had attacked a human. Renee peered at her hands. They'd been red before - covered in blood.

"Why am I yours?" she asked, staring into his amber eyes.

"Because you always were." His fingers traced the side of her face. "Because I love you."

Renee held her breath, not sure she'd heard him right. "You... you love me?"

"Only you."

Deciding to shut off her higher thinking, she leaned forward and captured Zane's lips. He loved her, only her. Her heart swooned at his words. Hearing someone declare their love in real life was absolutely better than reading about it. Perhaps he was an undead creature, but he was still a beautiful one, equal to, if not better, than some magical being from one of her beloved books.

Renee needed to show him she cared about him too. She twisted her body and straddled him. He responded but seemed almost hesitant. Her fingers traced his sculpted chest and abs as she used her body weight and climbed him until they toppled back onto the bed. He laughed at her antics and gently broke their kiss.

"You need time. This can wait. I don't want to, but you're more important."

Her heart twisted in her chest, giving her more reason to want him. "No. I've already waited. You told me when we got somewhere else..."

"I know, but a lot has happened." His fingers threaded into her hair.

"Yeah, I hurt someone to protect you. That's gotta get me something, right?" she asked in a playful tone.

"Yes, okay." He laughed and kissed her.

Renee's fingers went to his pants and undid the button. His hand clasped hers to stop her. She smacked his hand and bit his lip.

"I'm naked, so you have to be too."

He grinned and tugged off his pants along with his boxer briefs. He didn't know it yet, but Renee wasn't taking no for an answer. Zane kept proving he cared about her, and she would care for him in the only way she knew how at the moment.

Her fingernails dug into his shoulder as she had another mind-blowing orgasm from only his touch. Being the gentleman he was, he repositioned them to cuddle, but Renee shoved him on his back and climbed on top of him. Her heated core brushed against his hard shaft.

"Renee," he said in a strained voice and shook his head.

"You said you loved me."

"That's why I'm saying we can't." His chest rumbled with his words.

Renee delighted in the vibrations that her fingertips sensed as he spoke. "You're the only one who makes me feel this way. The only one I need or want like this."

Shamelessly, she rubbed herself over him, coating him in her wetness as he groaned. "Make me yours, Zane, in every way, forever."

Something broke in his eyes. He growled like he did when he ripped something apart. Damn, that was hot. It used to terrify her, but now it triggered her desperation for him. His fingers dug into her hips before he flipped them, so he hovered over her.

"You'll always be mine," he said in a monstrous voice that made her nipples sharpen to points.

"Always," she echoed back.

Renee's breath hitched as he eased into her. She hadn't realized his size, not really, but she did now. It was the most incredible sensation, and he hadn't even moved yet, as he waited for her walls to stretch to accommodate him. With slow, gentle strokes, he opened her and claimed her. Tore her soul wide open and captured a piece of it to tuck away as his forever. In return, she snatched a portion of his for herself, hiding it deep inside her heart so no one could take him from her. As long as they had each other, they would be whole.

Her fingers touched his silky hair as their eyes locked. With Zane, she was better than safe. She'd finally found a home – a place she could let her guard down and remember. *Remember?* Before her mind focused, his fingers rubbed her tiny bud. Her eyes slid shut as she moaned, and her hips bucked.

"Come for me," he commanded.

Renee cried out as her core clutched him tight. He hissed but kept going. She gasped as she was torn from her body and scattered among the stars. Reborn with his love. Her eyes burned with unshed tears. She wanted to see his face but didn't want to make him feel weird. Instead, she drew his mouth to hers and kissed him.

Zane's movements quickened, becoming more frenzied. He broke their kiss and buried his face in her neck as she screamed and tightened around him again. He groaned and thickened inside her. His lips kissed her neck as she twitched under him, still coming down from the high.

"That was," Renee tried to catch her breath. "Oh my god, that was amazing."

He chuckled and propped up on his elbows. "I wanted to do better." His fingers brushed the hair from her face.

Better? She wasn't sure if she could handle, better. Who knew the king of the undead was so skilled? Her brows pinched. *Did* anyone know?

"What are you thinking?"

"Do you have sex with other..." She didn't want to say zombies because it was really gross and also made her furious to think he did.

"No." He brushed his lips across hers. "I've never touched any of the undead. I haven't had sex since I've been... this."

"I didn't know zombies could have sex." Shit, was she going to get something because she'd done this? It dawned on her that they hadn't even used protection. Panic filled her.

"It's okay. You don't need to be worried."

"But you said..." As far as she knew, no human had ever even considered being intimate with a zombie, so it wasn't like there was a rulebook for any of what they'd just done.

"You said you trusted me."

"I do," she insisted.

"Then trust me when I tell you it's okay. I would never hurt you or put you at risk."

Renee exhaled. "Okay. I didn't mean to make you feel weird."

"Us talking about this isn't what's making me feel weird."

"Then what is?"

"All the possibilities since you became a part of my life. Nothing is the same anymore." His fingers caressed her jaw. With him on top of her, not only did she see and hear his words, but she felt every one of them reverberate against her skin. It was enthralling.

"Yeah, nothing's the same, but that's not terrible. I mean, you're here with me."

"Do you honestly believe that?" His head tilted to the side.

"Yeah, I do," she admitted. Perhaps she was a turncoat to her own species, but she didn't care anymore. This insane and maybe sick love made her whole and strengthened her.

"Why did you run again?"

She looked away. "I wasn't running from you or Brie. I couldn't stand all the death, the violence."

"I know."

"You do? Is that why you keep forgiving me?"

"No, that's why I understand. I keep forgiving you because I love you."

He said it again. Her heart threatened to burst out of her chest.

"If you love me," she paused. "And you wanted to do better..." Her lips shifted into an impish grin as she raised her hips.

He laughed but lowered his mouth to hers. Hours later, spent from Zane insisting he could do better two more times, Renee drifted off to sleep. She'd never been happier in her entire life.

Chapter 28

With a yawn, Renee padded into the joined bathroom. She stretched her arms and shuddered when a twinge of pain crept up from her core. It didn't matter, that had been the best night of her life. She washed her face and stopped before she left. Tempted for the first time in years to look at herself.

When was the last time she'd felt anything resembling happiness? Probably before the zombies. But those memories were distant and more like a dream. It had been that way for years. She thought those memories might seem so far away because it hurt too much to think about them, so she let them go.

When she had a good dream, she assumed those were her memories drifting into her thoughts. But now she had Zane and could make new memories with him. Good memories. Well, when it was just them, and he wasn't the king of the undead, he was just Zane. Her Zane. Still mixed up but finally feeling hopeful, she slowly raised her eyes to the mirror.

Her mouth dropped open as she stumbled backward.

Not real.

That wasn't her.

Renee blinked several times and waved her hands around, watching how the movements in the mirror matched hers. Pale, bright, glowing, green irises peered back in her reflection. Her entire naked body on display was sickly white and thin, with almost translucent skin. Violet and blue veins mapped over her form. Her long, wild, dark hair starkly contrasted everything else.

She stared in the mirror and raised her hand to her neck. A chunk was missing. *Had been missing.* The indentation was so old it had healed over with ashen-colored skin. Is that why she hadn't tied her hair back like she used to? The subconscious was weird. Renee thought about her strange interactions with both Brie and Zane. How he kept asking her if she remembered what'd happened.

She'd been dead since the day the horde attacked Baltimore.

Dead when she had tried running the first time.

Dead when he told her he owned her because he owned the entire horde.

He was their king - *her king.*

The bathroom door opened slowly. Zane's face fell when he caught her expression.

"Renee."

"Don't. Go away. Leave me alone."

"Please, let me help you."

"Help me? Your horde did this to me! Get away from me!" She flung herself at him and hit him repeatedly.

Zane caught her wrists and tried to hug her, comfort her, but she wouldn't let him.

"You don't love me. You just own me because I'm part of your army."

Her chest ached. It was as if an invisible hand had reached into her chest cavity and ruthlessly torn her heart out, tossing it on the cold tiles beneath her bare feet.

"That's not true. Please let me explain."

"There's nothing to explain." She ripped herself out of his arms. "Do you fuck all your new recruits? Or am I special because I'm less chewed up?"

Zane said nothing and just stared at her with a tormented expression. His Adam's apple bobbed up and down in his throat.

"Did I do what you wanted when I killed that woman? I murdered someone." She bent over, gasping for breath. "I murdered someone to protect you because you're my king. I don't have a choice, do I?" Renee started laughing and crying at the same time, then collapsed on the tiled floor.

He stepped closer but paused when she spoke.

"Get away from me. I hate you. You and your horde took everything from me."

His eyes were damp when he backed up. "I'll send Brie to get you later." He turned and left.

Renee laid on the floor and wept, staring at where she imagined her discarded heart would be, hers that slowed with each second. Lies. Everything had been a lie. Had she done anything because she wanted to? Or was everything because he willed it; was she anything more than a puppet?

Chapter 29

Renee cried until there wasn't anything left and then lain on the bathroom floor even longer. Months ago, her heart had stopped. She was dead, but not the way her body already was. It was worse because even the death of her brother hadn't destroyed her like that revelation had. Tore out the only part of her that was worth a damn and made it useless.

Iris' words crept into her mind. *They found people often and never, ever left survivors. Sometimes they'd eat until there was nothing but bones. That group is more dangerous because they aren't just zombies, not like the others. They have an intelligence about them.*

Renee had tried to go back and get her brother's body so she could bury it, except there was nothing left - only bones.

Bones. Just like Iris said. Just like she'd witnessed herself while traveling with them.

Perhaps it wasn't Zane's fault her brother died, but his horde had devoured him, taking away her opportunity for closure. And she'd slept with him. Idiot. The worst part was, even understanding that didn't take away her agony. It didn't remove the hole in her chest from her ripped-out heart because she had cared. Crap, maybe she still did, which made her the absolute worst person and sister ever.

"Renny, please don't die. Don't leave me with those assholes," the voice of a ghost whispered in the silent bathroom.

Renee snapped her eyes shut. Damn it Liam. She bit her lip. She couldn't handle a conversation with her brother. Balling up her fists and trying to ignore his nudges, she needed to get up and keep fighting. She'd promised him she wouldn't give up, that she would survive for him. Keep fighting until her dying breath. The problem was, she was already dead – another failure.

I'm sorry, Liam.

She knew Liam was not mad at her. He was probably happy she had a friend and people, even if those people were undead. Hell, he probably wouldn't have judged her for loving Zane, either. She laughed as tears rolled down her cheeks. He should have lived, not her. Granted, she wasn't really living.

"I told you, princess, it was my job to protect you. It's okay. Let me go."

Renee sobbed until she dry-heaved. It'd been so long since she let herself remember her brother's last moments. The misery of losing him was still fresh. He'd been gone for years, and it didn't make any difference. Every time she was reminded of him, it was like the hole that had been left inside her from his absence grew, devouring more of who she was. She hit her head against the tiles.

Frustrated with everything but mostly herself, she clamored off the floor and stumbled out of the bathroom to the closet she had found earlier. She picked through the closet and dressers and got dressed, tucking a few extra outfits in her backpack since there wasn't any water left. Did she even need water? She sat on the bed and studied her hands. How could she not have noticed how pale they were before? Stupid, always so stupid. Her brow wrinkled. Someone used to say that to her all the time, but she couldn't place the voice.

The door opened, and Brie peered at her. Her wan, pretty face frowned. Quiet as a mouse, she sat beside her on the bed. Embarrassed for so many actions and words with Brie, she couldn't look at her. When Brie's arm wrapped around her shoulders, Renee leaned into her friend. Brie was the last person she'd ever expected to be kind to her about her recent realization. She indeed was her friend.

"You don't have to hide here. He left with a scouting group to check the other settlement nearby."

"He left?"

"Yeah, he was pretty pissed off, too. Not sure what you two argued about, but it must've been intense. I haven't seen him like that in years. It was like the old him. Before all this, I mean." Brie adjusted her lilac print dress.

Renee's head snapped in Brie's direction. "You knew him before?"

"Yeah, it was a long time ago. Doesn't matter now."

But it mattered. It mattered so much. She knew nothing about Zane, except he was king of the undead and claimed to care about her. He hinted he knew or understood her. It wasn't fair, but it didn't matter anymore. Nothing had been real.

"So, you know... I mean about yourself. I don't have to pretend anymore?" Brie asked.

Renee averted her burning eyes. "Yeah. Not sure if I'm crazy or just dumb. I don't know how I could have not realized."

"I was wondering the same thing. But he told me if I even hinted, he'd rip my arms off. I've seen him deal out punishments before. No way was I going to risk it."

Renee turned to Brie. "Are you really afraid of him?"

"Yeah, and with good reason. He's never acted like he has since you showed up."

"Really?"

"Yeah... it's annoying. He's supposed to lead us, not try to... protect you? Romance you?" Brie shrugged.

"So, all these years, you've gone from place-to-place and..."

"Ate every living thing, yes. And now you will too."

Renee shook her head. "I won't. I don't want to."

"Doesn't matter. You don't have a choice. Even if he didn't make you, you'd do it, anyway. If you wait too long, it makes you crazy and breaks down your body. Some shamblers didn't used to be shamblers."

Once again, it occurred to Renee how her knowledge of the undead was still lacking. "What do you mean he makes you?"

Brie narrowed her eyes and studied her before she answered. "If he orders it, you do it."

"They follow orders," Renee whispered, recalling Zane's words. "Because he owns you, all of you, and you have to do what he says."

"As fucked up as that is, yeah. You understand why you can't run now?"

"Because he'll always come back for me?"

Brie jerked like she'd slapped her. "He would, wouldn't he?" she asked in a nasty tone.

Renee shrugged. "That's what he said."

Brie averted her eyes, but not before Renee caught the distress and the torment lurking there.

"What did I say? I don't want you to be upset. Brie, I don't know what to do anymore. I can't be around him, but I can't leave."

Brie turned to Renee. "Because you argued?"

"Yes. No. I can't - things are complicated. If I have to stay, I just want to be part of the horde. I don't have to talk to him to get orders, right?"

Brie narrowed her eyes again. "No. They can come through me if needed, but you really don't want to be around him?"

"No. I already packed my bag." Renee pointed to her bag.

"He's going to get angrier."

Renee jutted her chin out. "Too bad."

Brie raised her eyebrows. "Okay. Well, let's head downstairs. Most of the chosen are there. Now that you understand things better, you can meet them."

"The chosen? Really?" Renee perked up at the idea of finally meeting them.

"It's not that big of a deal. You're chosen too." Brie shrugged as she stood.

"I am?" Renee bolted up.

"You're talking to me, and you can talk to him, so yeah. Plus, look at you. Barely a scratch on you."

"Wait. I'm confused. What makes a chosen, a *chosen*?"

Brie huffed and drew a deep breath. "I was never great at this stuff. A chosen, is someone who was turned intentionally. Chosen versus some random attack. You can't be chosen unless you're turned by another chosen or him."

"Does he tell the chosen who to turn?"

"Yeah, mostly. The chosen don't get hurt as easily. We're faster and stronger." Brie walked ahead of her, out of the room.

The quick zombies, they must all be these "chosen" Brie referred to. Zane had brought her to a decent apartment. Clean and didn't smell of rot like a lot of the others did. A tiny part of her didn't want to leave. Her idiotic heart was pleading with her to stay, to hear him out. *Shut up, you're dead,* Renee snapped at it.

"We can talk like this but also understand the others. We're always the leaders because we can still think and plan. We're dead but not." She laughed.

Renee liked the more relaxed version of Brie. Maybe she was like this because she didn't have to lie to her anymore, which had been Zane's fault. They descended several flights of stairs.

"The chosen don't have to eat as much or as frequently. We're more connected to him and can understand what he wants better than the others." Brie turned left into a large open lobby, where many of the horde milled around.

These undead seemed more like Brie, dead but not quite. They were all dressed and had less of a disheveled appearance. They were also all engaged in conversation. It was similar to what she'd witnessed when they were deep in the horde but this had to be next level. It was almost human.

Renee glanced at Brie. No matter how much Brie downplayed her looks, she was still more beautiful than most. She always looked like a movie star to Renee, with her willowy body, long, pale, blonde hair, flowy, floral clothes, and graceful movements.

"What?" Brie asked when she caught her looking.

Renee leaned closer to whisper. "You told me they were just as pretty as you, but they aren't."

Brie laughed, really laughed. When she smiled, it lit up her entire face, and for a second, Renee could see past the corpse-like coloring and see what she had been.

"You're the silliest friend I have ever had," she told her again. "Let's go meet the crew."

Chapter 30

Brie took Renee around and introduced her to so many chosen Renee couldn't remember half their names. Most of them didn't use their human names and instead chose things they identified with more now. It varied from terms or objects that sounded like something from a movie to words or phrases that made little sense.

Renee particularly liked the one who'd taken the name Mace. Not only because his name sounded cool, but he was hilarious and went out of his way to make her laugh and feel welcome. Although Mace was a giant creature towering over the others with a scraggly beard, he reminded her of a giant stuffed teddy bear. She wouldn't tell him how bizarre a juxtaposition he was because Brie said he was a good berserker for them, and he'd probably be offended being compared to something soft and squishy.

Renee was stunned when Mace introduced her to his wife, who was half his size and also a chosen because he'd accidentally turned her after he'd become a zombie. Daisy, who named herself after her favorite flower, wasn't angry about it at all. Daisy told Mace and the others she now had more time with the man she loved unless their human prey were successful and killed them. The verbal exchange somewhat grossed Renee out, but she didn't comment.

Renee wouldn't classify the interactions she had with the other chosen as *normal*, in the manner it would've been with humans, but it wasn't as weird as she thought it would be, probably because she was one of them.

Hearing them speculate about the state of things in the horde was fascinating. The chosen considered themselves something akin to the shepherds of the masses. Their duties included leading, protecting, and providing for them, but with no expectation of anything other than loyalty in return. How was it that a bunch of zombies seemed more honorable than humans?

"Shouldn't we be heading south?" Hatchet asked and scratched at her neck. Although clean, her clothes were a bit rough and needed to be replaced.

Renee's head was on overload trying to remember all the unfamiliar names and faces, so she remained quiet and listened to them all speak. It was odd to Renee that they all spoke so well. She had no issues understanding them, although the cadence differed from humans or Brie.

The king, well, he was in a class of his own. His deep voice was a treat to her senses because she didn't just see or hear it, she always *felt* it. It made it easier to understand him. Her mouth twisted at the thought of him. She wasn't supposed to be thinking about him.

Brie's lips flattened. "We go where he leads."

"I know, but the temperature is shifting faster this year. It's going to be a hard winter." Hatchet answered. Hatchet wasn't particularly tall or short. She was of average height and very muscular. Her threadbare clothing clung to her well-toned form. Renee wondered if she'd been an athlete in her former life as a human from her style of clothing and well-built physique.

"Tell me about it. The nights have been brutal," Hawk complained.

Renee wasn't sure if he was called Hawk because of his sharp facial features or his shock of white hair, maybe both.

"That's because you're too thin." Hatchet smacked him on his back and laughed.

Hawk was thin, but as Renee's eyes scanned the room, most of the chosen were. It made sense, depending on when they were recruited. If it had been a couple of years after the downfall, when food was scarce and tough to scavenge, any remaining humans lost any extra fat they may have been storing as their bodies went into survival mode.

"We will endure, as we always have," Brie commented.

Renee's eyes flicked to her friend. Something in her voice was off. It sounded like Brie, but not, at the same time. Listening to Brie's voice shift reminded Renee how Zane sounded when he said awful things about humanity or when he would comment about the superiority of zombies.

"I know, but there are still problems with some of the families. If food gets scant, you know how that will turn out." Hawk's tone sounded grim before his entire body shook, then he straightened.

Renee studied the odd movement and found it reminded her how a bird would shake and ruffle its feathers.

"There are always problems with *certain* families," Hatchet said with a frown.

"It won't m-matter. If it gets too loud..." Nail said and twitched beside Renee.

Nail was an interesting creature. Taller and gaunt like most of them, he reminded Renee of the old pictures her mom would show her of her aunt, her mom's wild and rebellious sister, also the only fun aunt she'd had. Nail's dark brown hair was long, to the middle of his shoulder blades, with both sides shaved. His black jeans, concert tee, sleeveless jean jacket covered in metal band buttons and patches, tattooed arms and neck, wrapped with a spiked choker and numerous leather studded bracelets, gave him an intimidating appearance but when he spoke, his voice was always soft, and he seemed unsure of his words. He was the least threatening zombie she'd met.

Renee almost asked what conflicts zombies could have within a horde, but of course, it was over food. No, that wasn't fair. It was about food, but it was *more* than that. Apparently, a couple of the groups within the larger group of the horde, believed other families had taken more than they needed, and others were suffering because of it. Renee paid close attention when Nail spoke. He had a pleasant, calming voice, it reminded her of Liam's.

"I j-just mean-" Nail began but was cut off by Hawk.

"We can move them toward the rear, though if Flint realizes why his group was moved, you know how he'll react."

"I get that, but we can't have them bickering. If *he* finds out, you know what will happen to *all* of them." Hatchet said and leveled her gaze at Hawk.

"Or maybe us if we're involved," Nail whispered. His right hand drifted to the studded bracelets on his left wrist and he fidgeted with them.

He? Were they talking about Zane? The only thing they seemed reluctant to voice was anything to do with their king. They were every bit afraid of him as Brie seemed to be. Movement from the corner of Renee's eye drew her attention. It was the chosen she'd spotted several times before.

Every time Renee tried to look at him, he migrated away yet still seemed interested in her. He was only a few inches taller than she was, with a lithe frame and long, straight, black hair. His mouth appeared wider than it should've been, which enhanced his already feral appearance. Long claw-like nails were at the end of each finger. Oddly, as threatening as he looked, he seemed shy and wouldn't meet her gaze. Maybe he wanted to be her friend. Renee turned to search for him as he blended into the crowd when Brie spoke.

"Move them toward the rear. If Flint starts shit, tell me as *soon* as it starts. Don't try to fix it. I'll take care of him," Brie said sternly.

The others nodded, but still seemed nervous about the idea.

"He'll fall in line, or he'll get left behind." Brie averted her eyes.

Hawk lowered his head as Hatchet slid her eyes aside. Renee scanned the group and realized that Mace and Daisy had shuffled away during the discussion about Flint's group. She wondered if they were friends with Flint or just didn't want to be involved.

Renee tried to control her curiosity, but the words tumbled from her mouth before she could stop them. "What do you mean, left behind?"

Brie turned her head toward her and grimaced. "It's punishment. The horde's survival is above all else. If certain... members don't comply, they're locked away somewhere or chained to something to starve until they turn into shamblers. Eventually, they'll rot until they die."

Renee's hand flew up to her mouth at the idea. "Will they know what's happening?"

"For the most part, yes. Especially if they are chosen," Brie answered.

"We can tell when we're slipping if we don't eat," Hatchet added.

"Yeah, even in the haze of hunger, you can sense your mind going. I guess it's sort of like what used to happen to older people?" Hawk's face twisted in concentration, which only sharpened the edges of his cheekbones.

"But... the one whose arms were ripped off..." Renee started, but then stopped, unsure how to phrase her question.

"As long as someone fed them, they'd still keep their thoughts. Although, that'd hurt like a motherfucker." Hatchet chuckled.

Renee didn't see the humor at all.

"The virus tries to keep us alive at all costs, for as long as possible." Hawk ran his fingers through his white hair.

"Hawk, shut up," Brie snapped.

"What?" His tone sounded almost offended.

Brie slid her eyes towards Renee as Hawk pressed his lips together. Why weren't they allowed to talk about "the virus" in front of her?

"I'll tell you about our plans for the next few months as soon as he decides and gives his commands," Brie told him in a very formal tone that didn't sound like her as she backed up, gesturing for Renee to follow her.

"It was great to meet you. I can't wait till we can hang out again." Renee glanced at everyone in turn, giving them her best smile, which probably wasn't great. Liam always told her she had a "model's smile," but Renee was pretty sure he was only trying to make her feel more confident.

Hawk stared at Renee like he didn't have a clue how to respond to her departing remarks. Nail cracked a tiny grin, and Hatchet laughed. Damn it, she was screwing this up too.

Hatchet moved around to her and smacked her back several times. It knocked the breath from her lungs. "Our *king, as we heard you like to call him,* picked a friendly thing, didn't he? I think you'll be a good influence on all of us."

Renee didn't know what to make of Hatchet's statement, but Renee sensed the heat in her cheeks as she waved and wandered a few feet from them. She was still processing the conversation when Brie's words interrupted her thoughts.

"Do you want to stay with me for now?"

Her words tightened Renee's chest, and she threw her arms around her friend, ignoring how uncomfortable it made her. "Yes, thank you so much."

"We're going to have to work on how friendly you are. It's freaking everyone out. Nail looks like he's gonna pass out, and I've yet to see one of us end up unconscious," Brie told her with levity.

Renee squeezed her hand, then released it. Sure enough, Nail frowned at her words before he cracked a smile and shook his head. He also had claws like the shy chosen she'd lost track of. Probably making a fool of herself, she waved to everyone as they left. Not probably, definitely... she definitely looked a bit unhinged.

Chapter 31

They spent the rest of the day exploring the now-safe city. Renee tried not to think about how it was safe because it was full of zombies. Brie took her to any place she wanted to go, which was great since she'd never had the luxury of searching for supplies without fear of being discovered and eaten by zombies. It was almost relaxing as she scavenged.

It was always the same when she'd been with various groups before traveling with the horde. Either by herself, almost pissing her pants in fear as she looked for scraps, or almost pissing her pants searching for whatever she'd been told to find by whatever group she traveled with. She'd been useless to most groups, so she understood when they sent her out. They didn't care if she returned. She was deadweight in their minds.

So, when they'd approached a city, she was always among the first to go in. After traveling with the horde, it only highlighted how lucky she'd been. *No.* It hadn't been luck. She was a coward, which was always how she'd survived. The first sign of violence she'd panic and hide. If there was an escape route, she'd run. Positive she'd been the reason for many, many deaths of her traveling companions, for even if they called for help - she never answered. Either everything in her would shut down, and she'd enter a catatonic-like state while she hid, or she'd take off and run until her legs gave out. It was why Renee never argued when groups made her enter cities first, she deserved it for all the lives she'd taken. Perhaps she hadn't been the zombie that killed them, but she also hadn't lifted a finger to save them.

"Black t-shirts?" Brie's voice ended her self-degradation.

"They aren't for me," Renee answered. Her fingers brushed against the fabric. These were softer than the ones Zane had worn before. Tempted to take them for him, but then she remembered their last conversation and how upset she still was, she put the t-shirts back on the shelf. Stupid heart, trying to betray her - again. It was dead, just like her. Its insistence that it wasn't dead, just wounded, made her angry.

"It's weird; when I used to forage, I would grab anything I could carry. Especially if it was food, water, or clothing. Now, I'm not sure what to get."

"We don't need food or water. Although you drank a lot for the first couple of weeks." Brie picked two flowery blouses from hangars in the small department store they were ransacking.

"So, no one else drank like that before?"

"No. Others had issues with sunlight hurting their eyes, but no one ever wanted water like you did. He told me not to say a word and made sure we had a steady supply for you." Brie held a flared black skirt against her.

"I really *was* thirsty all the time," Renee said in a quiet voice. Her inner bitch hissed that she was broken. Broken when she was a human and now broken as a zombie.

Brie grabbed the skirt and a pink one of the same style. "It's probably a genetic thing. Some of us get nails like claws or better vision or hearing. Could have something to do with our cells changing? We don't really know why. Not like there's a scientist to tell us." Brie laughed and picked out several pairs of panties.

Renee brightened when she realized there were at least three untouched tables of underwear. Not that the zombies cared, at least the main horde, but the ability to take time and find essentials was a comfort she hadn't had in years. She snatched up several weeks' worth and also decided to upgrade her backpack to a bigger one.

"Does anyone ever *want* to know about the changes we went through when we turned?"

Brie paused as she picked up a hairbrush. "Maybe, but we don't talk about it. I'm not sure how to explain it, but we feel weird if we start digging or thinking too hard about what we are."

"All of you?"

"Yeah. That much we all agreed on." Brie peeked at the hair accessories.

Renee's fingers wrapped around an intricate, purple handle on a brush next to the one Brie had chosen. Renee's mind raced, speculating why the horde would feel strange wondering about their origins or the changes that occurred when one transitioned from human to zombie. Her gut told her something was off, but the longer she focused on the "why" of it all, the strangest *feeling* nudged at her to leave the questions alone. Renee chewed on her lip. It didn't make sense. Viruses couldn't "talk" or make someone *feel* any way. Could they?

"Do you want to go anywhere else?"

Her stomach tightened until it hurt. "No. I'm good. Thank you."

•   •   •

After sunset, they returned to the apartment building Zane picked out as their unofficial undead headquarters, intent on returning to Brie's apartment. Renee was curious if she obtained decent accommodations, but then Renee's thoughts were distracted by the scouting group that had returned, which meant Zane was back.

Shit. She wasn't ready to face him yet. Still feeling too mixed up about everything that happened, Renee tried to get Brie to leave with her, but she refused and said she needed more information to prepare for an upcoming attack. Renee still wasn't ready for that part yet, attacking and massacring groups of people.

Renee sensed Zane before she saw him. It seemed as soon as he was within a certain radius, her body hummed with energy and longing. She straightened and squared her shoulders as soon as he stepped into the room, his eyes locked on hers. She tried to stay focused, but everything blurred around them until it was only her and Zane. Renee exercised all her willpower not to go to him. To run, and jump up, and latch herself onto him. It was where she was always meant to be. But was it because he owned her like he did the rest of the horde?

Thankfully something, or someone, redirected his attention from her, and she drew several ragged breaths to recenter herself. He was talking to the other chosen, telling them what the scouting group found. The food they'd returned with. Was the encampment near the city destroyed already? It was then Renee really looked at Zane and found him covered in human remains again, irises bright. She turned her head, mumbling a quick goodbye to Brie, and wandered down the hall.

Chapter 32

Jerked back and shoved against the wall, Renee was not surprised when she saw Zane's shining, amber eyes glaring at her.

"You're not staying with Brie."

"Yes, I am." She raised her chin.

"I'm trying to be patient-" he began.

"Go to hell. You can't tell me what to do even if you think you have the right to."

"Don't test me, Renee," he warned.

"Or what? What will you do to me that hasn't already been done on your order? What else can you take?" She shoved against his chest. "It's not enough? You want my friend now, too? I can't even have a friend?" Her voice was shrill at the end, but she couldn't help it.

"I'm not trying to take anything away." He gritted his teeth. The feral side of him raged to get out. Not a great idea to argue with him so close after a killing spree. "You don't understand. You think you do because you realize what you are, but-"

"But what? What am I missing, Zane?"

He'd been vague about so many things since she'd been with him. His fingers dug into her arms as he flashed his teeth. She'd gone too far, pushed him too much. Brie tried to warn her. Would he rip off her arms? No, Zane would never hurt her, but the fury in his eyes didn't look like Zane at all. He looked like the zombie king. The zombie king who'd ripped someone in half with no hesitation.

"I think it's best if she stayed with me tonight," Brie's voice said from beside him.

"You dare defy me?" he snapped at her.

"No, think about it. It's what you'd want me to do." Brie crossed her arms and slanted her eyes to Renee.

Zane growled and released Renee before turning to Brie. "Don't disappoint me. We leave in the morning."

"I will guard her with my life," Brie told him, tugging Renee down the hall.

Once in her temporary apartment, Brie released Renee and placed her hands on her hips. "What the fuck is going on with you two? Are you a thing now? Like dating or whatever the fuck we would do if we did shit like that?"

"No, well maybe. I don't know!" Renee threw her hands up.

"He told you his name," Brie said somberly.

"Yeah, at the cabin."

Brie sat on the beaten couch. "At the cabin," She repeated in a defeated tone.

Renee sat next to her. "Brie, what's wrong?"

"Renee, I like you. I shouldn't, but I do." She shook her head. "You're going to get us all killed."

"I don't understand."

"I know, fuck I know. You're making him crazy."

"But I didn't do anything. I didn't chase him. He wouldn't leave me alone."

"I get that. Believe me, I know more than anyone. I should've fucking realized. I thought he fixated on you because-" Brie stopped and turned her head to the side.

"Because why?"

"Because you pissed him off the first day when you ran. It got his attention."

"Well, you said if I kept pushing him away, he'd never leave me alone."

"Good job listening," Brie replied sarcastically.

Shit. She'd done the opposite. Especially tonight. She put her face in her hands. Now he'd be worse. What could she do? Zane didn't seem to understand the concept of someone needing space to sort things out.

"What should I do?" Renee asked.

"Fuck if I know. This is all screwed up. As your friend, I want you to do whatever's right for you. He can be a bastard, so I get you don't want to be around him. But for the horde, I need you to make-up or whatever, so he'll chill out and fucking focus."

"You honestly think it will risk everyone if we aren't getting along?"

"He slaughtered that encampment. That wasn't the plan. It's great he had the scouts carry the food back, but it screws things up. We needed to wait, like he said, to keep the horde healthy."

Brie cared about them more than Zane did. She was their leader... their *queen*.

"Why did he destroy the encampment?" Renee dared to ask.

"Why the hell do you think? Whatever happened between the two of you before he left really got under his skin and messed with his head."

Renee didn't say anything since she had now been responsible for more human deaths. She had been so happy only hours ago, and now all she wanted was for everything to stop. Renee needed a second to breathe so that she could process everything.

"You want to sleep? I don't most of the time. The chosen don't need as much. It's why we guard at night."

Renee nodded. She was not tired, though. It was the first time since she'd started marching with the horde that she didn't want to sleep, though she did want to disappear. Since that wasn't an option, she'd lay there and shut off her mind for a while.

Brie took Renee to a room with a bed that didn't look nearly as nice as the one she'd left. Renee crawled beneath the covers and cried. As distraught as she was, she missed Zane. She'd driven him away, but it wasn't because she didn't care. It was because she did.

Chapter 33

The next day Brie greeted her the same way she always did. "Get up. We need to leave." She turned away, applying her red lipstick, and walked out of the room.

"Okay. I'm up." Renee rolled out of bed and grabbed her backpack. She rubbed her eyes unsure if she actually dozed off because her mind had cycled all night with thoughts about Zane, the horde, her brother, and how many mistakes she had made. They trudged downstairs and waded into the mass of the horde.

"I thought we'd be with the chosen," Renee said.

"You want to be near him?"

"Oh. No. He's always up near them?"

"Yeah, we're his... generals, remember?" Brie said, using Renee's titles.

"Right. Hey, that makes me a general too," Renee said with a smile.

Brie chuckled and shook her head.

"How far do we have to go today?"

"I don't know. He's still in a mood and changed the route we were supposed to take. I think he picked the city we're headed to because he just wants to kill more humans." Brie snapped her head toward Renee. "I meant-" She paused and grimaced.

"No, you were telling the truth. He's punishing others because he's mad at me."

Great, he was even worse than yesterday, Renee was learning more about who Zane was. He might have treated her like she was precious, but it didn't seem like anything or anyone else was. Apparently, he was a bastard like she'd accused him of being and wanted to make others suffer, especially if she was the reason.

"Yeah, maybe." Brie tried to lie. "Anyway, everyone is full enough since he brought food and there's less of us, so we can probably make it without too much trouble. Anything we find on the way has to go to the horde to keep them functional and calm. We'll have to go without till we get to a city."

We'll. She meant the chosen, which now included Renee. Part of Renee enjoyed hearing Brie say that because she was included, not only as part of the horde but also as a friend. A real friend. It kinda sucked too, because Renee was already hungry, and that meant it'd be days before she had anything to eat. Zane wouldn't worry about her anymore, not after how she treated him.

As the day passed, she and Brie talked about nothing in particular, but now that Brie could be more open, she spoke of her life before being one of the undead without being so guarded. She *was* popular. Her parents had been well off, so she got to do cool things like ride horses for fun. Brie didn't understand why Renee was so enamored by equestrian skills but indulged her with a few stories of competitions, nonetheless. Renee adored animals and would have loved to have had hobbies that included various kinds.

When she was young, before her implants, when her brother was her only friend, animals were there too. They didn't judge her for being deaf. They accepted her exactly as she was. She couldn't hear, but still felt she understood animals better since she had to focus on their body language to understand what they were communicating.

She frowned; she was lazy now. Had been for years because she got used to hearing, she still noticed nuanced movements, but it wasn't the same. Now, she had to remind herself to pay attention, whereas before it was by default.

Brie changed topics to daily life in the horde. Thankfully, she didn't focus on stalking humans or eating them. She spoke more about the friendships and families within the horde. From what Renee could tell, there weren't romances, relationships, or couples per se, but there were husbands, wives, and children. Some units acted like, and called themselves, family.

She recalled when the chosen referred to horde members having families too. They watched out for each other and cared for one another, not because Zane ordered it, but because they cared for each other. Or some kind of emotion that evoked compassion and empathy. Not quite to the level of the chosen but there seemed to be bonds between those in the horde. Renee had a million questions but tried to be patient and let Brie explain the dynamics in her own way.

"Do they... do they use the word family?" Renee asked.

"Sometimes. Sometimes not. It depends on who it is." Brie's eyes darted around checking for some unseen threat.

Renee couldn't imagine anything would be a threat to a zombie horde of this size, but she couldn't help but notice how often Brie scanned the area. Plus, with thousands of zombies, it would be impossible to go unseen by at least one of them if there was a threat. What was Brie looking for? Renee wanted to ask but kept her mouth closed and let Brie educate her.

"Those that do, though, are usually closer to one another than the others. Occasionally they get upset when they lose members of their specific group within the horde," Brie explained. "Some of them call themselves a pack, but those are usually the more feral ones, the ones that seem to think more like animals than humans. Regardless if a chosen is feral or not, many of us also show rage if one of us is lost from our specific group."

How had zombies evolved so quickly? *It's the nature of evolution.* Zane's words echoed in her head. Did that mean he knew they were like this and still didn't care? They were just the horde to him? He said they didn't matter. Except, from what Brie implied, he did care. Renee really needed to talk to Zane about the seemingly obvious changes zombies in his horde had experienced. Her eyes flicked to the front, hoping to catch a glimpse of him, but it was only an endless sea of bodies.

No wonder food was such an issue. They wouldn't need so much food if the army wasn't so big. Otherwise, as Zane had explained, to keep the horde from transitioning into shamblers, they'd have to eat every couple of days, which didn't seem bad until you considered the sheer numbers, meaning they had to move all the time, as well as understanding what or *who* they were eating. Renee's brow furrowed. At the time, it seemed more like he was talking about himself, but had he really meant the horde?

"Did you hear me?" Brie asked beside her.

"Sorry, I was trying to think about everything you said."

"Except what I just said," Brie chuckled. "I said I needed to go up front later to see if we're staying on course and wanted to know if you'd be okay."

"Oh, yeah. I'll be fine." She was one of them now and Renee was slowly starting to accept her new reality. She had nothing to fear from the horde. Unless it was time for a culling, then everyone was on the table.

"Okay. You staying with me again tonight?"

"Yeah, nothing has changed."

"Tell me about it." Brie's tone was filled with sarcasm. "All right, I'm heading up since the sun's setting. Stay here and don't cause trouble."

"I won't. I'm definitely not going anywhere now."

"It'd be great if that was the only trouble you caused." Brie turned to the approaching chosen with long, black hair, Renee had glimpsed him in the lobby. He appeared cleaner, fresher, and rather intelligent.

"Keep an eye on her," Brie tilted her head to Renee.

The chosen declined his head respectfully and fell in beside Renee. He'd had to have brushed his long hair because it looked like silk. She peered at her tangled locks and frowned. Brie propelled through the herd like water through rock and disappeared from her sight.

"She's so good at that, fast too."

The chosen nodded.

"I don't think we've met. I'm Renee. I'm new, obviously," she said awkwardly.

He nodded again.

"If I talk too much, you can tell me. I talk when I get nervous. Or mad... or, well, it's just a lot."

The chosen gave her a brief grin but didn't reply. Damn it, she was trying not to be so cringe, she felt her minimal social graces failing her.

"You don't talk?"

He shook his head.

"But you understand me?"

He nodded. Renee wanted to ask why but understood he couldn't explain, and she probably couldn't guess.

"I'm glad you're here and I'm happy to meet you. It's nice to know people. I mean, people you live with."

He nodded and scanned the surrounding area. Renee noticed every minute or so he'd do that. Look at her, then scan their surroundings. She wondered if they were passing through a dangerous area, which could have explained why everyone seemed to be on high alert.

"Are you one of the guards? Like at night?"

He smiled and seemed to be proud of his position within the horde.

"Wow, that's cool. You're like a sentinel of the night."

He tilted his head to the side.

"Okay, you probably don't have an official title. But now you do. Sentinel of the Night sounds legit, right?"

He nodded.

"Yep, an elite guard who protects all of us and serves the king." She smiled at him and gave him a quick side hug. "Thanks for ensuring safety so we can rest."

Her touch made him stiffen, and he stopped walking for a minute before he smiled. He pulled his shoulders back and shifted closer to her as they walked. Renee rambled on about random things he probably didn't care about until she noticed that some of the surrounding horde seemed to have shuffled closer to listen to her talk.

Her eyes flicked around her. Did they understand her, too? She thought only the chosen could communicate in whatever way they did and not like the chosen. The sun had set, night was falling, so perhaps she was sleepy and misunderstood the situation. They veered toward a wooded area. How many miles had they covered? It seemed like a lot, since she realized her legs were tired.

Brie advanced toward them with a grim expression. She dismissed Renee's sentinel without words. He gave Renee a brief bow before he blended into the horde.

"What the fuck was that? Did he bow to you?"

"Yeah, it's kinda a joke between us," Renee said dismissively. "What's wrong?"

Brie still stared after the guard.

"Brie?"

She shook her head. "I have bad news, and I need you not to overreact. Think about the others, not yourself."

"You want me to think about the horde?"

"Yeah, I do."

"Okay, you're freaking me out a little. What is it?"

"You're not staying with me tonight." She took a breath. "Or any other night."

"That bastard!"

"I'm sorry, Renee, but you have to do this. Not for him, for the horde."

"Are you kidding me? What the fuck is his problem? He doesn't own me!"

Brie glanced around them nervously. Some of the horde watched them. "Yeah, he does. We're all his, it's just the way it is."

"Don't start that again!"

"Don't fight him on this. It's not because he is being weird, not exactly. He doesn't trust anyone else with you."

"What's that supposed to mean?" Renee narrowed her eyes at Brie.

Brie took her by the arm and led her aside from the horde to a clearing. In the distance, Renee saw an old shed that looked like it was about to fall over. Great, probably where she'd be sleeping.

"You're important to him, and he doesn't trust the others."

"He doesn't trust his own horde? They have to obey him, right?" Inside, part of Renee, was overjoyed that she was still important enough to him that he wouldn't trust others with her at night.

"Yeah, they do but there's a lot going on you don't know about yet, and I can't." She glanced at past the clearing. "I can't get into it right now."

Renee's mind raced back to when Brie constantly checked their surroundings and how the Night Sentinel did the same thing. She couldn't decide if Brie wouldn't tell her because Zane was being a dick or there was something larger happening and it was too risky to talk about. Oddly hoping it was only Zane being a jerk, since the possibility it was something more, made her nervous.

"Because he said you couldn't." Renee spat.

"Yeah, but that's not the only reason. Look, you just found out what you are, and you need time to adjust. You're my friend. Let me do this for you, okay? I promise you'll know everything soon enough, and you'll wish I hadn't said anything."

Damn it. It wasn't just Zane. Renee stepped forward and touched her arm. "Brie, are you okay?"

"I'm fine." She averted her eyes.

"Zane trusts you. You know way more than anyone else. I thought you were his queen, but he kept telling me no. Even now, I still think you might be more important than that."

"What?"

"You're his Knight Commander," Renee said in awe as her chest tightened. In the back of her mind, memories churned and threatened to force themselves to the forefront but she shoved them away. Now was not the time.

"What the fuck is that? You keep switching between military terms and old fantasy shit."

"Well, actually, even in the old days they had armies-" Renee started.

Brie laughed. "You're so fucking goofy." Her face grew serious again. "Please, for now, just stay with him. If he tries to get pervy or something, tell me, and I'll bash his face in. Or die trying. Otherwise, let him stare at you so he knows you're okay. For us."

Renee sighed. The problem was that she wasn't sure she wouldn't be the one to try to get pervy with him. As mad as she was, she was most afraid that she'd be around him for five minutes and not care about anything but him – being near him, letting him comfort her for ruining her life.

"Okay. Okay, fine for now. For the horde, Night Sentinels, and the Knight Commander, I'll suffer his company," Renee teased.

Brie rolled her eyes but smiled as she led her to the shed.

Chapter 34

Renee ignored Zane as she breezed by him and checked the shed for some place to set up her sleeping arrangements and avoid him. There was ol' trusty in the corner; who had been keeping track of her sleeping bag? Whatever. She went to it, plopped down, and picked out one of the books she took from the cabin. She was not speaking to him and certainly not going to look at him.

She opened the book but had difficulty concentrating. Even though she'd already read her romantasy book twice, it would hold her focus more. The next city they went to, she'd need to see if she could find the rest of the series. Perhaps see if there was a library like Zane had mentioned before. If there was, she had a good chance of finding plenty to read.

The moment in the hallway pointed out how weak she truly was. She'd always been weak, especially when it came to him. She had to push herself to keep overreacting and saying horrible things so he would be angry enough he'd want to back off. Because if he didn't, she knew she wouldn't push him away. She had been drawn to him even before they had sex and entwined their souls forever. She wanted to be entangled with him.

But it couldn't be real. It was all because he'd ordered one of his zombies to tear out a chunk of her throat. Compared to Brie's shoulder and a lot of other's wounds, Renee's was barely noticeable. It'd been a targeted, neat wound. Of course, since she had passed out from her head injury it wasn't like she could fight back. Which seemed somehow worse.

Staring at the pages in front of her, she wished it was another fantasy novel, the kind she could hide from the world in. Before the zombies' uprising, she thought she had problems and wanted to escape but they paled compared to what she was dealing with now. Before, she was lonely and dreamed of masquerade balls and finding her prince.

Of course, she knew her story would be dark and full of twists and turns. Her prince would be broody with dark hair and tragic backstory because most of the male characters in her books were like that. But with her, he would see that none of his past tribulations mattered anymore. Their love would heal them both. Remake them into something stronger, better.

Stupid. She'd been naïve and stupid.

She peered at Zane. Why had he chosen her? Because she'd been unconscious? He sat on the opposite side of the shed as he had before, one leg stretched out and the other propped up with his hand resting on it. She couldn't place his expression, but the anguish in his eyes made her stomach hurt. He was gazing at her, but it was like he saw through her, his thoughts a million miles away.

"Before you, this was all there was," he said in the darkness. "Violence, pride, pain."

Renee didn't respond though she did stop pretending to read.

"When I saw you suffering the violence you didn't deserve, the pain you never asked for, how hard you fought... something made me act. Maybe it was my guilt. Your refusal to give up. My pride? I don't know." He averted his eyes and balled his hand into a fist before flexing it.

"After that, I decided things would be different. I'd be different." He paused, rubbing his jaw. "There's nothing to this existence. Just more violence, pride, pain, and the need to consume."

"It must consume," she whispered.

"What I want doesn't matter. It never has. I wanted to believe..." He turned his glowing gold irises to her. "It doesn't matter. I'm only here to serve its needs."

Renee leaned forward. Again, he spoke in sad, cryptic statements that made her realize he was so lost. So alone. Surrounded by hundreds, thousands of creatures, he created and controlled yet wholly alone.

"Zane."

"I won't-" He swallowed. "I won't force you to be around me except at night, so I know you're safe. Brie will watch over you during the day and when we hunt. I can't free you from this new life, but I'll try to make this existence tolerable for you." Turning his head from her, he balled his hand into a fist again.

Shit. It's exactly what she said she wanted. He was backing off, giving her space. But it sounded more like they were ending whatever it was between them, breaking up. She flattened her lips. Breaking up though, meant they had actually been together. Excuses or not. She'd have to admit the lies she told herself were just that.

If they could be broken, then they'd been together.

It had been real.

"Zane, I-"

"Don't. I'm giving you the only thing I can. You're right, I did take everything. I was selfish because I wanted you."

"Okay, but-" She stared at him. "You're not only here to serve its needs."

"I wish that were true." His voice was haunting, barely above a whisper.

Chapter 35

"Wake up, princess. It's time to move."

The sound of Brie's voice warmed her after the cold, lonely night she had with Zane. They hadn't spoken after their brief conversation, and Renee couldn't shake the feeling that she'd royally messed things up, not only for them, but also with Zane. She'd broken something in him, and he wasn't going to be okay. And she didn't know what to do.

"Okay, okay. I'm up." Renee grabbed her bag and walked out. Reflecting on their conversation from the other day, she risked the question. "You mentioned others also had to wear sunglasses sometimes. What was that about?"

"Oh. When we turn and our eyes change, it can be tough for some of us. It doesn't happen to everyone, however the ones it hurts and gives headaches to, we discovered shades help. After a while, whatever's going on is done, and they don't need them."

That explained Renee's daily headaches that had disappeared. "Is that why our eyes are so light?"

Brie shrugged. "Not sure. Most of us ended up with corpse-like coloring, and I haven't seen one of us that doesn't have pale-colored eyes. Those of us who had brown eyes while human seem to have the most variety."

"Brown? But that's the most common eye color."

"Yeah, but something about when we die - it shifts. My eyes were always blue. Now they're just lighter. Yours were probably always green. Garren's look red now, but they used to be dark brown. Nail's were a lighter brown, and now they look kinda like coffee with too much milk." Brie chuckled. "Hatchet's reminded me of milk chocolate, fuck, I miss that. But she said hers were almost black when she was alive."

"So maybe it's whatever colors are mixed inside the brown?" Renee guessed.

"That's the working theory. I remember back in the day when I would go to the salon," Brie paused and sighed, her fingers trailing over her locks. "Anyway, one of the stylists there who did the clients' color would always shine this bright-ass LED light in someone's eyes before she would agree to a color. She insisted that people with brown eyes had a "base" color mixed into their eyes, and the highlights or coloring for their hair needed to match if someone wanted to pass it off as their natural color. I always thought she was nuts, but she was their best colorist." Brie picked up strands of her hair and narrowed her eyes at it.

"Did you ever dye your hair?" Renee hadn't ever considered coloring her hair natural-looking colors. If she would've dyed her hair, she'd have picked pink, purple, or maybe blue. A color one of the magical beings in her books may have chosen.

"No. I'd get highlights or lowlights, but it was always this." Brie frowned and let go of her hair. "I had an image to maintain for all the good it did me."

She wasn't sure how to interpret Brie's displeasure about her hair. Renee thought she enjoyed being stylish and fancy. In an attempt to improve Brie's mood, Renee changed the subject. "Are we going to the same location as before, or did he change his mind?"

"Nope, still headed to the city. It's supposed to be kinda like the one we just left. Full of food, but we'll need to fight for it. Some humans have taken parts of the city for themselves to keep us out because of the smaller settlements around it. It looks like they're trying to set up shop more permanently."

"Won't that be dangerous for the horde?"

"Yeah. We weren't supposed to go there until we had at least two more rounds of the culling and... enlisted more troops."

"But why-" Renee stopped and groaned. "I need to talk to him. We can't do it if we're not ready. We'll lose too many... of us." It was weird to say 'us' when she talked about zombies. She understood her reality but hadn't completely given up on humanity yet.

"Thought you wanted us gone?"

"Don't be a bitch. I haven't wanted you or Zane gone for a while."

"Aww, I rank, how sweet." Brie's red lips gave her an exaggerated smile.

"Brie."

"I'm just fucking with you. I know it's still messed up for you. I was trying to lighten the mood," Brie said as they joined the bulk of the horde.

"I know." Renee gave her a weak smile as they trudged on. "How long before we reach the other city?"

"A few days."

"Won't we need to... eat before then?"

"Yeah, tomorrow we take a minor detour. There should be an encampment and a large feral deer population ahead. The scouts reported to him right before I woke you up."

"That's... efficient."

"Yeah, he's pretty good at this. The military experience helps," Brie said with a shrug.

"Zane was in the military?"

"Yeah, before he turned. For five years."

Well, shit. Brie knew a lot about Zane. So much that it made Renee uncomfortable. The word queen shouted in her mind again.

"I didn't realize he planned so much."

"He kinda has to. There are so many of us. An army, remember?"

Renee tried to smile but couldn't manage it. Everything Zane said conflicted with what Brie told her about him. Brie had no reason to lie, granted, it didn't make sense for Zane to lie either. It was like he was their king but didn't want to be and didn't like them. He seemed to have felt some sort of responsibility for them because he made them. If he didn't want to be their king, why had he made them or ordered them to be made?

It must consume. Again, it repeated in her mind.

"After everyone... eats, I'm talking to Zane. We can't go to that city because he's upset. I don't want to risk-" She stopped. Did she even have any right to say any of this?

"You don't want to risk what? Zane? Yourself? Me? The horde?" Brie studied her.

"Anyone, I don't want to risk anyone for a lost cause. It's stupid." She looked away from Brie.

Renee thought about when they'd talked weeks ago. He told her he planned to devour the world until nothing was left, and they'd all eventually die.

"But if you keep traveling and eating all the humans, there won't be any left. You'll all die."

"Yes."

If his plan was to kill them all, her actions seemed to have sped things up.

Did Zane want to die?

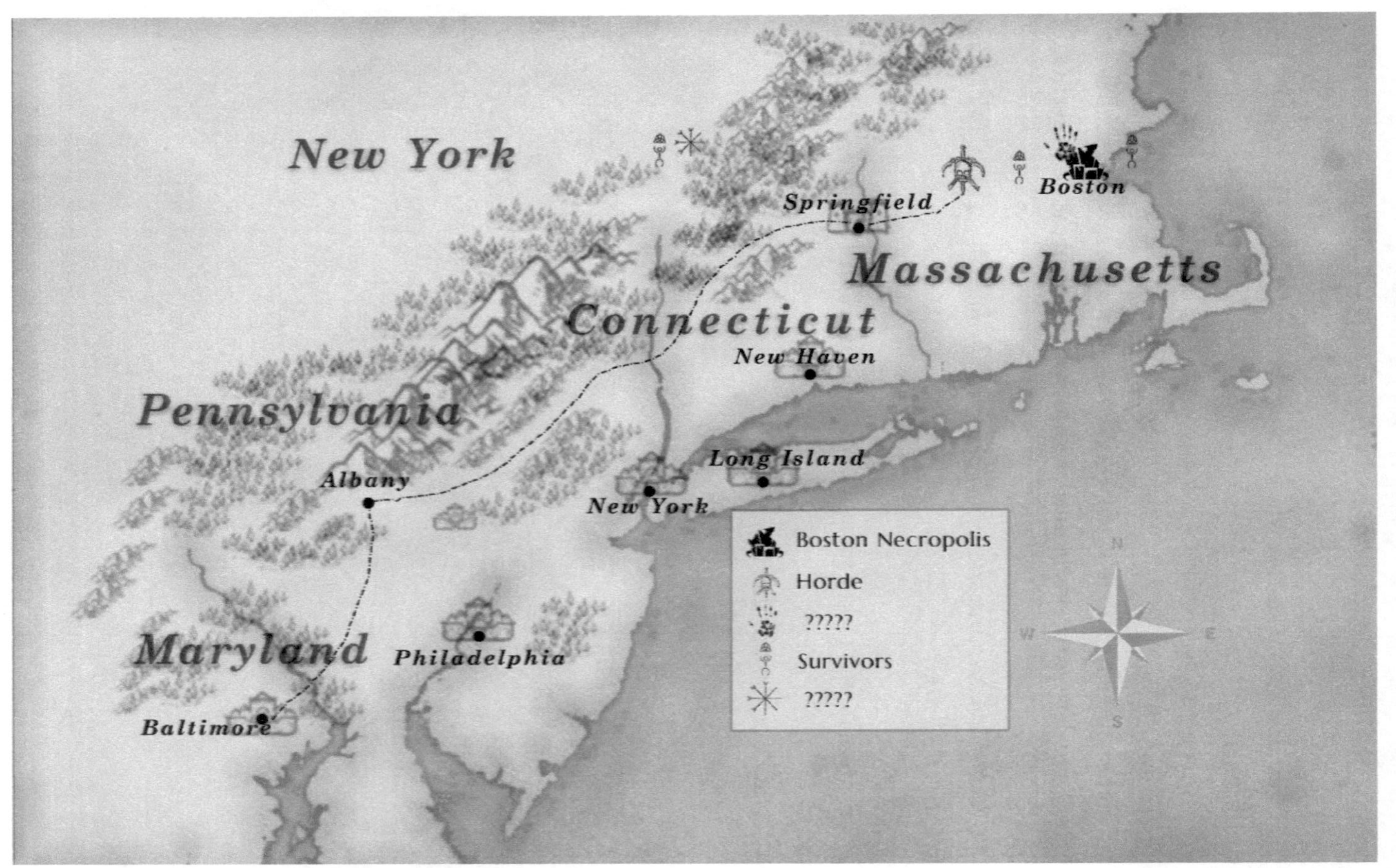
New York
Springfield
Boston
Massachusetts
Connecticut
New Haven
Pennsylvania
Long Island
Albany
New York
Maryland
Philadelphia
Baltimore
Boston Necropolis
Horde
?????
Survivors
?????
N
E
W
S

Chapter 36

After another uncomfortable night with Zane, with him refusing to speak to her and a long chilly day and night of marching, they entered a nice, wooded area. From the way the sky appeared, it wasn't too long before dawn.

Her mind kept circling, trying to figure out how she felt about Zane. How she could reconcile her new existence while somehow keeping her promise to her brother. Had she only developed feelings for Zane because she was one of his horde? That didn't seem right. After all, none of the other members seemed to get doe-eyed over their king.

She was now an enemy to humans, and although she didn't want to see them eradicated from the planet, she understood that they would never accept her again. Honestly, they hadn't really accepted her before. If she met them now, it would be identical to what happened in the city, even though that situation didn't make sense at the time. They would shoot first and ask questions later. They'd never see her as anything but an undead.

Brie barked orders at the horde and set up a perimeter. Renee was familiar with, and understood, how things ran when they set up camp. Not a human base, but it had some similarities with perimeters, guards, and a central social location - something that somewhat resembled a gathering of friends.

It hadn't occurred to Renee what a massive undertaking effectively moving this many bodies was, probably since she had been kept away, when they set up camp. Now that she knew, or at least recognized, the chosen, she understood the responsibility they bore for the horde. Although Brie was giving orders, many of the chosen had already started their tasks, and those in the horde who seemed confused or lost, received guidance from one of the chosen. Zane's horde worked like a well-oiled machine. If the humans witnessed this, they'd shit their pants where they stood.

Renee tried to be helpful but wasn't sure what to do. Hatchet was kind and let her tag along to gather wood. Although Hatchet was annoyed when Renee paused to say "hi" to Garren who was working with the other guards to establish the camps' boundary.

"Sorry," Renee mumbled when she returned to Hatchet's side.

Hatchet chuckled. "I called it before, you're friendly. It'll take the others some time to get used to it."

"I'll try to be better about it," Renee vowed and shifted position to cradle the wood better.

Hatchet lifted the wood from Renee's arms. "You don't need to be better. Just don't forget what we are."

"Zombies?" It was hard for her to get the word out because she wasn't sure if it was offensive to them or not.

"Monsters. We can play nice, but we are what we are. Our king, as you like to call him, is the worst one since he controls all of us." Hatchet frowned at her own words.

Renee's stomach twisted. She wanted to disagree but couldn't, unless it involved her. He *was* a monster. Cold and without remorse.

Hatchet studied her for a moment. "Although you're different."

Her heart sped up as her hands got clammy. "No, not really." Unsure why, but she was fairly certain, if the horde viewed her as different, it would make things more dangerous.

"You definitely are, in a good way." Hatchet's eyes glanced at the old cabin. "I hope you don't change."

"Seeing as I'll be a good influence?" Renee said with a grin, trying to lighten the mood.

Hatchet laughed and smacked her on the shoulder. Ouch. She was really strong.

"Mace will love that!" Hatchet said through her laughter.

"Hatchet." Brie's tone was irritated.

Hatchet stopped and wiped the smile from her face. The two women stared at each other long enough that it made Renee uneasy. She wasn't sure why Brie didn't like Hatchet being friendly towards her, but she'd considered it progress until the moment Brie interrupted.

"Are you done?" Brie asked and rested one of her hands on her hip.

"No, we need more wood."

"Then go get it." Brie's tone was strange again. It sounded cold like it had when Renee had first met her months ago.

Hatchet handed Brie the wood and glanced at Renee before she stomped off without another word. Brie took the timber and dumped it into a pile where other chosen were starting fires.

"Come on," Brie said and tugged on her arm.

"Why can't I talk to the others?"

Brie slowed her steps as her eyes darted around. "You can, but not when we set up camp. Too many eyes paying attention to what you do."

Taking in Brie's defensive posture and hushed voice, she knew she was acting like this because she was afraid of something. Or someone. Her face held a grim expression as they approached the cabin.

"Do you mean *him*?" She whispered.

"Yeah, but..." Brie's steps were even more sluggish. "There are other... just listen to me, okay?"

Renee breathed in frustration because every time she felt like she'd finally found her bearings in this new life, either Brie or Zane would ruin it with cryptic statements that explained nothing, and they didn't offer enough for her to figure it out.

"Tomorrow's the hunt. You should try to take part. With the animals, I mean. Learn how to get food in case you're in a bind." Brie said as they stopped in front of the porch that desperately needed repair.

"Yeah... maybe. See you tomorrow," Renee said as she opened the door to a smaller, rougher cabin than the one from weeks ago. The interior housed only a table, some stools, and random pieces of broken furniture. Part of her was relieved that it didn't resemble the other cabin; thinking about her time there with Zane gutted her.

Her eyes roved over the sparse accommodations. Damn, she missed beds. Her sleeping bag was on the floor. He always remembered it and ensured it was there when she arrived. She wanted to be near him but went to the sleeping bag and sat. He rested against a wall while staring into space. His sorrow ate at her, consumed her the way the horde consumed every living thing.

"I really miss you." Her voice trembled as she spoke.

"Why would you say that to me?" The hurt made his voice raw.

"Because it's the truth. It doesn't change anything, but it's true."

He sighed and rubbed his forehead.

She swallowed. "I can't figure you out, but I know I'm not right for you. In some ways, you're too good for me."

"Too good?" He looked at her like she had two heads.

"Yeah, only with relationship stuff. You're a total dick otherwise."

He laughed, a real laugh, and damn, she'd missed it. In the end, he seemed even more miserable.

"Renee, you'll never stop being too good for me, in all ways."

His words devastated her because she knew he meant them. She still couldn't understand how he continued to put her on a pedestal after their arguments, all the times she was so hateful.

"No. I'm hot-tempered and bitchy and say mean things when I shouldn't. I hurt the only people who've been good to me. You said you loved me, and I shit all over it. You keep proving you do, and I keep screwing up." She wiped her eyes. "I don't think I understand how to be in a relationship. I'm angry and confused. I don't want to break up, but I don't want to keep hurting you, either."

"Break up?" He shifted and leaned forward.

"Did I mention I'm immature? Apparently, the world ending when I was in high school fucked me up." She laughed at her own grim humor. She'd always wondered if the world going to shit had somehow frozen her brain and kept her from developing past teenager, even though she was an adult now.

Zane got up and perched beside her on the sleeping bag. He brushed the hair off her neck. "You think there's hope? That we're together?"

"Well, no. You kinda dumped me the other night. I figured that much out. I get you were doing it because I said I didn't want to be around you anymore, but I was overreacting and-"

His lips silenced her words when they covered hers, making her dizzy. Her arms wrapped around his neck and touched his soft hair. Zane kissed her like he was in pieces, and she was the only thing that held him together. His kiss was usually gentle, but this one was desperate, fierce, and all-consuming. It was like he was trying to crawl inside her or pull her into himself.

"Stay with me," he said against her mouth.

"I did. I am." She broke their kiss gently. "I am."

He cupped her face. "There is nothing without you. Nothing. *I* am nothing."

"Don't say that. You're their king, and that's important. You protect them, feed them, lead them."

He averted his eyes. She hoped that if she reminded him how essential he was to the horde's survival, he would stop feeling that way about himself. Then again, when his expression shifted, and she saw his pinched mouth as he scowled, she realized resentment was the dominating emotion.

"You resent them. Your duty to them, even though you created them."

Zane said nothing, dropping his hands and refusing to look at her.

"You told me once if I kept my word to you, then you'd give me almost anything I wanted."

He turned to her with narrowed eyes.

"I can promise to stay now and truly mean it. I'm done running, Zane. From this life, and from you. I can accept it. I accept you."

Flickers of hope made his face soften. Zane reached for her but swallowed and dropped his hand to his lap. "I don't think you understand what you're saying."

"Maybe not. And I can't promise I won't screw up again because I probably will, but I don't want to lose you. When I-" She paused and drew a breath. "When I killed that woman because she threatened you, I didn't know what I was then. I only knew she wanted to take you from me, and I wanted to stay with you."

Renee touched his gorgeous face once again, delighted by the cool smooth skin. Not all zombies were handsome, but Zane... was sheer perfection. "I wanted to stay with the king of the dead even when I thought I was the thing he and all his minions ate for dinner."

"Do you remember what happened?" he whispered.

"If you mean do I remember when your chosen took a chunk out of me? No. I guess I was unconscious."

Zane picked up her hand and kissed her fingers before putting it over his heart. "If I had realized how much this would disgust and scare you, I wouldn't have done this to you. I was selfish."

"Stop." She put her fingers over his lips. "I don't care anymore. I told you I accept this new life. I accept you."

He closed his eyes and moved her hand away. "I need to tell you something."

"Okay, but first, I need to ask you to do something for me, for us."

His eyes popped open. "What?"

"Don't attack the city."

Zane pulled back. The soft expression vanished. "What?"

"Please, not that city. We can go somewhere else. Anywhere else."

"You don't even know where we're going." He narrowed his eyes at her again.

"Well, I don't know the name, but-"

"Stop. Why are you asking me this? Did Brie say something to you?"

Shit. Shit. She didn't want Brie to get into trouble. "No, it wasn't Brie. It's making the horde nervous and-"

"How would you know that?" His tone was accusing as his face shifted to less Zane and more king, as though he was about to do something horrible.

"Because I've been traveling with them for weeks. They don't want to do it, and they're just afraid to defy you," she blurted out because it was true.

Zane stared at her for a long time before he spoke again, "You're asking me for the good of the horde? Not some personal agenda?"

His words made her pause because they sounded ridiculous. Why would she have a personal agenda? And more than that, even if she did, how would that even work? He was the king, and it had been made abundantly clear that he called the shots, *all of them*. It didn't matter who she spoke to, they all had the same mantra over and over. Zane was the king, and he decided everything that happened in the horde. There were no personal agendas allowed.

"Personal agenda? I don't have a personal agenda. This isn't about me. This is about them. It's our job to look out for them, and you're leading them into danger. If we entered this city, it would kill a lot of them. You're their king and are supposed to care about them!" Her words tumbled from her lips before she considered what she was saying.

Zane sat back and furrowed his brow. "*Our* job to look out for them?"

When Zane repeated her words, she shrank back and felt lightheaded. Shit. Why'd she say that? She was angry he was being so selfish because of her and wanted to hurt others or himself. With little to no experience dealing with someone who had acted like this, she didn't know what to do.

"Do you want to die, Zane?"

His face became all sharp angles with irritation before it morphed into despair. He turned his head aside. "I already told you I can't die."

"Because *it* won't let you."

"Yes." His jaw worked. So much bitterness in that word.

"But it doesn't change that maybe-" She swallowed. "You wish you could."

Zane turned and grabbed her shoulders. "Why would it matter to you?"

"Because I care about you. I care what happens." Renee wished she was brave enough to tell him she loved him.

"And you care about the horde? Enough to ask me not to take the city?"

"Yes, because they're yours. We're *all* yours."

Zane let her go. "I don't want you to be mine because you're part of the horde." He stood.

Renee jumped up and yanked him to her when he tried to walk away. "That's *not* why I'm yours. And it isn't because you were a jerk and told me I was." Her arms slid up around his neck. "I'm yours because you *don't* make me do whatever you want. You let me say what I want and act stupid even when it hurts you."

She brushed her lips against his in a feathery kiss, but he was still hesitant. "I thought maybe I only felt this way about you because I was part of the horde, but it's not. I've been around them, including Brie, for a while now, and it's different."

"How is it different?" His glowing irises bored into her, like he was afraid to believe her words.

"It's different because I've never felt this way with anyone. I couldn't leave you, even if I weren't dead. How I feel is not about me now being undead or being part of the horde. It's about you." She pressed her lips to his, hoping he felt how much she loved him. "It's you, Zane. I want to be with *you*."

She sensed when he stopped fighting his internal struggle, when he gave in to her. To them. His mouth moved over hers and teased her lips open. She moaned into his mouth and leaned into him. God, she'd missed this. Missed him. It was only when they were locked together that things were right.

Not sure when things heated to the point, they were on the floor on top of her sleeping bag, but the next thing she knew, they clawed at each other until they were naked on the dirty floor with him hovering over her.

He broke their kiss and drew a shaky breath. "I can't do this again. I mean, we can't." He stopped.

"What's wrong?"

"I can't do this. Be with you if you're going to push me away." The misery in his eyes tore her open. Eviscerated her.

"I'm sorry." She drew his mouth to hers. "I'm sorry. I won't do that again."

"I don't trust myself anymore. You're right." He breathed out as his jaw ticked.

"I'm right?"

"About the city. About me." He buried his face in her hair. "I shouldn't be their leader; except I don't have a choice."

"No. That isn't what I meant. Look at me."

He raised up on his elbows and peered at her. So much vulnerability played on his features. He was so defeated by his crown, believing he hadn't made correct choices for the horde when it was evident he had. Perhaps he wasn't kind, personable, or attentive to anything but their basic needs. However, they were strong because of him, because of his forethought, his strategy, and his planning. Many of them had survived for years and were healthy, well as healthy as zombies could be. They were able to *evolve* because of him. The tiny part of her humanity that lingered didn't like he was a decent king because it probably meant doom for any humans who survived.

She refused to let her lingering emotions toward humans dominate her mind. It wasn't about them; it was about Zane. "Until I showed up, you were a good king. Look at how powerful your army is. It's me that caused the problems."

His body tensed against hers. "Don't say that. You're the reason I care at all."

"That's not true. You took care of them, made them strong."

"You've been talking to Brie too much." He looked away. "It wasn't me, not really it was... I wasn't really me until I saw you."

"I don't understand."

He turned his golden eyes back to her. "You breathed life into me."

Holy shit. What could she say to that? Again, laying on the fucking ground and swooning.

"We won't attack the city yet." He told her resolutely. His expression relaxed, and he kissed her cheek and then her neck before whispering into her ear, "Stop listening to everything Brie tells you." His playful tone made the butterflies in her stomach flutter and dance.

"Okay, but then you have to explain things to me."

He gave her a wolfish grin. "Have I explained how I thought about you every night since we were together?"

She laughed. "Pervert."

"Only for you." He captured her mouth again.

Chapter 37

Brie glanced at Renee again as they walked. Perhaps it was because Renee wasn't marching so much as strolling. It could be because as much as she tried, Renee couldn't help but smile when she mused about the morning.

"Don't think your head's in the game today," Brie commented as she finished the braid at the side of her own head.

"Yeah, sorry. I'm hungry, but I still don't like the idea of hunting, even if it's animals." She'd insisted on going with Brie today to hunt, even when Zane told her she didn't have to. That he would make sure she never had to hunt anything, animals or humans, considering violence bothered her so much. Still, she'd pushed back and told him she needed to know how to feed herself if things got tough.

"Not so much what I meant."

"What?"

"Fuck, this is weird for a lot of reasons." Brie's lips pinched as she pointed to Renee's neck. "I think... I don't want to ask but it's killing me."

"What?" Renee touched her neck where the bite was. Did it look weird?

"No. Not that side. Do you have a hickey?"

Heat rose in her cheeks. Shit. Could zombies get hickeys? She cleared her throat. Flashes of Zane sucking on her neck as he thrust into her clouded her thoughts.

"Oh, my fucking god, it is. You made up by making out? What the hell? We don't even have those urges anymore." Brie stopped. Her face caught between anger, shock, and curiosity.

"I, we, um…" Renee's eyes darted around her to see if any of the others were paying attention. Much to her relief, they were too busy focusing on finding food. "It's not what it looks like," she finished weakly.

"It looks like you fucked him, but I know that doesn't happen, which only leaves you two having made out."

Renee wanted to correct her but didn't. She'd ask Zane later why Brie didn't think it was possible, the draw between them, the very clear and strong, lustful urges.

"Did he make you do that?" Brie's tone changed to the same one she'd used when she vowed, she'd beat him if he got pervy, and it made Renee smile.

"No. It's okay. We talked and things just-" Renee floundered, unsure of what to say.

"Oh god. Stop. I don't want to hear how you two made out."

"He agreed not to attack the city. We're supposed to get food to feed the horde and go somewhere different. He's going to talk to you when we get back."

"Did you only make out with him to get him to agree?" Brie's tone was accusatory as she crossed her arms and tapped her foot.

"No! It wasn't like that."

"So, you *are* a thing now?" Brie's tone was clipped.

"Yeah, I think so. Are you mad at me because I said I wanted to get away from him?" Renee stepped closer to Brie.

"No. As long as he isn't forcing you then, whatever. We need to go. We're falling behind." Brie turned and peered at the horde.

Something wasn't right. Renee wasn't sure why, but Brie didn't like that she and Zane were together. She hoped Brie didn't think she was a threat to her being the Knight Commander, because she wasn't. Especially since she had zero interest in battle planning or strategizing a city takeover. But even if she had a desire to take on that role, she'd never take it from her friend. Renee doubted anyone could beat Brie in combat, anyway. She was amazing.

The rest of the day, Brie was in a foul mood, but she still taught Renee how to stalk and hide. Renee was awesome at hiding but not so much at stalking something. She'd spent most of the apocalypse running away, so hiding was almost second nature to her now.

They hunted deer, wild pigs, and other feral animals. Unsuccessful at catching any of them, Renee carried several carcasses for the horde. Initially, she thought she wouldn't be able to handle it, that the dead animals would make her sick to her stomach. Instead, it made her hungry, which she ignored because she couldn't deal with it.

They stopped on their way back so some of the chosen could eat. Brie explained that several of them had gone without and needed to eat immediately. It had been exactly as Brie had described, although they ate, it was a normal human portion, and sure they were a bit food aggressive, it was nothing like she'd witnessed in the past with the horde or during the culling. Renee wondered if she could suggest they try to be a bit more civilized and sit at a table or use cutlery but then felt dumb and figured they'd be offended.

However, staring at the scene before her, it would be a long time before even the chosen would be ready for sitting at tables with cutlery. Mace smacked Toad on the back of the head. His huge palm was as large as Toad's head. Brie cleared her throat and stared at the young chosen, Toad.

Renee remained quiet but studied Toad's features. He looked nothing like a toad but he could leap great distances, as she witnessed during one of the hunts. He also had an abnormally long tongue, which he was using to nervously lick the corners of his mouth, removing all traces of blood. His shoulders were slumped and his expression was contrite. If Renee had to guess, she would say Toad was just barely eighteen when he turned and his demeanor still seemed very childlike.

The reason Toad was in trouble was for taking another's meal and eating it himself. From the way it went down she was scared they were going to turn on Toad and eat him.

"It's good, it's j-just us... *his* punishments are more... hardcore," Nail whispered beside her and twitched.

Nail had surprised Renee during the hunts because he was far scarier than she thought he might be. As soon as Toad swiped the piece from

Rabbit, known for her speed and acute hearing, everyone got angry; Nail shut down. He reverted into the uneasy, shy person she'd met back in the lobby. It was interesting to Renee that as predatory and fierce as Nail could be, as soon as the need to consume was gone, he seemed conflict-avoidant and didn't seem drawn to any violence.

"You are a chosen, so you understand how things work. What happens if you don't fall in line..." Brie began and crossed her arms over her chest. "What do all horde members do?"

"Serve the horde," Toad said in a subdued voice.

Brie drummed her fingers on her arms. "And the chosen?"

"Protect the horde. Above all, the horde and *he* must survive." Toad lowered his chin.

"Do you take from yourself?" Brie snapped.

Renee froze at Brie's tone. Again, it sounded too harsh. Not as it had when she first met Brie and Renee's very presence irritated her. It was that odd tone that was almost... disconnected? Toad shook his head.

"Then why did you?" Brie dropped her arms and stepped closer.

Toad flinched. "I... was hungry." His lips trembled.

Brie moved closer until their faces were inches apart. "We're always hungry. We always want to feed. But we are *chosen*. We must control our cravings because we are *more*. Do you understand?"

It was hard for Renee not to speak, but it was also the first instance she'd even seen the chosen interact like this or seen how Brie interacted with them in a disciplinary way. It was troubling to hear how single-minded they seemed to be on Zane's survival. Of course, she wanted him to live but the way it was worded sounded a bit cult-like to Renee. They feared him but almost worshiped him at the same time. That couldn't be healthy but then technically he *was* their creator.

Toad nodded enthusiastically but kept his head tilted down.

"Good. Apologize now." To her relief Brie's tone sounded like her again.

"Sorry, Mace," Toad mumbled.

"It's alright kid, don't do it again or we'll be having you for dinner." Mace chuckled and rubbed Toad's back. When his large hand touched Toad's back he leaned into it until Mace gave him a side hug.

Renee's eyes bulged from the sight. Brie had told her they didn't hug like she did. Granted it was a side hug, but it was still friendly contact and Toad seemed to be looking for it. Perhaps they were part of a family grouping? Or were the chosen evolving before her eyes?

Brie retrieved another feeding portion for Mace and had a few words with both of them as he ate. Renee turned away because part of her still didn't like seeing raw meat being eaten. She peered at Nail who still stood beside her. He was twisting one of his bracelets around, careful not to cut the leather with his claws.

"What's the standard punishment if someone takes your... food?" she asked in a low voice.

"The punishment for taking others' food... is death," Nail responded, letting his bracelet go. "Or worse, depending on whose it was and when it happened."

"Always?"

"Yeah, you can't take from yourself." He lifted a shoulder.

"Is that why it's bad if some families take more than they should?" she whispered.

Rabbit turned her head toward them but didn't make a sound. She blinked her large moss-green eyes as she studied them.

Nail nodded. "We all s-serve the horde to keep us s-strong," he managed and chewed on the side of his mouth.

Renee slowly reached out, so Nail could see her movement and it wouldn't scare him until her fingers brushed against his arm. She gently squeezed.

"We have to stay strong," she whispered in the most reassuring tone she could muster, sensing that was the correct response.

He visibly relaxed. After her conversation with Hatchet earlier, she had to be sure she didn't draw attention and make herself seem too different from them. She wasn't even sure why she was different, at least not yet.

Brie strutted over to them. Her gaze dropped to Renee's hand still on Nail. Renee pulled her fingers off his arm and balled her hand.

"Let's get moving. The horde's waiting on us." She picked up a carcass and started walking.

Brie was so good at hunting and leading the various packs within the horde, regardless of if they were chosen or just regular horde members. When they made a coordinated attack, they caught almost everything they targeted. It only reinforced Renee's faith in Brie as the horde's Knight Commander.

While Zane told them what to do, Brie solicited their input and then chose the best option for success. They followed her orders as well as his, but the difference was they weren't *hers* and didn't *have* to listen to her, they *chose* to.

Renee couldn't fathom how Brie thought she had nothing to offer. She hadn't known Brie when she was alive. Although if she was this awesome dead, she absolutely had more to offer than her good looks when she breathed. She tried to compliment her, but Brie brushed her off.

Unsurprisingly, as soon as they made it to camp, Brie said her farewells and left. Disheartened, Renee went to the tiny cabin and waited for Zane. They had made up, at least in part, but they still needed to talk about things. He'd mentioned he had to check on a few things in the horde, which usually took a few hours since the horde was so large, but she thought he'd be back by the time they returned from hunting.

Chapter 38

Renee paced the tiny space. Her mind was racing from her interactions with him the night before and from the hunt earlier that day. When Zane opened the door, she wanted to ask him about what she and Brie had spoken about, along with a million other things. Only when their eyes locked, all thoughts flew out of her head.

They collided with each other, both trying to consume the other with kisses and touches. Everything in her demanded they be joined immediately. Every cell screamed for him to fill her, twist their bodies and souls together until they were one. They were meant to be one, always.

Zane broke their kiss when she got his pants unbuttoned and unzipped. They both peered at each other with heavy breaths.

"I didn't mean-" he began.

"Don't apologize. If you hadn't stopped me, you'd be naked right now. I don't know what's wrong with me. I'm not usually this horny. It's like every time I see you, I can't wait for us to be like this."

His body stiffened, and his expression became distant.

"It's the only time I feel like everything's right. When we're close, it's like nothing else matters. I know it's all going to be okay because we're together." She threaded her fingers into his hair.

He lowered his forehead to hers and closed his eyes. Renee waited for him to say something because she felt pretty vulnerable and raw after she had just disclosed such intimate thoughts and feelings, but he didn't. He just held her tighter. Zane shifted them until he crushed her in a hug.

Had she said something wrong? Why was he holding her like she was going to disappear if he let go?

"Zane?"

"Stay with me," he whispered.

Renee's head spun. Her vision blurred, and she thought she might pass out. Something about the way he'd said that. He'd said that to her before, but this time he sounded scared and broken, like he believed she might not. The tone and words struck something inside her and made her legs wobbly. A sharp ache in her head caused her to inhale sharply.

"Zane," she muttered as her vision went dark.

•   •   •

Renee dragged herself up and placed her palm against the windowpane. The bloody scene in front of her wasn't any different from anything she'd seen in the past, but it still left her heartbroken. No escape. Even Renee knew her time was up. She got away because they'd assumed she was already dead and had moved on to the still-live prey. They preferred meat with a heartbeat.

She'd fallen and hit her head on a concrete curb just outside the hotel she was hiding in. She only managed to make her way two floors up because dizziness was overtaking her sense of direction and ability to balance. Her fingers gripped the windowsill of the window in the room she was hiding in while her palm, flat on the glass, kept her from swaying. Something tickled the side of her face, but she ignored it, unable to look away from the death in front of her.

Maybe it was better she couldn't hear the screams, gunfire, or explosions. Renee shivered. Most places had no power, and it was only fall, so she shouldn't have been as cold as she was. It was just after nightfall. She closed her eyes even though it was stupid to close them, leaving herself open to attacks, but what did it matter anymore?

The city was overrun. All of her family and friends were long dead. Any new alliances she'd made - gone. After fighting so hard over the last seven years, she was alone, again. The last of her food was depleted days ago. Out of water. No reason to try anymore. Humanity had lost.

As soon as they stepped foot in the city, Renee knew they'd made a colossal mistake. It was too barren, too quiet. She swore she even felt the undead watching her. It didn't make sense - zombies didn't watch anything; they didn't plan. They came in waves and devoured everything until there were only piles of bones.

The image of the tall, menacing zombie filled her mind. Renee had seen him in the shadows as she neared the harbor. At first, she hadn't realized he was undead because the dim light obscured his features. Even after, when everyone was running for their lives and she'd seen him again, he didn't look quite dead. He was too clean, too fresh looking - almost human.

Renee put her forehead against the glass and gripped the windowpane tighter. Nausea threatened to make her throw up what little fluid she still had left in her body. The hair on the back of her neck stood. She bit her lip. They were here. It was only a matter of time.

A light touch on her back made her stiffen and tremble. It was a hand, a cold hand. It slid up to her neck and gently squeezed. She froze. Not a zombie. Confused, she opened her eyes and glanced at the reflection in the window.

Her mouth dropped open, and she gasped, trembling even more. It was him. His odd, bloodshot, amber-colored irises stared back at her in the window's glass. It must've been a trick of the light because they seemed to glow. Blood covered his mouth and chin. Tears cascaded down her cheeks, but she didn't fight him even when he turned her to face him. His eyes moved over her face.

Renee's lips quivered as he continued to hold her by the neck. Her eyes flicked to his arm, covered in blood and gore. She snapped her lips shut to keep from retching. His other hand came up and reached for her face. Instinctively, she shuddered. He advanced until his body touched hers and showed his teeth.

Yanking her head to the side, his fingers stroked the side of her head. Definitely not what she had been expecting. His touch was light, the way it had been when he'd touched her spine seconds earlier. She recoiled when his fingers grazed the spot on her head that she'd hit. His odd eyes flicked to her face. Renee wanted to scream or possibly tell him to go to hell. However, her lips stayed sealed.

He moved his hand and brushed the hair over her shoulder. Why hadn't he killed her? No other undead had ever acted like this. Come to think of it, no other zombie had acted like anything. They were murdering machines, period. Renee thought about shoving him away and making a run for it, but his expression changed, surprising her.

He looked heartbroken. Genuinely bereft and lonely. Lonely, she understood. What the hell was she thinking? Maybe she was already dead and in purgatory. When her shaking hand reached up and touched his face, no one was more shocked than her. His brows pinched. Something in those almost gold eyes shifted, growing more resolute.

He pulled her head to the side and brought his mouth to her neck. Shit, this was it. He would tear out her throat because she offered it to him. Tingles covered her when his lips planted a kiss there. Her hand snaked around his waist and tugged him closer. When his teeth sunk into her neck, she almost welcomed the bite. Renee was glad as her flesh was torn from her. She couldn't live with herself knowing she'd willingly offered herself to a zombie, that she went out on her terms.

•   •   •

Renee's eyes fluttered open and found Zane holding her. Concern wrinkled his brow and made his face tight. His glowing, amber eyes looked troubled as he gazed at her. Distressed, the same way he had appeared when he'd killed her.

Zane, *her Zane*, killed her. He'd told her over and over he was selfish. He agreed with her, when she said he took everything from her, including her life. He hadn't ordered it. He'd done it himself. But even then, he hadn't wanted to hurt her. It pained him to do it.

"Why?" she choked out.

With watery eyes, he eased her to the sleeping bag and pulled his hands from her. "You remember." He withdrew so he no longer touched her and averted his gaze.

"You didn't order them. It was you."

He nodded, still not meeting her eyes.

"I wasn't in the street. I was in a hotel hiding. You found me," she said as the memory sharpened.

"Yes."

"Did you search for me?" Renee remembered seeing him several times before he found her. He'd been watching her.

"Yes."

"Why?" she whispered.

"I told you, I'm selfish." His tone filled with the self-hate she recognized. Not sure what he was like before he'd turned her, but since then, every time he talked about himself, his voice was always filled with contempt. And she despised it. Someone had turned him too, made him undead. He wasn't evil. He was doing what was in his nature now, and what would be in her nature too.

"Okay, but why?"

"I don't know, maybe because I'm a dick like you said."

Renee scooted toward Zane until her legs touched him and reached out. His body tensed as her fingers touched his face. She turned him to her.

"Why?"

"Because..." He paused as his eyes moistened again. "Because you're mine."

Renee wondered if he kept telling her that since he felt responsible for her death, although it didn't make any sense. He'd decided that before she was dead. She brushed his hair back.

"You were so gentle, like you wanted to comfort me." With her other hand, she threaded their fingers together. "It's like you didn't want to turn me. Why did you? And don't tell me it's because you're selfish. That isn't why."

"It is. I could've let you die, be at peace but I couldn't let go." He blinked, and a few tears escaped his eyes.

"Let me die?"

Zane raised his fingers and touched the side of her head. Renee remembered he'd done that same motion then, too.

"You were dying. I only meant to be with you so you wouldn't die alone."

"I was dying from when I hit my head?"

He nodded and withdrew his hand before turning his face away again. "You didn't have long. When you touched me, I thought... I'm a bastard. You hate everything about this existence."

"Not everything."

He turned his watery eyes to her.

"I don't hate you. You saved me."

"I damned you."

"No." She brushed her lips against his. "You saved me. I would've died if you hadn't bitten me."

"I made you into *this*. You hate everything it means to be undead."

"Yeah, I do, but I get to be with you. If I have to exist like this, then I accept it," Renee said, and meant it. She was done questioning everything about them, especially their relationship. She'd never experienced anything like their connection before, with anyone. Something that twisted her up and challenged her constantly while also giving meaning to everything.

"You can't. It's not enough. I'm not enough to make it worth it."

"Stop!" She cupped his face. "You told me there was nothing without me. Don't you get it? Zane, there's nothing for me without you. I love you."

His eyes widened. "You love me?"

"Of course I do. Did you think I'd be mad when I remembered?"

"I thought you would hate me, think everything was a lie."

"Well, I don't. I'm not angry. I'm happy you made me, because it means we get to be together." Renee moved until she straddled his lap.

"But you can't stand the violence, the death." His hands traveled up her sides.

"Are you trying to ruin my moment?" she quipped.

"Your moment?"

"I'm going to strangle you," she said with levity, recalling when she'd attacked him on the roof. "I'm trying to be romantic like you usually are and profess my love, and you're screwing it all up." Renee wrapped her arms around his neck, wondering how he would feel if she suggested he read the book he found for her so he could get these moments right in the future.

"This is my fairytale, remember? Kings, queens, armies... this is the part where you're supposed to say something that sweeps me off my feet. Then we kiss, so it all ends up happily ever after."

"You could be happy with me, even in this world?"

"I could *only* be happy in this world, with you."

His lips quirked up before they broke into a smile. "Then I will spend the rest of my life making you as happy as I can, my queen."

"Queen?" Renee smiled because he used her words.

"You did say I was their king," he laughed.

"Don't let it go to your head."

"Then you have to stay with me. Keep me in my place." He drew her closer until their hearts beat against one another's.

"Always, my king." Renee sealed her promise with a kiss. Because this time, she knew she'd never run again. Her place was with Zane, her king of the dead.

Epilogue

Eric peered at Lucy, who shivered beside him. Even with her six layers of clothing that gave her an unusual appearance, like her head was too small for her body, she was still cold. Caleb and Zaila scanned and sniffed the area, searching for threats. Zaila was just up ahead of Eric, with Lucy and Valen slightly behind him. Caleb remained in the back of the group with Seth.

Eric was the one who had decided they would go on this mission to find the necessary medicine. And although they were lucky to find more antibiotics to take back to their settlement, it wasn't as successful as they'd hoped. Still, Eric was happy they were headed back, and so far, no one had been gravely wounded. Wounded, sure, but not bad enough to prevent self-healing or be healed by Lucy.

They'd been living in this hell on earth for over seven years and still weren't sure how to stop the zombies. Thankfully, they were able to destroy the gate that Father Cornell had opened, but not before everyone and everything in their hometown had been destroyed. Eric's only goal had been, and still was, to keep his family safe. They were all one another had in this world, and it was his job to keep them together and alive.

Lucy and Valen had insisted they try to work with other people to establish safe areas for survivors because they had gifts and abilities others didn't to better defend the territories. Both Eric and Caleb had pushed back, but eventually gave in.

"Hey, get closer to one another. I'm going to put up a barrier, so Lucy isn't so cold," Valen said.

"It's okay. I'm okay." Lucy insisted, her big eyes locked on Valen.

"No, you're not. Let me help. I haven't used any spells today. It's fine." Valen assured Lucy and tossed her long black hair over her shoulder.

Eric's chest tightened. He'd never get over how gorgeous Valen was. Her smooth, sepia skin was lighter because it was winter, and she was his. It had been years, and he still couldn't believe how lucky he was that she wanted to be with him. With a quick grin at him, she put her arm around Lucy and tugged her closer.

With a few words and a wave of Valen's hand, everything shimmered for a few seconds around them and then appeared normal again. Even though none of them, except Valen, could see the magic she used, he knew it had worked from the chilled breeze that no longer assaulted them.

Zaila's hand went up before she balled it into a fist, which meant she sensed a threat. They all remained motionless. Seth and Caleb moved from behind them to flank Zaila. Eric narrowed his eyes and peered into the darkness. His vision was the best out of the group, but he'd agreed that letting them take point to keep Lucy and Valen safe was smarter.

Something was moving toward them in the distance, something substantial, only he couldn't make out what. He considered calling on his powers, but it was dangerous to use them unless he could control the environment. So many had died since the undead had taken over the earth. If he picked the wrong place to use his ability, he'd quickly be overwhelmed.

"Undead." Seth's gravelly voice said.

Eric zeroed in on the moment. Crap. Seth was right. That was why the movement didn't make sense. It wasn't one big thing; it was many human-sized things moving as a unit. Seth turned his head and locked eyes with Lucy. She signed *I love you* to him before she and Valen clustered together.

Valen and Lucy scooted behind him as he pulled out his rifle and aimed, as everyone moved into their familiar formation. The cracks and pops of Zaila and Caleb shifting were still unsettling but didn't bother him the way they used to. They hadn't fully shifted and were in their wolf-human hybrid forms. Terrifying to others who hadn't witnessed it before. Seth pushed the hood down on his oversized hoodie, letting his long, straight, black hair free. He flexed his hands, his jagged claws already popping through his fingertips.

"They've caught our scent," Caleb growled at them.

"I'll trip some of them when they come at us," Valen's voice said behind him.

Eric set the rifle against his shoulder and focused on a patch of wooded area in front of them. Seconds later, the zombies were visible. He scanned them to see which was the biggest, most fresh, or fastest. He exhaled before pulling the trigger. The taller undead fell to the ground. As always, he never missed, and he always shot to kill.

Roots shot up from the ground and tripped up the faster creatures barreling toward them. Some branches in the trees shot out and knocked more down. Seth took off into the fray, leaping into the air and landing on one of the faster zombies, toppling it before springing up and jumping on the back nearest to him. Wasting no time, he sunk his lethal claws into the creature's neck and tore its head off.

Caleb and Zaila crouched low, their hands barely touching the ground in the event they needed to push off it, their muscles tensing as they both growled, saliva dripping from their mouths in anticipation. Eric aimed and dropped three more undead before the big group reached Caleb and Zaila. Behind them were even more zombies. Damn it, they hadn't encountered a group this large in a while.

Caleb and Zaila tore through the group with savage satisfaction. The two worked together fluidly executing a deadly dance as they tore apart their enemies. A gust of wind blew into the creatures bringing up the rear, knocking them into each other. Eric reloaded and continued to take down the undead.

"There's more behind those zombies. We may need to leave." Valen's tone was heavy with warning.

Just as Eric was about to reply, a howl ripped through the noise of the battle. It made him freeze as terror ran down his spine. His always steady hands shook, and the urge to use the bathroom made him twitch. Shit, they were in trouble. Caleb turned his head to Eric as he ripped the zombie he held in half and nodded, confirming his fear that another werewolf had just shown up.

Werewolves were rare, especially since many had died during the initial fight to survive seven years ago. It was hard to predict how dangerous a werewolf was or what type they were. Some werewolves were like Caleb and Zalia. They controlled the shift and didn't lose themselves to the beast. Others were raging, mindless creatures.

Given Eric's reaction to the howl, it meant this werewolf was capable of using its howl to incapacitate others. Zaila had taught them a lot about werewolves. Seth ran towards them with an arm in his teeth, he pulled pieces off to eat as he joined them. They went into a defensive formation, back-to-back in a circle, as all the zombies froze and became silent.

"Why did they stop?" Lucy whispered.

"Why is there a werewolf?" Valen asked.

A giant honey-brown werewolf burst through the tree line, knocking down several trees, and snapping its jaws at them. It ignored the unmoving undead surrounding it, as it sniffed at the air and growled.

Eric gripped the rifle, lining up a perfect shot. The problem was, the bullets weren't silver, and he wasn't able to move again. Damn it, this werewolf was powerful. A tall, emaciated, almost skeletal man with dark brown hair that fell down to the middle of his back, strode into the clearing, unconcerned by the situation.

The wolf padded closer to them, moving towards the thin man. As the man neared the group, it became more apparent he was not just another survivor. Confidence, strength, and corruption oozed off of him. His complexion was almost corpse-like, his gaunt face showing every sharp angle, with tattoos covering every visible inch of his skin except his face. What drew Eric's attention most were his eyes. They were glowing and were two different colors. One was an illuminated cornflower blue, and the other was a bright, deep green due to the glow it emanated.

The rail-thin man cocked his head to the side and studied them before he spoke. "What have we discovered? They are not human. Can you sense what they are?" He turned to the monstrous wolf.

The wolf continued to growl at them, probably so Eric wouldn't shoot the man in the head. Or to keep them all immobile with its ability. The man strolled around them slowly, but the werewolf's gaze remained trained on Caleb, Seth, and Lucy. Skeleton-man paused and peered at Valen.

"You have power." He waved his hand in front of them. "Ah, you are a witch." Dropping his hand, he narrowed his eyes at Lucy before he continued to Eric. He waved his palm in front of him, a crease forming between his brows.

"You want me to tell you what he is? You *should* know," a gruff disembodied female voice said from beside the man.

Eric strained to see who had spoken. A breath later, he knew he'd made a mistake. The muted, almost colorless spirit floated closer to Eric. She was an older, petite woman who reminded him of Valen's grandmother, only much smaller in frame. He hadn't meant to use his ability. He could only assume his fear of the werewolf had triggered his ability to see and speak with ghosts.

The man frowned at the ghost's words. Eric stopped breathing. Behind the man, still visible, were the zombies. Except something was wrong. Something was *very* wrong. They weren't dead. Their spirits stared at Eric with a hallowed look.

"He can see and hear me," the female ghost taunted.

"You see shades?" The thin man's voice was softer, almost kind.

Eric didn't know what to make of the man, his questions, or his companions, but what he was positive of was, he and his friends didn't need to fight this fight if they could avoid it. Caleb, Zalia, and Seth would be agitated, but he was the one who made the final calls. Eric sweat from the pain of the small movement as he forced a tiny, almost indecipherable nod.

Turning to the werewolf, the man's fingers twitched at his side and he tilted his head left. The werewolf huffed at him while circling back and stopping in front of Lucy and Valen. As soon as the paralyzing effect wore off, Caleb, Zalia, and Seth turned to face the intimidating trio before them. The man waved his hand and spoke some sort of gibberish. They fell to their knees and groaned in pain. Eric steadied the rifle to take his shot.

"Do not be foolish. You sense my power. Your companions meant to attack, and I cannot allow that. I want to speak with you," he shifted his gaze to Eric.

"Are they hurt?" Eric demanded.

"They are not human and will heal."

"That's not what I asked." Eric was ready to pull the trigger. The man didn't understand. He never missed. His shots were always killing shots. He wouldn't survive, but... Eric wasn't certain the thin man in front of him was human either.

"You are young," Skeleton-man glanced at the rest of them. "You are all young. If you are intelligent, you will leave here tonight with your lives. I only wish to speak to you. Can you control them?" He gestured to Caleb, Seth, and Zalia.

"Yeah, but you and your... wolf, must agree not to attack us." The werewolf's head reached the man's chest. Eric had never witnessed such a creature on all fours.

The enormous wolf's eyes flashed brighter, the amber irises shifting to a molten steel for a few seconds before returning to the goldish color. The man reached his hand to stroke the wolf behind his ear.

"You must restrain yourself. I need information," he told the werewolf.

"Good luck keeping him from raging," the older woman's spirit cackled.

Eric shot her a glare. When she noticed him looking at her, she smiled at him. Eric kept the barrel aimed at the thin man's skull as he spoke.

"Stay calm," Eric told them, counting on years of friendship and experience for them to understand the true meaning. Which was to stay calm until it was time to fight. His eyes darted around to the zombies, all with spirits attached to them. "Why did they stop?"

"Lower your ineffective weapon. You cannot harm us." Skinny-man's tone was arrogant, but he was probably right.

Eric lowered his rifle and stepped closer to Valen and Lucy.

"I will not harm any of you unless needed. Although you destroyed many of my creatures."

"The zombies are yours?"

"Yes. I control them." His voice and face were filled with indifference.

"But they're... they're not dead."

Valen's eyes widened at his comment, even as Lucy nodded like she already knew.

"I bound their souls to their forms. It was necessary to control them. I need their souls, otherwise they are useless to me."

The strange man's words confirmed Eric's fears. They'd only come across one necromancer before and barely escaped with their lives. Caleb and Zaila's low growls filled the surrounding space. The man chuckled.

"Yes, yes, I know the undead and myself are an abomination to you. Calm yourselves. With time you can build a tolerance and learn the self-control that will keep you and your companions alive." Again, his words were flat. His face hadn't changed even when he chuckled. It was like even if his voice changed octaves like it should, nothing else did. Eric wondered if he was also one of the undead.

"Still, if you bound their souls... aren't they aware of what's happening? Even if they can't exactly feel it?" Valen asked.

His glowing eyes shifted to her. "Yes."

"That's worse than death - you're a monster." She hissed.

"I am more than a monster. I am a void in the shape of a man. I control souls, not dead bodies. If you displease me, you will join them."

His words were a direct threat, yet something in Eric's gut told him he was posturing. Perhaps he wanted to seem like the ultimate evil to intimidate them.

"Now, you admitted to perceiving shades. Tell me what she tells you." He tilted his head toward the floating ghost that hovered near him.

"You can tell him he's an arrogant shit that doesn't appreciate me even in death." She shook her head as she spoke.

"I... she said..." Eric faltered. He was pretty sure if he said that the necromancer would kill them.

"You got no balls, kid. He's a powerful, evil bastard, although that's not all he is. You can reason with him. Stop being so scared. You got two werewolves, and whatever the fuck that kid is," she pointed to Seth, "so just tell him his name. His name is Ander. And then tell him to stop fucking with your heads."

The man's jaw tightened as she spoke. Eric could tell he wanted to respond, which likely meant she was telling the truth. He cleared his throat.

"Ander, your name is Ander."

"Indeed. You are useful to me." He turned to Valen. "You could be useful, too. However, you must move past your narrow views." He gazed at Lucy. "You are a mystery but... have a connection to life and death, which also makes you useful."

Ander's gaze locked on Seth. "You are also an enigma, not human, but not quite anything else, either." The werewolf huffed again and smacked its paw against the ground three times. "Yes, I sense that as well, but I would need to examine him further to be certain."

Eric wondered if he was psychic because he seemed to understand the wolf. "What do you want with us?"

His mismatched eyes moved back to him. "Your group attacked mine. Destroyed my minions. I did not seek you - you engaged me. We are traveling to find answers."

"Okay, what answers do you want from us?" Eric countered.

Ander's gaze was so intense it was hard for Eric not to look away. Silence consumed the area while they waited for him to speak again. After what seemed like an eternity, he took one step closer. Before Eric could react, Ander snatched his hand, pressing something into his palm. Eric's heart thundered in his ears, terrified, as his eyes dropped to their clasped hands. When Ander lifted his, a pink flower necklace rested in his palm. Eric lifted his head, confused.

"We are seeking a female. The one who used to wear that necklace. She is a shade now." Ander's tone had shifted back to the softer one he used earlier, and his face morphed to a more humane expression. A human in agony. As if the words had ripped open a wound so profound it would never heal.

Eric hadn't considered what it would be like for someone who controls spirits to lose someone they cared for. Their group had been through a lot, but they still had each other, which was almost unheard of in this world. Most survivors they came across had lost those they loved along the way. The wolf hung its head and whimpered, dragging its front paws against the ground.

"I told you this is a fool's errand. You need to let go," the female spirit said.

In response, the wolf growled at her and showed teeth.

Ander's eyes flashed. "If you repeat that one more time, I will bind you to the necklace. Do not test me."

"I'd... I'd need to know what her name was and what she looked like, but if she's been gone a long time, she won't be herself," Eric spoke before anyone lashed out.

"It matters not. I will mend her if needed." His fingers stroked the wolf's gigantic head. "Her name is..." he paused and clutched the wolf's fur. "Her name is Maeve. She is the most beautiful creature to have ever graced this plane of existence." His expression softened. "She is five feet nine inches, with long, dark brown hair that contains red undertones, her skin is alabaster white, and she has deep, bottomless eyes that delve into your soul. Her voluptuous form is perfection, but it is her heart that truly identifies her. She is the most giving, compassionate soul that exists. None compare to her."

The more he spoke, the more grounded and alive he seemed. The wolf made grunts of agreement. Shit. How could he begin to explain how hard it would be to find an unknown person when so many ghosts were haunting everywhere now? He pinched his brow. Surely Ander knew, or he wouldn't be asking for his help.

"Is she - should she be around here?" Eric asked.

Ander sighed. "We are certain she is on the east coast. Over the years, we have narrowed the search area to two states."

"We're in New York. What other state?"

"She is here or in Massachusetts."

Damn it. They were on their way to Massachusetts. What shit luck. Eric ran his thumb over the flower, trying to figure out the best way to deal with Ander. All necromancers were bad, and he seemed almost irrational. Definitely unstable.

"Okay, I'll look for her. It would be easier if I had a picture."

He nodded and reached into a pocket in his black cargo pants. "Yes, I should have shown you this before. Perhaps I am not thinking clearly." He muttered and pushed the side of the phone.

Eric's mouth dropped open. He had a cell phone? One that powered up? There were no working cell phones, there hadn't been in years. There wasn't a point anyway since most of the towers didn't work. The screen lit dimly as he slid his fingers over the glass. Valen shot an expression of disbelief at him.

Ander lifted the necklace from Eric's hand and lowered the screen to reveal a woman in her twenties grinning at the camera. It looked like she was in a bed inside a log cabin. It reminded Eric of when he used to go hunting with his dad. She was pretty, but he wouldn't say the most beautiful woman in the world, that was his girl, Valen. However, he had described her accurately.

The wolf padded over and pushed its snout against his side of the phone until Ander showed the screen to the wolf. The wolf whined and nuzzled against the phone before Ander pulled it back and turned it off, tucking it away again.

"How will I contact you if I find her?"

"That is the question, is it not?" Ander stared at nothing for so long it was uncomfortable.

Caleb and Zaila inched closer toward the man until his eyes swung to them, and he shook his head.

"Things are going well. Do not test me." His tone shifted back into the hard one he'd used when he arrived.

"Can you control any zombie?" Eric asked, mostly to distract him.

"Yes." He turned his attention back to him and then frowned. "No. I could control any I encountered as long as I bound their souls or a soul to the corpse. Recently though, I have not been as successful. Some are *different*. Have you also noticed this?"

Eric nodded. They had. Ever since zombies had started grouping up, their behaviors were slowly changing. Some of the bigger groups seemed to have an almost a mob mentality, moving as one versus a bunch of uncoordinated zombies.

"It is puzzling to me, at times infuriating. A mystery I must resolve. Not more important than her, but a secondary goal."

"That's the only goal you should be focused on. You're not a god, Ander. No matter how much power you gain, you're still the same person-"

Ander whipped his head to the spirit. Sweat broke out on Eric's back despite the cold temperatures when he watched all of Ander's arteries and veins turn black. They'd learned the hard way what that meant with the other necromancer they had encountered. He recited a spell and, to Eric's surprise, he recognized some Latin words, just not the others. The spirit shrieked.

"You evil bastard! Stop!" the woman cried out.

"I told you not to push me. Cease your nonsense and be grateful I preserved you. I make the choices now, not you. Accept it or move on."

"I'm done!" the ghost said with heavy breaths.

"Yeah, we've noticed the changes when they are grouped up. They're more dangerous now." Eric said once again, hoping to distract Ander.

"Exactly. The singular undead are no threat, even if there are a large number of them." He waved his hand dismissively, and the surrounding zombies twitched with life before they shuffled to create a circle around them. "They will keep watch while we speak. You need not be fearful."

Eric grimaced. The damn zombies weren't the thing that was unsettling any of them.

"Where are you traveling? And do not lie to me. I may not be as I once was, but I still can discern a lie, even a small white lie."

Eric didn't want to tell him anything. He wanted to get his people the hell away from this sickly looking man, his wolf, enslaved ghost, and mass of zombies. But he also believed Ander's words.

"Boston."

Valen gave him the stink eye, and Caleb huffed behind him.

An evil grin crossed Ander's mouth as the wolf nudged his side again. "Yes, of course. Let me finish." He petted the giant wolf and took another step closer.

Eric wasn't like Valen and couldn't pick up on someone else's magic unless they used it before him. But it was impossible not to feel the weight of his power as he approached.

"It appears our goals are aligned. Tell me your names as we will travel together."

The female ghost shot him a sympathetic look and shook her head.

"I'm Eric, though I think it would be better if-"

"Your consent is not necessary, but I would prefer not to force you. I would like it if we could travel as companions instead of enslaving you. Do you not wish that as well?"

Eric's eyes flicked to Valen. Could this strange man enslave them if they were still alive? Her mouth was a thin line. She rolled her shoulders back. "I'm Valen. We'll travel with you, but only if you swear not to hurt or enslave any of us - no matter what happens - even if we piss you off. If you try, I'll die trying to kill that wolf of yours."

His wolf? Ander's mouth twitched in amusement until she mentioned his wolf. Then his gaze turned into a glare.

"Then we understand each other. You agree, and we won't make a move against you - right Eric?" She turned her dark eyes to him.

"Yeah. I'll keep us calm and help you look for her, but we must go to Boston."

"We also are traveling to Boston. There is a large concentration of undead in that area I must study. Are you going to the human settlement outside of Boston?" Ander asked Eric.

"Yeah, we're the scouting party." If they were to stay with this crazy bastard, he'd know the truth soon enough, anyway.

"I see. Curious, the humans allow you to remain with them." His glowing orbs moved over Caleb, Zaila, and Seth. "Regardless. Are you, their leader? If so, we must enter an agreement."

"Yeah," Eric answered, speculating what the hell an agreement meant with a necromancer.

"Step forward."

Eric took a breath and moved in front of him.

"Put out your hand," Ander said and put out his right one.

"Eric-" Valen's worried tone made his insides tremble.

Eric raised his left hand. Ander clasped his wrist as Eric grabbed the necromancer's wrist. His hand, wrist, and arm were covered in strange symbols that held a dim glow.

"We will travel as companions until we reach Boston. We will work together to achieve success and safety for all of us." His voice deepened and an odd, warm sensation enveloped Eric.

"And we won't hurt or enslave each other," Eric added.

"As you have requested. Do we have an agreement?" Ander asked.

"Yeah."

As soon as he responded, the marks on Ander's skin brightened until Eric squinted. Ander spoke some additional words. None were Latin, so he couldn't tell what was said. Eric's eyes darted to Ander's, which made him squint more. It was like staring at the sun. More warmth enveloped him as his hand tingled.

"It is done." Ander released his hand and stepped back. He glanced at the night sky. "We should find somewhere for you to rest. It is late for most humans. We can discuss the path forward tomorrow."

The circle of zombies parted to let Ander and his wolf pass through. Eric hurried to Valen's side. She snatched his hand into hers and lifted it, turning it over to examine his palm. Her full lips flattened again. Ander strode forward without concern for anything around him. His wolf showed its teeth to them and joined the necromancer.

Lucy hurried to Seth and touched his face, healing the skin that had started to sag before she pulled his lips to hers. His claws retracted as he threaded his fingers into her hair. Caleb and Zaila shifted back to their human forms before Eric approached him.

"That wasn't a good idea," Caleb said in a hushed tone.

"What did you want me to do? If we fought him, not all of us would make it. I'm not willing to lose any of us, and neither are you," Eric fired back.

"Still, you let him cast some spell," Caleb sneered at Ander's back.

"I'd do it again if it protected us. I'll manage it. You manage your rage."

"How are we going to be free of him?" Caleb adjusted his eye patch.

"It doesn't matter until we get to Boston. At least this way we don't have to worry about zombies, right?" Eric tried to think of the positive outcomes. No random, wandering undead would surprise them, and if they crossed more dangerous creatures like demons, vampires, or shifters, they stood a much better chance with a necromancer at their side.

"I don't trust him," Caleb grumbled.

"Neither do I, and he doesn't trust us. Although, for now, it is what it is. It's not the first time we've had to deal with assholes. Let's just get to Boston, okay?"

"Fine. He moves to hurt any of us-"

"I know, man," Eric patted Caleb's shoulder.

Ander and the wolf stopped and peered at them, waiting. Eric stepped forward and tugged Valen with him. Good idea or not, for now, they were teamed up with a necromancer.

To be continued in...
Queen of the Dead
coming soon!

Acknowledgements

From the beginning, when I saw Zane chasing Renee in the city in my head, I wanted to figure out what was going on. Then that moment, right before he turned, it stayed with me for months. My brain kept asking: how could a zombie think? How could an undead be gentle? Finally, I asked myself what if this was a love story, but instead of being told from the survivors' point of view - what if it was the zombies who told the tale?

The idea invaded my days and nights, slowly crafting itself into what you just read. This series is so much more than a dystopian zombie story. It's more than a love story. I hope you continue the series to experience the true heart of it - what it's really about and enjoy the journey.

I want to thank the horde of people who've helped me bring this story to life. If I miss anyone, it wasn't intentional. I wouldn't have been able to bring this to life without you.

Sam, I wasn't sure if others would like this story, but your support and passion kept me going. Your unwavering love for the king helped me develop him into the cinnamon roll he is.

Chey, thank you for your insight and suggestions to make Renee better and the story stronger. Thank you so much.

Next Joyce, my knight in shining armor, no - Knight Commander for taking this rough story and polishing it until it became the gem it is. Without your insight and dedication, it wouldn't be what it is and I will forever be grateful.

Thea - your support with this story, with these characters, more than that - for all of my work - I can't tell you how much it means to me. Your art is a reflection of you and how beautiful your heart is. I'm so glad to have met you.

And to my friend, inspiration, PA, and the best cover artist, Gee. Without you, I would be adrift. I appreciate you so much. Even when faced with tight deadlines, you always manage to make both small and herculean tasks look effortless. Your talent and eye for what looks good never ceases to amaze me. You bring so much to this dark world, in both literal and metaphorical senses.

Thank you to the book bloggers who took a chance on this different idea and all the bookstagrammers who helped this story find its readers. Sending a shout out to my beta readers and ARC reviewers!! Thank you for your feedback and for loving these broken characters.

Finally, thank you to all of my readers, for taking a chance on me and my unique stories. I hope you enjoyed it. If you did, please consider leaving a review.

This is far from over....
Ryana

About the Author

Ryana writes compelling dark stories to remind the world of things forgotten and challenge their perception of reality, relationships, and beyond by giving voices to characters that are not mainstream. She is a neurodivergent author working in prose and comic books. Drawn to flaws and darkness, she finds honesty and depth lurking there, believing our most interesting stories are hidden behind our protective day-to-day facade. She scratches at the surface, flips the coin over, and keeps digging until she finds the soul of a story.

Ryana lives in a small island town in the wilds of the East Coast. When she's not writing or enthralling people with oral storytelling, she can be found relaxing with a cup of coffee, designing house layouts or painting with diamonds.

Do you want to stalk me?

Instagram: https://www.instagram.com/ryanahunter23/
Website: www.ryanahunter.com

Goodreads:
https://www.goodreads.com/author/show/22954808.Ryana_Hunter

Want more? Sign up for the newsletter for announcements, exclusive content, sneak peeks, and more! To sign up visit my website or use this QR code.

Other Titles by Ryana Hunter

<u>Haunted Legacies Series</u>
Savage Petal - <u>available on Amazon</u>
Cruel Orchid - <u>available on Amazon</u>
Cursed Soil - Val, Dev, Ren, Gideon, Bela & Madoc will return in 2026.

<u>Kingdom of the Dead Series</u>
King of the Dead
Queen of the Dead - coming 2025

<u>Shadows & Scar Series</u>
Shadowed Moon – coming Spring of 2025
Grim Echoes - coming Summer of 2025

Note from Ryana Hunter

Word-of-mouth is crucial for any author to succeed. If you enjoyed *King of the Dead*, please leave a review online—anywhere you are able. Even if it's just a sentence or two. It would make all the difference and would be very much appreciated.

Thanks!
Ryana Hunter

We hope you enjoyed reading this title from:

BLACK ROSE writing™

www.blackrosewriting.com

Subscribe to our mailing list – *The Rosevine* – and receive **FREE** books, daily deals, and stay current with news about upcoming releases and our hottest authors.
Scan the QR code below to sign up.

Already a subscriber? Please accept a sincere thank you for being a fan of Black Rose Writing authors.

View other Black Rose Writing titles at
www.blackrosewriting.com/books and use promo code
PRINT to receive a **20% discount** when purchasing.

www.ingramcontent.com/pod-product-compliance
Lightning Source LLC
Chambersburg PA
CBHW030821210726
48290CB00002B/691